PRAISE FOR TERMINUS

"Joshua Graham's TERMINUS is a fantastic read in every definition of that word. If Tom Clancy had written a novel of fallen angels and creatures that go bump in the night, this would be it: blisteringly paced, high-tension suspense, characters you bleed with. I can't wait to read more!"

—James Rollins, New York Times bestseller of The Blood Gospel

…A fast paced, adrenaline pumping, spiritual epic…
…Terminus will have you gasping for air, yelling at the characters, and questioning everything you thought you knew about angels…

—*Suspense Magazine*

…Highly recommended!
… Powerful and fascinating…
…will keep you riveted while you're reading and then keep you thinking long after you've turned the last page.

—*International Bestseller, M.J. Rose*

…Graham has taken stories of old and given them a new spin.
…The characters are richly developed
…Graham left the door open for more stories within this world, and I for one look forward to it with eager anticipation.

—*Rhodes Review*

ACCOLADES FOR JOSHUA GRAHAM

"...A riveting legal thriller.... breaking new ground with a vengeance... demonically entertaining and surprisingly inspiring."
(BEYOND JUSTICE)

—*PUBLISHERS WEEKLY*

"... A heart-pounding thriller...This gripping novel has it all: faith, hope, conspiracy, legal thrills, heart-pounding scenes..." (*Darkroom)*

—*The Washington Post*

"...Action, political intrigue and well-rounded characters. Graham has created a novel that thriller fans will devour. *(Darkroom)*

—*CBS News Entertainment*

"Darkroom is a haunting tale"

—*Toledo News Now*

"*Darkroom* is a fascinating, fast-paced, beautifully written story of love and war, murder, terrorism, and a dark conspiracy."

—Douglas Preston, *New York Times* bestselling coauthor of *Cold Vengeance* and *The Monster of Florence*

"*Darkroom* comes complete with a great mystery, unearthed secrets, and beguiling adventure. Joshua Graham mines an emotional landscape through an entourage of fascinating characters. Read this one—and take a walk on the perilous side."

—Steve Berry, *New York Times* bestselling author of *The Jefferson Key*

AWARDS AND HONORS

1st Prize Winner of the Forward National Literature Award.
1ˢᵗ Prize Winner of the International Book Award
Suspense Magazine's Best of 2010 list

TERMINUS

JOSHUA GRAHAM

REDHAVEN BOOKS

For Katie, my angel and my good thing…

TERMINUS

"Death—the undiscover'd country, from whose bourn
No traveller returns..."

HAMLET (ACT III), William Shakespeare

PRELUDE

THREE SECONDS. THAT WAS ALL.

The man in the black leather jacket had looked down for just three seconds to read a text message on his phone. And in the interim, his five-year-old Houdini of a stepdaughter Chloe had unstrapped herself, climbed out of her car seat, and slipped out of sight—nowhere near the doorway of the office where he was to meet his contact.

Just three lousy seconds!

His mouth went dry.

He scanned the streets, sidewalk, between cars, to the left then right then a quick three-sixty. Despite the thorough sweep, which took all of two seconds, he didn't see her.

"Chloe!"

She didn't answer, but he spotted her. Way down the street, her auburn pigtails bouncing with each step.

"Chloe! Wait!"

He slammed shut the back door of his Focus. Didn't bother to lock it. Ran up the sidewalk—fast. But the little stinker was fixated on a black cat luring her across the imaginary border that separated the gentrified arts district of Carleton Village and the slums of East Brentwood.

The cat bolted around the corner at the sound of the man's agitated shouts. Both hands outstretched, Chloe giggled and ran even faster.

"Kitty!"

He nearly tripped over an uneven seam in the sidewalk as he ran, his heart going faster than his feet.

A pair of SDPD squad cars with flashing red and blue beacons raced past Birch and came to a screeching halt somewhere around the corner of Lamont.

The little girl turned the same corner and vanished behind the red bricks of the apartment building. Straight onto Lamont.

"Stop, Chloe!" He'd gained but was still several steps behind.

The sound of a policeman shouting filled his head. Could things get any worse? He ran even harder.

It all happened within a matter of seconds.

Three lousy seconds.

That's what it took for him to round the corner and make out the figure fleeing the pimped-out Honda Civic that had crashed into a hydrant. The gunman shot at the cops, who now stood behind the open doors of their angled cars.

The man in the black leather jacket leapt at Chloe.

"Get down!"

Over his shout, the shouts of the police, the screams of frightened pedestrians, came a deafening *pop!* whose impact toppled him.

Chloe screamed.

A sudden chill overtook him as a crimson pool expanded around his face, now planted on the cold concrete sidewalk. He tried to speak, stretched his fingers towards Chloe. Felt nothing but the cold pumping though his entire body.

Life didn't flash before his eyes.

He heard more gunshots.

The last thing he saw was Chloe lurching back, her pigtails flailing to the side. As though in slow motion, she was falling.

Falling...

He never saw her hit the ground.

1

AS A REAPER OF THE THIRD LEGION, Nikolai—Nick, as he preferred to be called these days—had attended to more human deaths over the last thousand years than he cared to. Countless lives and memories snuffed out like the wick of a candle. It had all become routine, meaningless.

Vanitas vanitatum.

The ability to traverse the entire planet in the blink of a human eye had long grown commonplace, its charm lost somewhere between King Malcolm II's victory in The Battle of Mortlach and Guttenberg's invention of moveable type. These days he spent most of his time assigned to the northern hemisphere, one of the least active territories on earth.

As for leaving the planet, he typically only did that on days when he escorted a soul to the Terminus.

A day like today.

Nick waited while the OR surgeon continued trying to save the little girl from multiple gunshot wounds.

"My husband was killed," the beautiful woman standing in the door said, her voice breaking. "She's all I have."

"We can't keep her going like this," the surgeon said gently.

"She's not even five."

"I'm truly sorry. But it's time to let her go."

"No!" The mother rushed forward, knocking over a metal tray and all its equipment as she reached out to her daughter. The nurse caught hold of her arms and held her back.

"Please, don't let the last few moments of your daughter's life end like this. Let her go with some dignity," the surgeon said.

Nick tuned out the mother's voice as she got hold of herself. Having to watch this sort of thing was perhaps the worst part of his punishment. Far worse than his demotion. Worse than when he was a guardian a millennium ago. He'd seen tens of thousands die horrific deaths on battlegrounds in the physical realm—even intervened and partaken in sanctioned kills himself. But at least he'd been helping rid the planet of those who'd deserved it.

This was much worse.

Nick's reflection didn't show in the mirror, but in it he could see the surgeon calling the time of death and switching off the EKG machine, the little girl lying pale and still, the lovely mother weeping.

And now the warm golden light that only Nick could perceive filled the room, enveloping the body. It was about to happen.

The little girl's ethereal form sat up and separated from her expired mortal body. She looked to her mother, confused.

"Mama? Why're you crying?"

Her mother didn't respond. How could she?

Callous as Nick's heart had grown over the years, these moments always wrenched it.

"It's okay, little girl."

She turned to him and stepped off the operating table. Had she been older, she might have reacted with panic as most do when they see the blood on the sheets, the surroundings, the grief-stricken loved ones standing over their body. But she was too young to understand. She smiled and tried to touch her mother's head. Her hand passed right through it. She giggled and did it again.

"That's funny, Mommy."

Nick hated this. He should never have to take a child this young and innocent to the Terminus. He forced a smile and approached her.

"What's your name, love?"

"Chloe." Again she giggled, now prancing around the OR passing her hands through cabinets, walls, chairs, her mother. "Funny!"

Nick put his hand on her shoulder and her smile faded. This was the part he hated most. An expression common to people much older than Chloe replaced it. A look of recognition. Finality.

She's too young.

She looked back to her mother, still weeping over the empty shell that had been Chloe's body. Then she turned back to Nick with tears in her eyes.

"It's time to leave, isn't it?"

"Come, say goodbye to your mum. She'll feel it, and it'll make her happy—if only for a moment."

"Okay." She reached up, put her tiny hand in Nick's. Like an electrical current, a twinge that originated from the core of her spirit flowed into his. By now he should have been used to it, but he wasn't.

"Come on, then."

Chloe didn't seem to pay any mind to the fact that her mother could neither see nor hear her. She leaned over and kissed her mother's auburn hair, tried to stroke it without her hand passing through.

"It's okay, Mommy."

And in that moment, her mother stopped crying, sniffled, and looked up, her eyes incongruously hopeful.

"Sweetie?"

Chloe choked back a little sob and tried to wrap her arms around her mother's neck.

"I love you, Mommy. Have to go bye-bye now."

Her mother blinked. Nick waited a couple of seconds, then gave Chloe's shoulder a gentle squeeze.

"The last bit, love. Go on."

She nodded, understanding what he meant—spirits always seemed to know this instinctively when first separated from their bodies. Placing her forehead against her mother's, she joined her with shut eyes and poured out the very last of her mortal memories, the essence of their all too brief life together.

No matter how many times Tamara had tried to explain the human need for closure, to Nick's mind it was still sentimental. Nonetheless, he waited patiently for Chloe's spirit to converge for a moment with that of her mother's.

Her mother smiled, her eyes closed. It was only a moment, but she seemed at peace. When she began to cry again, Chloe kissed the top of her head and returned to Nick, sadness briefly tugging the corners of her mouth down. Then her eyes and face began to glow.

She took Nick's hand.

Her mother's tears and sobs penetrated the emotional barrier he tried to forge. His hand began to glow—how simple it would have been to use his healing ability and restore the little girl's mortal life. *Just one touch.*

But it was not allowed.

Nick had learned—the hard way, in England, a century ago. But what good was such an ability if it could not be used where needed?

What's the point of my existence, for that matter?

He started walking out of the room, an entirely human and unnecessary habit he'd developed from mingling with mortals over the years.

"Ready, Chloe?"

"I miss her."

"She'll miss you a lot more."

"How come?"

"Because mortals don't know what it's like on this side." For them, time was a driving tyrant: linear, merciless, flowing in one and only one direction. Why would anyone want to go through a short pittance of a life with all its sorrows—seventy, maybe ninety years—only to grow feeble and stupid towards the end? At least Chloe had been spared that.

Yet something about this premature departure troubled him unreasonably. He'd reaped the souls of children before, never liked doing it, but in Chloe's case the pain was quite a bit more acute.

As memories from the past surfaced, Nick without thinking released Chloe's hand and floated freely in the room. Before he knew it, he found himself standing beside her mother. The auburn hair falling over emerald eyes shimmering with tears made her look achingly beautiful.

Her weeping subsided. Her lips moved ever so subtly.

She was praying.

Again without thinking, Nick stretched out his hand, gently reached toward her face with his fingertips, taking pains not to touch her so she wouldn't perceive his presence.

Or would she?

She gasped with a start, her face lighting up.

Damn. Nick had inadvertently touched her hair and revealed himself.

Idiot!

He instantly slipped out of her perception. It had lasted only a second, but she had felt his presence. Seen his face.

She bolted to her feet and looked around the room, returned to her seat when she saw no one.

"Let's go, Chloe." Nick took her hand.

"What happened?"

"She'll be all right." He led Chloe to the door, hoping he hadn't just lied to her.

Chloe turned back to see her mother, waved, and said, "Bye-bye, Mama."

Nick, against his better judgment, turned and looked at the mother too. Any trace of that brief moment of euphoria mortals experience the first time they encounter an angel had been replaced by deep grief. He'd seen such pain far too often, but this was the strongest he'd felt it himself in a long time.

Human emotions.

As though they were his own.

He hated it. Hated the fact that he was starting to feel them again.

They were alien, perverse, just...wrong!

With a shudder, he held Chloe's hand and crossed the divide.

2

IF QUANTIFIED IN HUMAN TERMS, the trip to the Terminus would have taken about three years at several times the speed of light, a trivial fact Nick had worked out just because he could. But to Nick—and Chloe, who now perceived time and space as he did—they seemed to arrive after a few seconds in a dark tunnel.

"Where are we?" Chloe still gripped his hand.

"The Terminus."

"It's so dark."

Of course it was. But this painfully obvious remark could be forgiven because Chloe was a child. Most of his other subjects would be blubbering at this point: *I lived a good life!* Assuming the worst: *I don't deserve this!*

The simple fact was that Nick didn't know the final destination of any of the souls he harvested, so he'd grown immune to their pleas. And bargaining, for pity's sake! It wasn't as though he had any decision-making power.

Chloe wrapped her little arms—trembling little arms—around Nick's forearm.

"I'm scared," she whispered.

Scared? If she knew he'd once been a warrior feared by humans and demons, her fear might be understandable. But now, as a reaper of the third legion? He was nothing but a cosmic chauffeur.

Nick sighed, took a deep breath, and snapped his fingers to form a construct for her. It started with a pinpoint of light, the size of the little dot the old picture-tube tellies displayed in the last seconds before you shut them off. But instead of shrinking, the dot grew into a white circle through which a torrent of sensory details flooded.

A rushing wind blew Chloe's hair back like a flag while all around them the construct perfected itself in both her perception and Nick's: throngs of people going to and fro, steel-framed skylights, a female voice announcing endless arrivals and departures, lighted schedule boards, and everywhere the stench of humanity.

Over to the left, an old woman laughed and wept with a young woman who had run up to her. To the right, a group of high school students gathered together with high-fives and fist-bumps and bear hugs that seemed decades overdue. Apparently Nick was not the only compassionate reaper.

But the sights did make him feel a bit sick.

"A train station?" Chloe said.

"I've created a construct to resemble the terminus at Victoria Station for you."

"Why?"

"So you can understand where we are. What it's like. Somewhat, anyway."

"Why?" She *could* be annoying.

"Picture says a thousand words, doesn't it?"

"But why?"

Something nearby caught his attention.

"Get your damn paws off of me, you bastards! This is just a dream! A freaking nightmare!" The man in a dark gray suit and red silk necktie thrashed about to no avail as two metro policemen started to drag him off. Nick winked his left eye and obscured the three from Chloe's perception just as the man started to berate the dark reapers with language Nick really didn't want her to hear.

"Who were they?" she said.

"Bother that, we've got to go, straightaway. Don't want to miss your train, do you?"

Chloe giggled. And when Nick knelt and fixed her collar at the platform, checked that her little Tigger backpack was properly shut, she was still giggling.

"What's so funny?" he said.

"You said *bother*." When she got to the word she giggled just a little, as though the word tickled. "That's what Winnie the Pooh says!"

"Right." Winnie the freaking Pooh. Good thing she was about to leave, he was starting to feel...it was just a good thing she was leaving, was all.

Chloe launched herself at him for a hug. The train was coming in.

"It's here, it's here!"

"So it is," Nick said.

"I have to go now, don't I?" Nick hadn't let go of her hand, and she was pulling him towards the train's door, and her tug felt like salt on an open wound.

"Yes."

The doors hissed open. Everyone was boarding except for some wearing black suits and dark glasses. Reapers. Angels never tarried at the Terminus, they simply brought their subjects and left. Lingering was a sign of weakness.

But Nick didn't let go of Chloe. For some reason, he didn't want to.

"I'm going now," she said.

He gave her his best smile, couldn't help it. Then he let her go. As she turned and began running toward the doors, he called out to her.

"Chloe!"

To his surprise, she stopped and turned around.

He tried to speak, but pain from that laceration in his memory inhibited him and he could only mouth a goodbye. And then, knowing where all this sentimental rot came from, he resolved to kick it out of his mind.

It *would* be here, in this construct—he'd never build one for this place again. Not this one, anyway.

The next thing he knew, Chloe had run back, wrapped her arms around his neck, and was squeezing him as hard as a five-year-old could.

"Thank you," she whispered.

Were those *tears* in his eyes? He hugged her back.

"Goodbye, Chloe."

She ran off again, turning once to wave.

Then the doors slid shut.

3

AS CHLOE'S TRAIN LEFT THE PLATFORM, Nick let the sounds and images of the construct evaporate and remained alone in the pitch blackness of the Terminus with the pain he'd resurrected and inflicted upon himself.

Victoria Station…

"Why must you do this to yourself, Nikolai?" A bright golden light outlined Tamara's frame, though shadows somewhat obscured her features.

"Spying on me?" Nick said, not turning to face her.

"It's my duty to keep an eye on you."

"Then you've been remiss."

Now he turned to face her directly. She smiled and gave him a maternal look. They were now standing in his construct of the boardroom of a corporate office building, staring out the window over endless clouds.

"Don't tell me you're upset that I've been away. It's only been a hundred years. Is that what this is all about, Nikolai? "

"I prefer Nick."

"Since when?"

"Mid twentieth century."

He wanted to leave. Tamara came over and put her hand on his shoulder.

"Oh, come now, I know what's bothering you."

"Do you, really?" He didn't want to discuss what had happened at Victoria Station. Hopefully she wouldn't bring it up.

"You're getting impatient. Isn't that it?"

"Not even remotely close." Not entirely true, but at least she was on the wrong track.

"This delay is not due to neglect." She pointed upwards. "As if anything could escape our Father's cognizance. There's always a reason, a purpose. This, like all trials, is a test of character. It's His way of preparing you. You especially should know this, from your observations of the mortals."

"Do you suppose you could dial back the condescension?"

"Sorry." She laughed. "What's really bothering you, *Nick*?" Her emerald eyes bore into him.

He wanted to open the window and just fly off. But where? He couldn't hide from Tamara any more than he could hide from the commander in chief—whom he'd never seen, yet like every angel referred to as Father.

"Do you know how many reapers I've watched get promoted?" he said. "Reapers hundreds of years my junior with little experience where it counts? I used to be a highly decorated guardian, and now..." He sighed. "I think I've more than proven myself. Isn't it high time we end the games and move forward?"

"What is it you want, really?"

"For one thing, I'm tired of this holding pattern between earth and the Terminus. I'm ready to cross the divide. I'm sick of this glass ceiling. Sick of spinning my blasted wheels."

"My, you *have* spent too much time with them."

"Them?"

"Mortals." Tamara's eyes narrowed. "The facial expressions, the syntax...You're even speaking like them now."

"I'm doing nothing of the sort." After a hundred years of probation, the last thing he wanted was for her to think he'd squandered that second chance she'd risked so much to get him. Yet before this meeting was over, he'd surely disappoint her.

"I'm concerned, Nikolai. Perhaps you should take a leave of absence. Gather your thoughts for a century or so. I've always found that a short break helps alleviate the effects of...oh, what do they call it down there..." She closed her eyes for a moment. "Burnout! Yes, that's it. Take a break, and when you come back this whole issue of the delay, your promotion, it'll all work out."

"I'm sorry, a hiatus won't help."

She started to protest, but the resolve in his face stopped her.

"Then what will?" she said.

Now that it was time to actually tell her, Nick found it even more difficult than he'd imagined.

"I'm sorry." It wasn't easy to keep his eyes on hers. "I can't do this anymore."

She looked at him for a long moment. And though she had always been the maternal figure, she now seemed like the child, bravely holding back her tears.

"I feared it might come to this. You're not the first, you know."

"I know."

Now her eyes were filled with sorrow—and concern for him.

"Please, won't you reconsider? Don't do anything in haste."

"I've had almost a hundred years to think this through."

"As I said, haste."

"Tamara..."

"Are you absolutely certain?"

"Yes. No. I'm not sure, at least not a hundred percent. I just have to try or I'll go through eternity never knowing what might have been." He stepped back and tried to smile. Poignantly. "I appreciate everything you've done, Tamara, more than I can say. But I have to try."

She nodded. This was every angel's choice. She could not take this right from him, could not forbid him.

"No matter what, Nikolai, you are loved with an everlasting love. And you can always come back."

"I doubt that." His heart ached even as he hardened it. "It's too late."

"It's never too late."

He kissed the top of her head.

"It is for me." And with that he walked out of the boardroom, leaving Tamara alone by the window.

4

THE ELEVATOR RIDE SHOULD HAVE TAKEN HIM to the lobby but went down a few levels further. Levels Nick didn't know existed. He stood ramrod straight and hardened his gaze at the door. The elevator, which had been pumping in cool air and what sounded like *Fliegt heim, ihr Raben* from Wagner's *Götterdämmerung*, seemed to have grown smaller. And warmer.

Brilliant. I hate opera.

Without a chime or any other indication as to where the elevator had landed, the music stopped.

The air conditioner's fan stopped.

The lights went out.

Nick remembered he was still inside his own construct and snapped his fingers, but the darkness prevailed.

He groped around.

Cold doors. Buttons on the panel.

Still inside the construct.

"Splendid." Trapped inside an elevator in the Corporate Office building, heaven knows how many levels beneath...

He pounded on the doors—was the elevator air growing stale?

"Hello?" Another finger snap. He pounded the door again. "Anyone out there?" He wedged his fingers in between the seams of the cold metal doors and pulled with all his might. The lights came on, the music resumed, the doors slid open.

A long hallway stretched before him, filled with light. Spotless white walls with no paintings, no markings, just pure white. At the end of the hallway one small sign hung above the white twin doors. He couldn't read it from this distance so he walked close enough to see the sign clearly. Two bold capital letters:

A.R.

Beneath them, in small print:

ANGEL RESOURCES: NO APPOINTMENT NECESSARY

Even before his knuckles reached the surface of the doors, they yawned open. The unmitigated whiteness enveloped everything within to the point that Nick couldn't see the floor, wall, ceiling, or anything in the room that seemed to have just swallowed him.

He spun around and could no longer see the door. A physically void space would not have fazed him ordinarily, but to return to the elevator he needed to find that door. In this room he could see nothing— couldn't even tell it was a room. But out of nowhere someone suddenly appeared to join him in it.

A bespectacled gentleman dressed in a white suit, white shirt, and white tie sat at a desk, his hands folded before him. He had a full head of white hair, and looked quite harmless, which made Nick suspicious.

"May I help you?" he said.

"I seemed to have come to the wrong level."

He lowered his bifocals and looked at Nick over the rims. "Ah, yes! Nikolai. We've been expecting you." He extended his hand. Nick shook it.

"Expecting?"

"Yes, of course." He pointed to Nick's left. "Won't you please make yourself comfortable?" A plush white chair appeared. Nick sat. "Your first time, I see."

Nick leaned back into the wonderfully soft upholstery.

"It appears so, Mr..." He craned his neck to read the brass name-plate on the desk. "Mr. Morloch?"

"Why don't you just call me Harold, hmmm? It's a lot easier to remember. Tea?"

"Thank you." The chair was so comfortable he felt he might actually fall asleep—whatever that was like. "Earl Grey, please."

A delicate porcelain cup and saucer appeared in his hands, the cup steaming with aromatic tea. The ability to enjoy it was perhaps a happy byproduct of "spending too much time" with mortals. He took a delicious sip, then leaned back into the chair, surprisingly soothed.

Harold sipped from an identical teacup, his little finger pointing as he tilted it to his lips, then set it down in its saucer on the desk.

"So, Nikolai, welcome to A.R."

Until now, he hadn't known such a division existed. At which point did this cease to be his construct and become someone else's, if indeed it were? He took a considerable sip of the Earl Grey and finished it. As he set the cup in its saucer, both vanished.

"You said you were expecting me?"

"Yes, well...Let's see now, how best to explain?" Harold steepled his fingers. "You've had countless centennial performance reviews, no?"

"Countless."

"A couple of millennial reviews?"

"And?"

"We're privy to more than just metrics, Nikolai. Your dossier contains data on your behavioral tendencies, noteworthy remarks, as well as your self-evals."

"I didn't plan on coming here."

Harold peered over his horn-rimmed eyeglasses.

"Didn't you?"

"Look, I've no time for games. What's this all about?"

"No time? Fascinating expression." For an instant Harold's eyes burned with thinly veiled annoyance. And then, just as quickly, they returned to their placid state. "I take it you're tired of the menial work."

"Wouldn't you be?"

"Fed up with the meaningless deaths."

Nick sat up straight and leaned forward.

"You got all this from my doss—"

"Done with watching your efforts go unrecognized while younger, less experienced reapers pass you up." His words accelerated. "You're a warrior of the cosmos, yet relegated to—"

"Non-corporeal babysitting." They said it at the same time.

"Precisely!" Nick said. "That's why I'm tendering my resig—"

"Tut-tut!" Harold held up a hand. "There's no need to resign, my young friend."

"Young? I'll have you know—"

"How would you like to get fast-tracked?"

This was clearly Harold's construct, the way he commanded every element—the furniture, the monitors, the tea.

"I'm listening," Nick said.

"Consider it a lateral move, initially. We'll get you out of that dead-end department."

"Oh?"

"For starters, how would you like to begin dealing with meaningful deaths?"

Interesting.

"I'd still be a reaper, though, wouldn't I?"

"Only in the interim. We'd promote you to more meaningful projects soon enough. You're sick of taking innocent children, good people who never did anything to deserve it. What if you took those who really do deserve it?"

Nick leaned back, crossed his arms. He liked it but wasn't ready to let that show.

"Go on."

Harold stood up, waved him over, and with two hands traced the outline of a large rectangle. A flat-screen television filled the space—looked like a 92-inch, 3D (rather, 4D or more), ultra high-def screen.

"Take a good look at all the people in the world who are dying, Nick."

The screen flashed by with scenes of earthquakes, tsunamis, war, disease. Starving children, deathly sick families in Africa, India, homeless people in the United States freezing to death in dark alleys...It was hard to discern relative time in someone else's construct, but as the scenes went by faster and faster Nick could swear that at one point a frame stood still for an extra nano-second: Victoria Station, where a little girl—

He blinked, and the screen showed image after image of evil people throughout history. From the likes of Adolph Hitler and Osama Bin Laden to a drug dealer, a child molester, a serial killer sitting amongst his trophy collection—

Harold passed a hand over the screen and it disappeared.

"All right, Nick. What did you see just now?"

"The scum of the earth, essentially."

"Those are the souls we take pleasure in harvesting."

It was brilliant. A transfer. No need to resign. Perhaps he had already passed probation. Perhaps the promise that *all things work together for the good* applied not only to humans but to angels, too. In any case, it beat the tar out of reaper work.

"*This* I can do."

"Splendid! You start immediately. Hands-on training will take place on the job. Sign the transfer docs and you're on your way." A thick stack of papers in a black leather binder appeared in Harold's hand. He set it down on the desk, pulled a black fountain pen from his breast pocket, handed it to Nick, and opened the contract to the last page.

"Sign here."

"I suppose I ought to read it first."

"Be my guest, Nick. We have all the time in the..." A sheepish grin. "We have time."

For the most part the terms, warranties, and stipulations looked acceptable. There was one clause that mentioned a temporary abdication of angelic methodology, explained in language so dense he found himself skimming it. Finally he reached the signature line, clicked the black fountain pen, signed his name—in red ink!—and handed the contract to Harold.

"Very good," Harold said after a close look at the final page. "This contract is hereby executed and binding."

"Yes. Now, there's one thing—"

"Thank you, Nikolai." He gave Nick's hand a quick shake. "You'll be hearing from your new supervisor shortly."

"But—"

"Goodbye."

5

HE NEVER SAW THE DOOR OPEN. Nor did he see Harold leave. Nick stood with the fountain pen in his left hand and looked around, trying to discern any spatial point of reference.

He couldn't.

Like Chloe's train, the entire construct began funneling into a small black circle with a whooshing sound that sounded like an industrial-strength shop vac. The black hole sucked in all the white around him and eventually seized Nick's leg, tilting him sideways.

He could do nothing to stop from getting siphoned into that tiny void. In the next ten seconds, or ten hours for all he knew, Nick found himself standing on something solid in the gloom. He cleared his throat, and the sound of it resounded as though in a cavern that stretched for miles. He heard a dissonant trickling that seemed to grow in texture and complexity. As it got louder, the darkness around him began to pull away like black curtains at the unveiling of a monument—

Not a monument, but the body of an unreasonably large man dressed in a black suit, with Gargoyle sunglasses masking his eyes and no expression whatsoever on his face. Nick fell back onto the cool surface of the ground. But all he could see before him were the pant legs of what looked like a giant.

"Watch yourself." The black-suited man's voice was a *basso profundo*. When Nick got to his feet, he realized that this man with the coffee complexion, muscular build, black goatee, and shining bald pate stood at least six inches taller than his own six-feet two. He looked sort of like a larger, beefier version of Samuel L. Jackson. With a walking stick.

"Wait, you can see me?" Nick said.

He took a step back since Goliath here neither spoke nor exhibited any sign of affording him personal space. All around, humans pushed past one another through the long halls, up and down the wide staircase, and under the semi-circular windows near the domed ceiling adorned with an astrological mural painted in gold.

Grand Central Station, New York.

Another terminus.

"Wonderful."

Goliath raised his shoulders slightly and exhaled with barely contained irritation. All the other briefcase-toting luggage-rolling humans either walked past or through him.

"So, you're my new supervisor," Nick said.

The corner of Goliath's mouth twitched under his mustache. Nothing else moved, not even his eyebrows. Nick stepped up to him.

"You're going to have to say something sooner or later if you expect me to—"

"You can still return to your previous position."

"Ah, so he *does* speak." Nick shook his head. "All right, Goliath—"

"Johann."

"Johann, right. Let's get one thing straight. I am never going back to that dead-end reaper business. This is my future."

One hand still resting on his walking stick, which now revealed a golden orb under his ebony-gloved fingers, Johann lowered his sunglasses and glared at Nick over the rims.

"What do you know of your future?" He replaced his Gargoyles and clicked his tongue. "Sophomoric reapers."

"And what're you, a blooming archangel?"

Johann snapped his fingers—how he did that wearing gloves was anyone's guess—and something resembling a human smartphone appeared in his hand. With his thumb he typed away and muttered something about signs of excess mingling with mortals.

"Hey!" Nick said. "To whom do you report?"

He tried to grab the smartphone, but Johann snapped his fingers again and it winked out of sight.

"You'd do best to go back, Nikolai. Your path has already been ordained."

"I said, to whom do you report?"

"Are. You. Going. Back?"

"When hell freezes over." A woman in a tan raincoat pulling a carry-on passed obliviously through them both, and Nick started to laugh. He thought of what he and his giant must look like—only nobody could see them. "You really ought to try laughing, Johann," he said. "It does wonders for constipation. You know, of the mind."

Both hands on his walking stick again, eyes hidden behind his shades, Johann said, "Be careful."

"Don't worry about me, buddy, I can..."   he was gone, suddenly "...look after myself."

Sensing his strength and aggression returning, Nick leaned back against the window with his hands behind his head, peered over the ledge, and considered his new career. With this transfer he'd been granted not only a break from the meaningless deaths but a chance to use his power for something that truly mattered on this pitiful planet.

For the first time in a hundred years or so, he smiled.

6

WITH A HEAVY HEART, CARLITO GUZMAN looked down at his bodyguard. Had he not been forced at gunpoint to his knees by Lito's two lieutenants, Alfonso would have stood six foot four—nearly a foot taller than Lito, sometimes called The Chihuahua, though never to his face. Thin lines webbed Alfonso's eyes, black and red blotches littered his face, his busted lips bled.

"Ten years, Alfonso!" Lito sighed. "Ten years, I trusted you with my life. You took a bullet for me at the Conroy shipyards. And now this?"

"You have to understand, Lito. I was—"

"Don't even try." Lito held up a hand. "It's embarrassing." He knew what had to be done. It was for the good of the family, the organization. For the good of Maria, though she'd never understand.

Lito's anger burned white hot, his voice dropped to a deadly whisper.

"I will not abide a traitor!"

"You don't understand!" The hulking bodyguard gagged from the blood in his throat. "Maria and me, we're in love! We're—"

"If your intentions had been honorable, you wouldn't have sneaked around behind my back!"

From outside his office, Maria banged on the door.

"Please, Lito. Don't hurt him!"

"I'm going to have a word with you too, *hermanita*. You wait there." He turned back to Alfonso. "I can forgive many things, you know that. But betrayal? Dishonoring my sister?"

Now Alfonso began to laugh. At first a subtle ripple from his chest, then a crescendo until the laughter became near maniacal.

"Oh, you find this amusing, do you?" Lito said.

The amusement sloughed off Alfonso's face, leaving in its place a dark, cruel expression that gave Lito pause.

"You will see it my way," he said.

For a moment, Lito remembered just how imposing Alfonso could be, how dangerous he was to anyone that dared cross his family's safety perimeter. Even on his knees with two strong men holding him down at gunpoint, he could intimidate with his eyes—Lito referred to it as Alfonso's being in the kill zone. He'd never expected to see it turned against him.

"If I didn't know you better," Lito said slowly, "I'd think you were threatening me."

"Threatening is such a harsh term. I call it informing you."

"You're in no position to—"

"I have leverage, Lito."

"You have nothing."

"Oh, but I do. Privileged information."

"So does the FBI. As far as they're concerned, I am above reproach."

Despite the gun now pressed into the back of his head, Alfonso smiled.

"Not about you, Chihuahua, about Maria. I know all about her past. About January 27th, 1992, Pablo and Antonia Suarez. What if she were to learn the truth?"

Lito froze. Stopped breathing for a minute and for too long couldn't speak a word. How could Alfonso possibly have found this out?

"And you say you love her?" he said finally.

"Oh, I do. But you wouldn't want her to learn the truth now—not when your family has kept it a secret her whole life. She will hate the very memory of your parents and despise you forever for carrying on the lie."

"It would hurt her to know! Do you not understand?"

"Oh, I can imagine the pain she'd feel, the betrayal. You wouldn't want to bring that upon her just because your men think they saw me talking with Gustavo Suarez, would you? I mean, what if they were mistaken? Come on, let's be reasonable. Just give me the Hernandez branch and we'll forget the whole thing, eh?"

Lito was familiar with the many operational wings of the family businesses, but Papi had only mentioned this one in passing, no details before he died. The truth was, Lito was at a disadvantage. Not that he'd let anyone get the impression he was less than completely in control.

"The Hernandez branch needs further evaluation before I turn it over to anybody."

"I promise, Lito, you put me in charge of that branch, I will take the *best* care of Maria." He smiled. "If not, I can't guarantee your precious little sister will remain innocent about her—"

"Alfonso, I warn you—"

"I can't guarantee her safety, either. Her neck is so soft, so fragile..."

Was this *hijo de puta* actually trying to use Maria's life to blackmail him? Alfonso was indeed dangerous. With all the weapons and assassins available to him, he could have her murdered and disposed of without anyone knowing about it, without lifting a finger.

He wanted to kill Alfonso right then, right there, but Lito had learned not to show his hand too soon.

"I see." He kept his expression neutral. "Perhaps we can come to an understanding."

"Just give me a chance, Lito, eh? I promise to take good care of the Hernandez branch *and* Maria." Which probably meant he'd treat her just a little better than the dozens of girls he perpetually abused both sexually and emotionally. "Don't worry, I won't let you down."

Lito was silent for a minute. Then he shrugged his shoulders.

"Well, now that you put it that way..."

A triumphant smile lit Alfonso's beaten face.

"Yes?"

"Give me a minute to consider your...proposal."

The sun painted the sky amber as it sank over the horizon at Imperial Beach. Between the Venetian blinds, slats of dying light cut through the dust of the dimming office. The only sounds were the ticking of an antique grandfather clock and Maria's soft weeping outside—so naive, so foolish. That was why Lito had to protect her.

This was not the life Mama had envisioned for any of them, especially baby Maria. But it was Papi, the infamous Victor Guzman—by whose side Mama stood until her own untimely death—who had brought this upon the Guzman family. Lito could still hear his raspy dying voice: *No use crying over fate. Blessed or cursed, you accept the hand you are dealt, and you fight!*

Then came the memories of all the good times he and Alfonso had shared since childhood, Lito only twelve and Alfonso seventeen when they first met. But thanks to his size and ferocity Alfonso had already been in security training, part of the family for all intents and purposes.

A twinge in Lito's chest clipped his reverie short. He patted his old bodyguard's face gently and smiled.

"Thank you for all your service to our family, Alfonso."

"Wait! Where are you going? WAIT!"

He walked to the door, opened it, and with a nod to his lieutenants, shut it behind him.

"Lito, no!"

Out in the hallway, he heard Alfonso's panicked cries. Maria pulled free from Eduardo and ran over with tears streaming down her cheeks. *"Ay dios mio!"*

Before she could say another word, two loud pops exploded behind the door.

Twice, Maria flinched.

Twice, she gasped.

"Maria." He kissed the top of her head—a sweet jasmine fragrance rose from her hair. "One day, you will understand," he said gently. "You may even forgive me."

7

THE JOURNEY ACROSS THE PACIFIC was worse than he had imagined. He'd agreed to this job thinking, what was the big deal? Air or sea, cargo is cargo, right? But now, after four weeks of mid-ocean ship transfers in the middle of the night, dodging international patrols, Yuri Kosolupov had to face the irony that he might die from sea sickness.

Hanging his head over the gunwale to heave what little of his lunch he had kept down, Yuri comforted himself with the thought of his wages for this "simple" operation—20 million euros for gathering up components from various locations (an abandoned warehouse in Volhynia, Ukraine, the back alley of an electronics component factory in Pyongyang) and transporting the entire package to the States via the Mexican Border. Five million of it was already in his account in Zurich as a retainer, the rest to be paid upon delivery.

And now, after all the trains, the armada of ships he and his precious cargo had transferred from countless times, he felt like he was going to die on this miserable fishing boat off the coast of Ensenada.

The sky turned a shade of green that probably matched his complexion. As a dark veil obscured the sun, the air turned frigid with threatening winds that agitated the waves.

Just what I need now.

"Hey, Yuri!" Tom Jonas, the boat's captain, came over and slapped him on the back. "Feeding the fish again?"

Yuri wiped his mouth.

The ship started to pitch, and his stomach clenched again. A distant howling announced the impending storm.

"How much longer?" Yuri asked.

"You're going to want to get below decks, unless you fancy getting soaked."

"Just get us to dry land, all right?"

"I'll do that." Jonas shook his head. "Just don't blame me if you go overboard in this storm. You fall in, I'm not coming after you. Not with that storm coming."

"Don't worry about it."

"You're a hoot, Koso...Kuso. Whatever."

"Yuri."

"Like I said, whatever." Jonas was a man who spent more time with dead fish than people. And dead fish didn't complain, nor did they vomit all over his deck. They only bled.

Soon after Jonas left, the sea began tossing the boat.

Yuri chose the path of prudence and went below decks to stay with the package while Jonas battled the storm. One benefit of impending doom was that it distracted him from the waves of nausea that rose and fell with the ocean's. He wrapped his arms around the splintery crate that held the package and cursed the wind, the boat, her captain, and the buckets of dead fish who were his only company in this dark hour.

I didn't come this far to die like one of these stinking fish!

Above the cargo hold, he heard Jonas preparing for the onslaught, swearing and laughing maniacally.

"Here it comes!" The idiot knew nothing of the concept of healthy fear. Or perhaps he dealt with it by mocking it, even as he went down with his ship.

Heavy blows rocked the boat—heavier, he'd be willing to bet, than if some great leviathan had attacked. Then came the pitching, the falling, the leaping of the vessel. The single light bulb dangling from the ceiling fizzled out.

Yuri cursed the darkness.

Not until the frigid water seeped through his pants and engulfed his hands did he realize the truth: he was going to drown.

Why had he agreed to this? Shouldn't it have bothered him that thousands would die? No, he was just a courier, what his client did with the package was not his responsibility. But what use would all that money do him and Irina now? She would probably wait a month, maybe two, but even if his body weren't eaten by sharks or returned to Kiev, she'd move on to the next man who made the same grandiose promises he had. She was stunningly beautiful but shallow as they come. And that had been fine with Yuri because like most young guys, he only thought with his loins.

Until death comes looking for you.

Up above, the water smashing down onto the deck sounded thunderous. Here below in the gloom, the water around Yuri rose. If the boat took on any more, the package might begin to float. Hard to maneuver in water—his head could get crushed between the crate and the hull.

"I'm not ready to go," he muttered as tears began to sting his eyes.

He thought of *Mommochka*, who had always believed in him, sacrificed so he would become a "concert violinist like Oistrakh." How disappointed she would be to see him in the hereafter, having lived the life he'd chosen instead. Not that he'd see her, where he was going. She would be in heaven, not him.

The boat lurched sideways at a dangerous pitch.

Any minute now it would capsize.

Never in his adult life had Yuri prayed, but now, what the hell? It was worth a chance. *Mommochka* always said there is no sin too big for God to forgive. Shivering and curling up into a ball, Yuri folded his hands and thought of what he might say to the only one who could help him now.

"If you're...if you're really there..."

As if in reply, something heavy struck his head.

A white flash ruptured the darkness.

And then everything went black.

8

PERCHED HIGH ABOVE GRAND CENTRAL TERMINAL, Nick skimmed through the headlines of the newspaper. Housing prices across the United States were back on the rise as was the price of petrol, major online retailers reported that ebook sales were steadily overtaking print books, and U.S. Navy Seals had issued a slightly fuller account about the killing of Osama Bin Laden yesterday.

"High time." Nick flipped the page and wondered what it would be like to be the reaper bringing this one to the Terminus. Terrorists, murderers, those were the people who should be plucked off the planet like—

"Hand me the sports section?"

The sudden materialization of the woman sitting next to him near the ceiling way above the terminal might have startled Nick, had he been human. But after several millennia working this side of the realms, almost nothing surprised him.

Nothing save the beauty of the creature who now sat next to him with her hand outstretched: glistening crimson lips, sapphire eyes, glowing olive skin, raven locks that fell gracefully over her shoulders and half over her lovely features.

"I was starting to wonder when you'd show up." He pulled out the requested section of the newspaper, placed it in her uncommonly warm hand, and ruffled a page he had been reading as if he were interested in the contents.

They sat side by side for a few minutes, Nick's curiosity fighting with his determination not to be the first to break the ice. Though he had a fairly good idea who she was, he couldn't be certain.

Finally, she spoke. "I have to say, I'm surprised."

"Are you?" He turned the page, still not looking at her.

"I'm surprised you accepted this position. Few angels of your caliber would."

"I'm not just any angel." He kept his expression neutral.

The sunlight entering the station momentarily backlit her outline like a halo of white gold. If mortal, she'd probably be in her mid-twenties. But the intensity of those sapphire eyes gave the impression of someone more wise than youthful.

"Pleased to meet you. I'm Lena."

He held her gaze and wondered if she might be his new supervisor's assistant. He reached out to shake her hand.

"Nick."

Without warning, she pushed him off the ledge with a shove in the shoulder. Surprised, he turned around while suspended over the oblivious mortals hurrying to and fro in the physical layer. Lena floated down to him.

"I've read some impressive things about you, Nikolai. But frankly, I wonder if you're not a bit rusty." She was grinning, her expression was mischievous.

"*You're* my new supervisor?"

"That depends."

"What do you mean?"

"I don't hire anyone based just on a hand-walked resume or a verbal recommendation."

Nick cocked an eyebrow. "That so? Then what do you—"

Before he could see it coming, she threw what looked like a ball of light at him. It struck him in the gut, sending him to the floor, sliding though the crowd. Everything around him flickered as his head hit the foot of a set of steps. She'd caused him to enter the physical layer of existence just long enough for him to feel the impact.

He got to his feet and dusted off his jacket.

"Cute."

"Just seeing if there's any merit to your dossier. It says you were a highly decorated guardian." She landed right in front of him, grabbed his arm, then with amazing force threw him clear across the promenade, under the American flag that fluttered as he passed beneath it, and straight for the tall windows. If he crashed through the glass, shards would rain down on all the people below.

And so, just in time, Nick forced himself to remain outside the physical layers of time and space. As he whisked through the window silently, it occurred to him that it had been centuries since he'd had the pleasure of sparring. Never mind that Tamara considered it childish— whether with another angel or in battle with a demon, it had always given him a rush.

Nick hovered over the traffic lights of 42nd Street, then launched himself back inside Grand Central. Lena was nowhere to be found.

"Hiding, are we?" He scanned the area. "Not quite as impressive as I might have—"

A loud grunt from his throat cut off his words. Lena, having just punched him in the gut, appeared right in front of him giggling like a schoolgirl. Then blew him a kiss.

"You *are* rusty, Nikolai."

"I'm taking it easy on you." He'd never sparred with an angel quite like her. "You do know I've signed an agreement to join your division?"

"Consider this your formal interview, or an audition."

"I've already been hired."

"We can forgo all this if you want to take an entry level position."

"Such as?"

Lena bent down, brushed some hair out of his face.

"Oh, something like a celestial janitor."

In a flash, Nick drove headlong into her midsection.

The two of them went flying across the terminal and passed through the windows, landing outside on the pavement of 42nd Street—beyond the scope of human perception. Nick had her pinned down, a mix of excitement and rage surging through him. His body began to give off a slight red glow, the glow of destructive energy he'd used in 1362 B.C. while protecting Akhenaten, a pharaoh under attack in Egypt for abolishing polytheism and enforcing the new state practice of monotheism. Good old Tut, his son, reversed all that in the end anyway.

How sharper than a serpent's tooth.

Still pinned beneath him, Lena flashed a sultry smile.

"Oh, you like it rough, hmmm?"

The next thing Nick knew, she was on top of him, now glowing red herself. For a moment, he didn't care what might happen if their destructive energies collided. He wanted to conquer, to defeat her utterly. Back in the day he had commanded thunder and lightning, brought down mountains upon legions of Hittites with destructive power that was, of course, reserved for inter-realm warfare. But now, the drive to see Lena destroyed was all but uncontrollable.

Fingers flashing with red lightning tendrils, he thrust them straight at her throat—

She grabbed his wrist with astonishing speed.

But what happened next was far more astonishing.

Lena *absorbed* his destructive energy: it discharged from him so rapidly and with such force he thought he might implode. Containing both of their destructive energies, her entire body glowed, changing from red to hot white, its light expanding.

From the glowing orb that encompassed them both, a beam blasted into the sky, piercing the clouds. A spiral fissure expanded.

Though the two of them remained outside the physical layers, the flash in the heavens and the ground-shaking explosion caused just about every human walking on the sidewalk or crossing the street to stop and look up.

From the center of the clouds, the fissure blew outward like a drop of oil dispersing in water. Crackling lightning encircled what resembled a nuclear mushroom cloud just above the planet's atmosphere.

Screams of horror, gasps of bewilderment, fresh New York expletives. But just as quickly as it had happened, it all vanished.

"What did you just do?" Nick felt drained and more than a little frightened. "I...I've never seen anything like it."

Breathing heavily, Lena, swung her face back down to him, allowing that glossy raven hair to fall into his face.

"Was it good for you, Nick?"

"How did you do that?"

She got up and pulled him to his feet.

"It's a simple matter of focusing the destructive energy coming at you and channeling it through the spiritual layers of existence. Goes a lot further and faster that way."

"But the mortals saw it."

"Only after I released it in space. Oh, it might have disrupted a satellite or two, but nothing too serious."

"You'll have to teach me that one day."

"Now that you've seen it and I've explained it, you'll probably figure it out for yourself—if you're as good as they say you are."

"As who says?"

"Your files."

How far back had she dug into his career? Shouldn't his most recent demotion have overshadowed any good he'd done in the past?

"I suppose you already know about—"

"Enough about the past." Lena snaked her arm around his. "Let's get on with it. Ready for your briefing?"

"Your construct or mine?"

She turned to face him with the lethal beauty of her smile.

9

"INTERESTING CONSTRUCT," NICK SAID, standing with Lena at the ledge of a skyscraper looking down on the city below.

"It's not a construct," Lena whispered in his ear.

As he gazed down on the people and cars and buses scurrying about, he felt a pounding in his chest, a clenching of his stomach—and cold moisture on his forehead. *Sweat.* That had never had happened before.

"You're not afraid, are you? Who ever heard of an acrophobic angel? After all..." Lena touched his back. A pair of glistening wings unfurled behind him. He was so used to hiding this part of his physiology they almost shocked him.

With her fingertips, she brushed the edge of his wings and they vanished behind his construct again.

"I was starting to think you truly *had* been among the humans too long."

"No more than your typical angel." Nick swallowed—another human mannerism he'd picked up. How much did she know about his past? He thought he'd done a fairly decent job of remaining incognito in the last human century.

"Just an expression, Nick. You're talking a lot like them, is all. Ready now?"

"Of course." And he was—as long as he didn't look down.

In an instant he found himself standing in an office inside the skyscraper with her. The office, judging by the layers of dust on the desk, had been unoccupied for months—perhaps years.

How much time had elapsed, just now? The sun no longer shone outside. Instead, moonlight infused the room with pallid light, enough of it on the desk to reveal dust undisturbed by Lena, who was sitting on it.

"Thought you enjoyed dramatic constructs," she said.

"So long as they're my own."

"What's with the nerves? I mean, you're an angel, for heaven's sakes." Lena covered her smile. "I've never seen anything like it."

"It's...nothing."

But it wasn't. He'd never before perspired, never felt anxiety like that. Perhaps he *had* spent too much time with them.

"Are you done playing?" he said.

"Oh, all right." She pointed to the wall, where a large whiteboard lit up like a hi-def TV set. The images of three people appeared onscreen.

One was a man in a navy blue suit with slick black hair, a red power necktie, and a smile so white it could blind you. The images were silent, as though someone had pushed a mute button, but the man was standing before a large auditorium, talking and gesturing and holding what appeared to be a Bible.

"Oh, great, a preacher," Nick said. "You'd think more of them would believe in our existence."

"You'd think."

The second was a disheveled young woman wearing stained, ragged clothes who sat in a chair rocking back and forth in what appeared to be a homeless shelter. Her chair wasn't a rocker, so her jerky movements in it seemed strange. Hard to tell what color her hair might have been if it were clean. She stared vacuously out the window, hugging her arms as she rocked, lips moving though nobody was there to listen to her. Looking at her, Nick felt a twinge he didn't understand.

"What exactly am I supposed to—"

"Hold on, we'll get to that." Lena pointed to the third frame. A young man with dark hair, a coppery complexion, and perhaps the most troubled eyes Nick had ever seen in a mortal paced back and forth in a dark warehouse, shouting into his cell phone. Every now and then he pounded a wall with his fist as if punctuating a sentence.

"Your assignment is simple," Lena said in an official tone. "These three are extremely dangerous. Each will have a hand at misguiding many thousands of people and in the process altering the future in disastrous ways. You will simply hasten them to the self-destructive ends they have chosen before they cause incalculable harm. "

"Truly?" He looked them over, all three. "Except for the angry young man, the others seem harmless."

"Looks are deceiving, you can never tell. Your assignment comes from this department's top office. If you reach your targets on this one, you'll get the promotion you've always wanted."

"All right. Give me the specifics."

Lena reached into her pocket and produced a shiny black smartphone. It looked like an iPhone but had no distinguishing markings.

"I've uploaded all the information you need here. Just tap the icon for any of your three subjects to open an entire portfolio. If you need anything—anything at all—call or text me. I'm on speed dial."

"Wait. Call? Text?"

"Get with the times, Nikolai."

"I won't need this."

"You have exactly two weeks to complete your task. We must prevent an event from occurring at Cabrillo Stadium in San Diego, California, an event that could mean a significant loss to our cause. Two of your assignments are preemptive in nature. But the most crucial element is to stop this event at all costs. Two weeks, Nick. Fourteen days."

"That's not a lot of time."

"Which is why you begin immediately." Her eyes brightened. "Oh, and by the way. How many other angels in your division—sorry, your *former* division—feel the same way you do?"

"About?"

"Unhappy about their work."

"I don't see how that matters."

"It does to me. Do you know?"

"Look, I still have questions about my assignment. Let's stay focused."

Lena sighed. "So you're not going to tell me about the other reapers."

"I don't know what they're thinking. And truth be told, I don't care."

The intensity in her gaze softened. Like a cat, she leaned against his shoulder and ran her fingers down his arm. Nick stood there and let her do her thing. She was an odd one, to say the least. He didn't know what to make of her.

"I've had my eye on you for some time now, Nick. You're special, that's why we called on you to join our division."

"You didn't call me, I came and applied."

"That's what everyone thinks, at first."

"It was my decision. No one influenced me."

"Come on, Nick. Are you going to tell me about the reapers?"

"I told you already, I don't know."

"And what about Tamara? She'd know, wouldn't she?"

"Are you looking to recruit her?"

Lena only smiled.

Nick returned the smile. "And here I was thinking I was special."

"Oh, but you are."

She touched his face, and he reacted—he wasn't quite sure exactly how, but it disturbed him. If nothing else it reminded him of the emotions mortals could feel.

"Nick, if I were to send you back, just to bring me some information..."

"Is this a requirement?"

Her shoulders slumped a bit. She moved away and leaned against the window.

"No, it's not. It's just that...well, you're not the only one looking for a change. If you could help me with the information I need, I might be able to impress my supervisor enough for him to promote me."

"Can't you send a simple request via interoffice?"

"It's never that simple," she said, her voice a dejected whisper. Something about her drew his sympathy. But nothing shy of showing himself to Tamara would get Lena what she wanted. All the information was in Tamara's office—her mind. Going back was not an option.

Not so soon, anyway.

Nick spoke softly into Lena's hair, which smelled like roses.

"Why don't we see how this assignment goes? Then we'll talk about all this other business."

Lena nodded. "Of course. Forgive me...I'm embarrassed."

"Don't be."

"Desperation can make you do strange things."

"Why is it so important?"

She shrugged and smiled, covering what he was sure was discouragement and a touch of annoyance.

"You'd best be off, Nick. You've got deadlines."

"About that. You know, I still don't—"

But she vanished before he could finish the sentence.

10

GETTING TO HIS FIRST ASSIGNMENT would have been instantaneous had Nick simply concentrated on the image of the subject's face and teleported to Long Beach. But he'd developed a certain taste for flying—not the way humans did, crammed in the bowels of an aircraft like sardines in a tin—but by himself through the sky with the wind in his hair, clouds misting his face, and flocks of startled birds exploding in every direction as he flew invisibly through their squadron at speeds only theoretical to humans.

A trip from New York to Los Angeles took him six exhilarating minutes. He arrived just outside the Aquarium of the Pacific, where the midday sun called for T-shirts, shorts, and sunglasses. Not that anyone could see Nick, but he had them on too. He always blended in well just in case he had to interact with the humans.

A cool breeze blew gently against his neck, and for some reason the sensation seemed more tangible than usual. He rather enjoyed it. Taking in the warmth, the breeze, and the people—mothers and fathers with their children going into the aquarium and coming out—he further surprised himself by smiling. A refreshing change from the business of death, untimely or otherwise.

His smartphone chimed.

A text from Lena.

> SUBJECT: Jonathan Hartwell, Long Beach, CA
> ASSIGNMENT: Research routines, family, lifestyle. Prevent subject from his daily studies and routines over the next two weeks.

Embedded in the text message was a photo of Hartwell, a good-looking bloke in his late thirties, dark brown hair, deep-set blue eyes, and the kind of smile that would make people want to talk with him about anything and everything over a cup of coffee. He looked as friendly and trustworthy as they came.

But Nick knew better.

He'd read the dossier.

The subject was a man of dangerous influence. Wildly popular in the media, invited often to the White House to open important meetings with prayer, a bestselling writer, popular talk-show guest. Unlike many a famous preacher before him, he was viewed by most Americans, believers or not, as a genuinely good person. But he would ultimately lead thousands astray, altering their future directly and even more indirectly.

Just then, a loud shriek pierced the air nearly causing Nick to drop his phone and become visible. Since his time in London at the beginning of the last century he'd been experiencing some difficulty on the invisible-to-mortals front. A sudden shock or stress could make him slip.

The shriek had been replaced by unbridled laughter. A little boy about five or six years old hung by his feet in the air, his father swinging him around upside down.

"Faster, Daddy! Faster!"

And the man swinging his son over the concrete? It was none other than Nick's subject: Jonathan Hartwell.

His wife Elaine made a shushing gesture with one hand while pressing a shiny white phone to her ear.

"Honestly, Lisa, I wouldn't pay him another cent! If you keep giving them what they ask, by this time next year you'll be paying a hundred dollars a week just to have them mow your lawn. It's robbery, and you don't want to—"

Another shriek.

Elaine spun around. "Jon, would you please put Matthew down? Stop this foolishness now before you break his neck!"

Hartwell complied. Matthew whined.

"Aw, Mom!"

Elaine put the phone back to her ear. "Sorry, sweetie. Call you back? Love you, bye!"

Hartwell and his son gave each other a furtive smile Elaine soon wiped off their faces.

"Did you ever think what people will say if the media gets footage of you making a fool of yourself in public?"

"Come on, hon," Hartwell said. "I get one day off to spend with my son, and—"

"You happen to be a celebrity. So what you do in public reflects on me, too." She grabbed Matthew's hand and dragged him off, leaving Jonathan by himself at the aquarium's exit.

It occurred to Nick that Elaine could easily do this job for him.

11

IT WAS THE UTTER CALM THAT STARTLED YURI back to consciousness. Just how many hours he'd been out, he couldn't tell—the face of his digital watch was smashed. The throbbing pain in the back of his head made him wonder if his skull had been too. He touched it, then looked at his fingers in the sunlight.

No blood.

And sunshine—the storm had passed.

He stood there for a long moment, feeling the knot that ran from the base of his head and into his left shoulder blade. A dagger of pain impaled his neck at the slightest turn of his head.

He let out a childish yelp. Hopefully Jonas hadn't heard it, or Yuri would never hear the end of it until they arrived in Ensenada.

How long until then?

All around, the stench of dead fish engulfed him to the point of nausea. He couldn't—

He saw the crate. Broken open and its contents missing.

The package.

Gone!

Despite the tense muscles that felt more like steel rods in his neck and spine, Yuri whirled around, his feet splashing in ankle-high water. Where was that suitcase? Could Jonas have broken into the crate and taken it? It made no sense for him to do that, but they were out at sea and he was the only other person on board.

The boat leaned slightly to starboard and creaked. He almost called out but instantly thought better of it. If Jonas had gotten greedy and decided to confiscate the package...

Yuri reached around his back for his gun.

It too was gone.

At least he still had a small knife strapped to his ankle, though he hoped not to use it. Knives were so much messier than guns.

He swore under his breath. Yuri's contact in Osaka had assured him Jonas was reliable, minded his own business relaying passengers discreetly across international waters. With no way of getting to dry land without him, Yuri was for the time being literally at Jonas's mercy. He'd have to be clever, gain a physical advantage, and compel Jonas to stick with the original terms of their arrangement. Then, when Yuri and the package safely arrived, he'd teach that slimy mercenary a lesson.

Pulling himself up, Yuri listened carefully for any sign above.

Nothing but the lapping of waves against the bow and the doleful lament of seagulls. Their dirge grew louder as he gripped the cold metal handrails and struggled to keep his footing on the steps that brought him up onto the deck.

It took a while for his eyes to adjust in the brightness, even though his back was turned to the warm sun. Careful not to make any sudden moves, he turned around and scanned the deck, slick with water.

"Jonas?"

No answer. No sign of the man needed to pilot the boat to shore. Yuri's stomach clenched at the thought of being stranded at sea—or, worse, being murdered, fed to the sharks so Jonas could sell the package's contents to the highest bidder.

He took a cautious step forward.

Something hard and round bumped against his toes. Glancing down, he noticed some uncoiled rope spread haphazardly across the deck. It seemed to thin out into a taut line right past where it bent around a leg of the chrome rail. Following it, Yuri saw that it went over the deck and down into the water.

He didn't know the first thing about boats, but it almost looked like Jonas had tied an anchor to the rope and cast it overboard. Yuri approached the edge of the deck, following the rope.

Then he saw it.

At the end of the rope, Jonas's pale corpse dangled, eyes wide with surprise, mouth agape, blue tongue hanging out. The rope was wrapped around his neck—which, judging by its perverse angle, was broken. During the storm, he'd somehow gotten tangled in the line and thrown overboard.

No longer concerned he might be heard, Yuri began to hyperventilate. He was not one to mourn the death of such a man as Jonas. But he had no idea how to pilot a boat. And in the vast ocean around it, not a trace of land could be seen.

12

THEY'D BEEN AT IT FOR HOURS, and Nick was sick of it.

Talking, muttering, whining, Elaine's voice rising in pitch, volume, and intensity, then Jon's voice catching up, eventually booming over hers. If they only understood just how short mortal life was, how little time they really had to get it right, they might think twice about arguing over money, control, sex, and other such minutiae.

The door to their bedroom slammed shut, but the shouting seemed every bit as loud as when it had been open. When Matthew scooped up Riley, their golden retriever puppy, and ran down to the foot of the white-carpeted stairs, Nick wondered why it had taken him so long.

He went over and sat next to Matthew, who sighed like an old man as he stroked the dog's ears.

No child should have a sigh like that.

Nick wanted to step in and chide Matthew's parents—*An innocent child's future is being irrevocably cast in a mold of your wrath and self-centredness!*

Stupid mortals.

But what could he do? He couldn't reveal himself—the interaction might complicate his assignment. The yelling continued. Now they were accusing each other of just about everything under the sun.

He looked upstairs and glowered at the shut door that did nothing to shield Matthew from the hatred spewing forth and bleeding into his spirit. He had to get him outside for some fresh toxin-free air.

Nick leaned over and whispered to Riley, "Want to go for a walk?"

Riley looked right at him, opened her mouth for a big puppy smile, and leapt down from Matthew's lap. Her tail swiped left-right, left-right, left-right. She looked up at both of them and barked.

"What is it, girl?" Matthew said.

Riley ran to the front door. Barked twice, then ran back and barked once.

Matthew pointed to the door. "You want to go out?"

The ongoing combat in his parents' room paused for a moment, and Matthew looked up.

Nick called out to Riley. "Out? Out?"

Riley started yapping incessantly. The yelling upstairs resumed. Matthew barely had the door open before Riley dashed out.

"Hey, wait up!" Matthew started out the door.

Just then, the door at the top of the stairs swung open.

"AND WHAT ABOUT MATTHEW!" Elaine screamed. "DO YOU THINK *HE* CAN RESPECT A MAN LIKE YOU?"

Matthew froze.

"Oh, for pity's sake," Nick muttered.

If only he could cover Matthew's ears. His blue eyes were about to fill up, and the doorknob rattled in his hand.

But Riley's barking outside alerted Matthew. He turned around to look.

"Riley, no!"

He bolted out the door, which shut before Nick could see what was happening.

Something felt wrong.

Nick rushed out and saw it all.

Barking excitedly at a white toy poodle across the two-way street, Riley ran between the parked cars and out into the oncoming traffic. Matthew ran after her.

"Stop, Riley! Come back!"

Knowing what was about to happen, Nick flew out after him.

Two cars coming from both directions came down the street. Matthew, focused on his puppy, didn't see them.

13

JUST AS NICK REACHED HIM, Matthew saw the car coming from the left and blasting its horn at him. With a terrified shriek he dove forward and out of the way.

He landed face down on the pavement in the opposite lane.

When she heard Matthew scream, Riley stopped barking and ran over to him.

But the car from the right was coming. Both the boy and dog were in the middle of the street. With the first car in the left lane and the curb blocked by parked cars, it had nowhere to swerve.

Ignoring all angel dictates and canon, Nick grabbed Matthew by the waist of his pants and yanked him over to the narrow yellow painted space between the two lanes.

The second car sped by, blaring its horn. To Nick's disgust, it didn't stop.

He set Matthew down.

He looked up at Nick—scared to death, and not just by the near accident. Matthew could see him!

Nick looked over to the first car, but the driver who'd seen Nick appear—out of thin air from her point of view—rolled up her window and sped off, not bothering to see if the little boy she'd almost killed was all right. *That's humans for you.*

Nick knelt down and touched Matthew's shoulder.

"You all right, little man?"

"I...I..." Then he turned around and looked into the lane Nick had just pulled him from. His face crumpled. "Riley!"

There she was, lying still about fifteen feet down the street. As if he'd forgotten everything that just happened, Matthew rushed to his puppy, calling her name. Nick went with him, watching for more oncoming traffic.

Matthew fell to his knees, crying. Riley had been hit and was gasping her final breaths—something Nick was all too familiar with. Matthew looked at his puppy, his face all tears and dirt and heart-wrenching despair.

"I'm sorry, Riley! This is all my fault!"

"It's not, Matthew. Not your—"

"I let her out without me. Oh, Riley...Riley, please don't die!" He turned back to Nick. "I messed up—I always mess up! That's why Mommy and Daddy don't want me."

"That's not true!" Nick made up his mind. The laws about unassigned healings couldn't be so inane as to apply to animals. And if they did, he didn't care.

He knelt down and placed his hands around Riley's head. His entire body tingled with a pulsating light that started from his heart and radiated to his fingertips, which glowed as he pressed them gently against the puppy's furry brow.

He shut his eyes.

Connected with Riley's soul.

It surprised him, how deep was the love a puppy felt for her master, how intense the memories. But there they were, strong as any human's if not stronger. He had to take care not to send too much light into so young a puppy.

A tear slid down Nick's cheek.

Joy and sadness.

"Get up, Riley," he whispered. The light left him. The puppy's breathing returned to normal, and she lifted her head.

"Riley?" Matthew's face was alight with joy and wonder. "Riley!"

She rolled to her feet and let out a happy bark. Tail wagging furiously, she leapt into Matthew's arms and proceeded to bathe his face with puppy kisses. Matthew finally managed to lower her enough to look up at Nick.

"Wow, mister! That was awesome!"

"Be careful crossing the street, okay?"

"Thanks for fixing up Riley. She's good as new." He smiled big and offered Nick an outstretched hand.

He'd already revealed himself, might as well. Nick shook his hand. "Don't mention it..." Just then, the Hartwell's front door opened. "*Really*, don't mention it."

"Matthew?" Elaine Hartwell called from across the street.

"Over here, Mom."

She started for the street. "What are you doing there? And who is that man?"

Nick straightened up. He'd have to remain visible now that they'd seen him too.

"It's all right, Mrs. Hartwell, I was just helping Matt—"

She reached them and took Matthew by the arm.   "I'm sorry, do I know you?"

"I don't think so."

"Then how do you know us? And what are you doing talking to my son?"

"Everyone knows you. From the television shows, the radio, your books—"

"What books? Nobody knows about that yet."

Oops.

"I mean your husband's books."

"He saved your son!" From a second-floor window an elderly woman pointed down to the street. "Your boy nearly got hit by a car. Twice! That nice man just came out of nowhere and pulled him out of the way and...Hey, your dog! I thought it got—"

"Thank you!" Nick called out. "But really, anybody would have done it. Have a nice day!"

Hartwell now joined them. While he and Elaine asked their son what had happened, Nick tried to slip away. But the preacher stopped him with a firm hand on his shoulder.

"Excuse me."

Nick sighed, then turned around to face him.

"Yes?"

"You're not from around here, are you?" Hartwell said. "England, Australia? Sorry, I always mix up the accents."

"It's you Americans who've got the accent."

Hartwell smiled. "I guess. Hey, Matthew just told me what you did."

"I assure you he's exaggerating."

He took Nick's hand and instead of shaking it held it firmly for a moment.

"I can't thank you enough. What you did for my son..."

And the dog? "Nothing any decent person wouldn't do."

"I don't know what we were thinking, how we let this happen. But thank you." A wet sniff. "I wish there was something we could do."

Nick took back his hand. "Keep an eye on him."

Hartwell laughed. "I'll do that. Hey, why don't you come on over? I'll fire up the grill and we'll have some burgers. I'd love to get to know the man who saved my son's life."

"Thank you, but—"

"I insist."

Matthew stepped away from his mother and walked up to them. "Please?"

Between Riley's and Matthew's puppy dog eyes, all was lost.

14

MARIA HAD DRIVEN ALMOST AN HOUR and a half from Chula Vista to San Clemente, where she was stuck in a log jam at the checkpoint on the I-5 north. For most of the drive she'd heard Alfonso's scream behind the door just before the gunshot that ended his life.

Lito hadn't pulled the trigger, but he might as well have.

If you kissed up to him, he'd throw thousands of dollars at you or take care of a problem for you. But watch out if you crossed him, lied to him, or broke his rules. Who did he think he was, God?

She'd probably benefit from seeing Dr. Kramer, but right now she was too upset. Her therapist would try to help her get perspective on what had happened, do the right thing, not let her emotions rule. Well, she was in no mood to do what was right, and she could no more control her emotions than she could stop the tide.

Gray clouds obscured the ordinarily bright sky that made the waves off the coast sparkle like diamonds. Like the diamonds on the ring Alfonso had given her last night at *Casa del Oro* in Old Town. Surrounded by a touristy Mariachi band, he got down on one knee and proposed. And of course she accepted, to a chorus of cheers and music and wine and...

Maria put her car in park and wiped her eyes. She'd tried to stop Alfonso's screams in her head by listening to a sermon by Jonathan Hartwell, whose event at Cabrillo Stadium she planned on attending—her first time hearing him speak live in San Diego. It hadn't worked. Today nothing could lift her from the turmoil into which Lito's pig-headed arrogance had cast her.

The ring on her finger, a symbol of Alfonso's devotion, now served only as a painful reminder of her brother's cruelty. She slammed the steering wheel over and over.

"Damn you, Lito! Damn you to hell!" All her life he'd been over-bearing, overprotective, with his overinflated sense of honor. According to him, he'd done everything "*for your own good, hermanita,*" but she knew damned well everything he did was for one reason.

Power.

He'd killed Alfonso just to assert his power. To demonstrate that no one better cross Lito Guzman or mess with his property. And that's all she was to him, right? Property. She might as well have been his dog, for all he cared. Maria had enough of Lito's control. Enough of his power trips, pathetic overcompensation for his short stature.

You're not the only Guzman who can get things done.

She reached inside the center console and grasped it: cold, hard, deadly. The feel of the gun sent a tingling chill from her fingertips straight to her scalp.

But a stolen weapon was not enough to get her the justice she need-ed. For that she'd decided to go to her cousin Joey Hernandez. He could help.

She took the gun out, caressed the barrel, felt the tension in the trigger. God should not mind one bit if she rid the planet of such a wicked man, even if he was her brother. And would Papi turn in his grave? Ha! Maybe he'd thank her.

Carefully, she laid the gun on the passenger seat. A white flash lit the pewter sky followed almost immediately by a thunderclap. Then a heavy downpour of rain, so heavy she didn't hear the CHP officer rapping on her window.

"Ma'am?"

She threw some papers over the gun, then opened the window.

"Is there a problem, officer?"

"You're parked."

Maria glanced over at the passenger seat. The papers only half concealed the gun.

"Parked?"

"You're holding up traffic, ma'am."

Glancing into her rearview, she noticed what had been there the last time she looked—an endless line of cars, their windshield wipers now whipping aside the rain.

Back to the officer: "But we've been this way for—"

"Ma'am, please?" While he looked in front of her car, pointing, Maria grabbed a sweater from the back seat and threw it on top of the gun and papers. Then she looked.

"Oh."

A wide open lane was ahead of her.

Now she could hear the horns honking behind her, the drivers annoyed at her stopping for what had to have been a few minutes.

"I'm sorry, I must have dozed off." She quickly shifted into drive.

"You going to be all right?" the officer asked.

"Yes...I just received some bad news.   Wasn't paying attention, that's all." Her heart pounded so hard she could feel it in her ears. But he couldn't see the gun.

"Be careful.   Freeway's going to be slick." He tipped his hat and started walking back to the checkpoint.

As she drove off, she turned on Jonathan Hartwell again.

"*...and I say to you now...Your best days are just ahead, and closer than you think*"

15

IT MADE LITTLE SENSE NOW, but the first thing Yuri did after seeing Jonas's corpse was to try and pull it back on board—until the sickening vibration of the dead skipper's neck bones deterred him. He rushed back down to the hold, sloshed around in the water, and found a flashlight in a toolbox that floated by and banged into his shin.

He swept the entire compartment from edge to edge. The water, he found, was deeper on one end and shifted each time the boat shifted. The flashlight beam disclosed several dead fish floating by his ankles, their eyes and mouths open wide in an expression that made him think of Jonas, still hanging on the side of the boat. With a shudder, he shook the image from his mind and continued to search the hold.

The crate which held his precious cargo must have broken open during last night's storm. The only thing in it was packing materials and splinters, one of which caught under his thumbnail. Yuri cussed in Russian.

I'm sorry, Mommochka.

She hated it when he used "vulgar" language because she believed, deep down, that he was good. Not so his stepfather—Sascha had beaten him almost every day of his childhood. *You're worthless, useless, you'll never amount to anything.* Deep down, he'd always believed Sascha.

He'd made ten-year-old Yuri steal liquor from the corner store, then forced him to watch dirty videos with him, taught him to drink, smoke, deal drugs, and worse. By the time he was fourteen, he'd experienced more debauchery than most men would in a lifetime.

And Mommochka knew.

But she couldn't do anything about it. Sascha blackmailed her with an ongoing threat to Yuri's life should she ever tell anybody, try to stop him, or leave. And with all the beatings she took from him, Yuri had no doubt he would kill her, too.

Naturally, the first person Yuri ever killed without being paid was Sascha. But it was too little, too late. His mother was dying in the hospital from lung cancer, Yuri holding her hand till her last breath, when he whispered with tears in his voice, "You're free at last, Mommochka."

Damn, he was *crying.*

He hadn't thought of his mother for so long, and now was no time to start looking to the past. He had to find the package, find a way to get this ridiculous boat back to dry land. *God, if you help me get to Mexico safe I promise this will be the last—*

Something gently bumped the back of his ankle.

He whirled around with the flashlight.

Floating like a rectangular life preserver was the suitcase containing the components for the package he was delivering.

"Thank you!" he cried, then grabbed the suitcase.

There was hope after all. Someone might rescue him if he could get onto Jonas's radio. He hurried up the steps to search for it.

Having gotten past the border authorities of at least four countries and survived the deathly grip of the Pacific Ocean, Yuri now felt invincible. Not even Jonas had survived—the madman of the seas now hung like some gruesome ornament from his own boat. Yes, Yuri would get to his destination, complete his job, and become obscenely rich in just a few days.

Nothing could stand in his way now.

Except for the large white ship with a large red diagonal stripe and a thin blue one that now stood at the fishing boat's bow with the words U.S. Coast Guard emblazoned on its hull.

16

HOW COULD SUCH A NICE BLOKE as Jonathan Hartwell be so dangerous an influence? Nick found it hard to see this loving father as a future threat to millions of people.

He'd read Matthew a bedtime story and put him to bed a couple of hours ago. Now he sat in his plush leather executive chair staring at the screensaver. Photos of the wedding. Elaine, the world's most beautiful bride. Matthew, sitting in a stroller at two.

Hartwell was thinking now, and some angels could discern human thoughts. "Listening in" wasn't one of Nick's outstanding abilities, like that ridiculous power of healing he was forbidden to use. But he could do it. In fact, he was finding himself able to hear more clearly than ever. Which was convenient if he was to prevent Hartwell from his daily studies and routines over the next two weeks.

Hartwell sighed. He thought. Remaining invisible, Nick heard.

// SHE'S RIGHT. IF I'M EVER GOING TO GET TO THAT NEXT LEVEL I'VE GOT TO TAKE THINGS MORE SERIOUSLY. //

He reached for his notebook and Bible.

His shoulders relaxed a bit.

// CAN'T BELIEVE I'VE LET THINGS SLIDE FOR SO LONG //

He was about to commence his daily studies. Nothing so terrible about that—especially since his materials included the Good Book. But Nick's assignment was clear.

A smile lit up Jon's face as he zipped open the leather cover of his Bible and began leafing through the pages.

Nick flicked a finger.

Hartwell's computer sounded an email alert chime. Not that the computer actually chimed, it was just a small auditory construct.

About to read the first lines of the sixth chapter of the gospel according to Matthew, Jon looked up for a second at the screen. He deliberated for all of two seconds.

// NO...EMAILS CAN WAIT //

"Oh, come on." He didn't feel right about getting in Hartwell's way at the moment, but—

Nick's phone rang.

And at the same moment, so did Hartwell's. The young preacher let it ring a few times before Nick answered Lena's call.

"Nikolai, are we having any difficulty with the assignment?" He could just see the smirk on her face.

"Of course not. As a matter of fact, I just—"

"Hold on..."

Before he knew it, she was standing before him.

"I don't need any hand-holding, Lena."

Shushing him, she looked over at Hartwell, who was still on his cell phone. Tension furrowed his brow.

Nick turned to Lena. "What are you doing here?"

"Saving you and your cute little angel butt from blowing it."

"I just got started!"

"If he even begins to read his Bible tonight, it's going to make both our jobs *much* more difficult down the line. I'm not about to let my director chew me out for your mistakes."

"I'm not making any. In fact, I already—hold on...Listen."

Hartwell walked over to his shoes and slipped them on while he talked.

"You sure?...I suppose so.... Well, it can't wait if she's that desperate."

Nick and Lena looked at each other.

"Again, what are you doing here?" Nick said.

"I've already done it. Just watch."

Elaine came to the door, her arms folded.

"Who're you talking to? And why in the world are you whispering?"

"It's all right," Hartwell said into his phone, "I'll be there right away."

"Jon?"

"Ten minutes, see you there."

"Jon, who are you talking to?"

He hung up, put on his jacket, and walked to the door.

"That was Carla. There's an emergency at church."

Elaine blocked the doorway.

"You're going out *now*?"

"It's an emergency."

"Jon, if you don't start valuing your own time, your family time, your

followers will never respect it. Trust your wife on this. Set some boundaries."

"Excuse me."

He took her wrist and gently began to pull it away from the door
frame.

Elaine jerked it out of his grip and slapped it back down, again
blocking the way.

"No. I'm insisting you stay. You're going to thank me one day for
this tough love, baby."

"What do you want from me!" Now, for the first time, Nick saw
healthy indignation in Jon's eyes. Elaine's, on the other hand, were
shimmering. Crocodile tears, no doubt.

Jon stood there, waiting.

"I...I just want..."

"What!"

"I just want you to set some boundaries!"

He took hold of her wrist again. This time he lifted it off the door
frame and put her hand down at her side.

"I'm setting some now: You don't control me or my schedule."

And without looking back, he left.

17

TRANSPORTED OUT OF THE HARTWELL'S HOUSE, he stood on the front lawn with Lena, who was massaging the back of his neck. Her fingers caused a prickling sensation he'd not experienced for a while. The rain had stopped.

"Nice work, Nikolai."

"I'd still prefer it if you call me Nick."

"Hope you don't mind my help on your first assignment."

He shrugged. "I didn't need it."

"You're welcome, anyway."

Hartwell's Audi backed out of the garage and sped down the street, engine roaring as though fueled by the anger Elaine had ignited in him.

"Remember," Lena said, "all you have to do is keep him distracted. As you can see, the land mines of his life will take care of themselves."

"Well, that's...grim."

"This from a reaper?"

"Ex-reaper."

"Whatever. Now, your next assignment—"

"About that," he said.

Lena's penetrating gaze made him uneasy.

"You're not getting cold feet, are you?"

"Of course not."

"Good. Because this one is the most important of the three."

She snapped her fingers and a three-dimensional image that looked like a holographic projection appeared before them: that same disheveled woman, oily hair snaking around her grimy face, eyes shut tight, lips moving like a crazy person's—and he had enough experience to know what those were like.

"Something about this subject make you uncomfortable?"

"Not at all," Nick said. "I just..."

"Her name is—"

"Don't tell me."

Lena's eyes opened wider for a moment and a curious smile pulled at the corners of her mouth. She snapped her fingers and the image of the subject winked out of sight.

"Why?"

"I mean, knowing her name would only make it more difficult. You see, ushering someone to the Terminus is one thing, but *causing* a human's death?"

Lena smiled. "You've got such a tender heart."

"I've nothing of the sort."

"I just adore that about you," she said, gently taking his hand.

A tingling warmth ran through his hand, arm, chest. But rather than alarm him because it was so physical, the touch brought him comfort.

"Doesn't sit well with me is all," he said.

"You've got to remember a couple of things—things you can learn from human wisdom." She drew quotation marks around the word *wis-dom*. "First, looks can be deceiving. And second, you're an accessory to a crime if you don't seize the opportunity to stop it."

"She's just a poor homeless woman."

"Nick, you're not causing her death, okay? It's suicide—her *own* doing. You're just keeping her on track."

"How?"

"By reminding her of what she feels about herself, her life. Look, she's already condemned herself. It's that simple. But if she talks herself out of it, if she lives, she'll destroy the future of innumerable souls by misguiding them." She stepped close and looked into his eyes, her red lips parted enough for him to see her pearly teeth, the tip of her tongue dancing as she spoke. "You don't want that on your record, do you?"

"I guess not."

"Come on, Nikolai. It's just like ushering them to the Terminus, only a little earlier."

For a brief moment his knees threatened to give out. His thoughts and feelings blurred, had no clarity. Lena's voice, her eyes, her lips— they weakened him.

Like a wound.

Lena blinked. "A wound?"

"Did I say that out loud?"

She gave him a queer look.

"I only meant...well, allowing a dangerous person like this unnamed subject to go unchecked would be like allowing a wound to fester."

"That really how you see it?"

"Is there any other way?"

"Good." Much to his surprise, she pulled his head down to her and brushed her lips against his ear as she whispered. "Then you're ready."

"As I'll ever be."

"Off you go, then." With a gentle nudge, she prodded him to the sidewalk. There she opened a portal mid-air and Nick, dazed, stepped inside without looking back.

Without noticing the wisps of the dark vapor that followed him in.

18

LENA BREATHED A SIGH OF RELIEF as Nick left. The assignments seemed simple enough, but why did Morloch consider them prerequisites for consideration of her proposal? Did he really believe two humans at one stadium event could create so much damage to the cause?

It didn't matter. Nick was more than capable of carrying out these orders, he just needed a bit of nudging and direction.

She turned to the house to find Elaine standing at the open window of her bedroom, gazing down at the street on which her husband had just driven away. She wore the expression of one who's been devalued, maimed by cruel words and insensitivity. Feelings that resounded in that catacomb of memories Lena tried to keep sealed but could not help allowing to reopen on occasion like the old wounds they were.

"You have to hang on—I'm going to get help."

"Be...strong, Punkin'..."

No! This is nothing like that.

A sob from the window brought Lena back to Elaine, her face laced with regret, sadness, guilt. This broken and contrite spirit within her could prove troublesome—better do something about it. Whispering to her soul, Lena projected the thoughts:

// WHO DOES HE THINK HE IS, JUST TOSSING YOU ASIDE LIKE
THAT?//

A sudden alertness lit Elaine's eyes. The sadness in her face yielded first to a neutral look, then a growing suspicion.

// IS HE REALLY GOING WHERE HE SAYS HE IS? //

It was working. Jealousy and suspicion were the silver bullets for this human. One last thought should do it.

// STOP KIDDING YOURSELF. IT'S ANOTHER WOMAN AND
YOU KNOW IT. //

Elaine grabbed the window and slammed it shut so hard it woke the neighbors' dogs into a chorus of barking.

Lena smiled. With Elaine duly directed, it wouldn't take much for Jonathan to fall into the final steps. Nick's success was all but ensured.

19

THE HALLWAY LIGHTS WERE DIMMED and the janitors were starting in the offices at True North, Jon's church. Seven thousand attended every Sunday, millions watched on television.

Carla looked up as he stepped into the reception area. Her eyes drooped from fatigue under the graying hair that made her look much older than her fifty-two years. She nodded at the door to the right of his office.

"In the conference room."

"What's going on now?"

"She's distraught. Says you're her only hope." Carla shrugged. "Not sure how serious she was about killing herself, she said it like she was joking. But she's real upset."

It had been a while since anyone had expressed any need for pastoral counsel, especially since the television broadcasts had begun. He'd gotten so used to having his staff handle things that it was gratifying to make this exception and see someone himself for a change. It was good to feel needed again, in a way so-called celebrities aren't.

"I'll need you in there with me—mind staying a bit longer?"

"I'm already late to feed Charlie." Carla's cat, her only companion, was notorious for exacting revenge if he had to wait too long for his supper.

"Please. For propriety's sake, Carla."

She sighed. Heavily.

"All right."

"Thanks, Carla. Let's see what's going on with her."

He pushed open the walnut door to find a woman seated with her back to them at the long table, her glossy black hair falling around her shoulders. Carla went to the mini-refrigerator and got bottles of water for them.

"Pastor Hartwell, this is Maria Guzman."

An unreasonably beautiful young woman stood up and turned to face him.

"I'm so sorry to bother you this late—it was raining, I couldn't find my hotel, I just happened to pass by your church and the lights were on...I'm sorry."

"Not a problem." He took her warm hand and shook it. "Please, have a seat."

Though she smiled, her eyes were full of something bitter, something dark that lay just beneath the surface. They sat opposite each other, Maria's hands in her lap.

"So how can I help, Ms. Guzman?"

"Maria, please." She glanced over at Carla, who was sitting at the far end of the table. "I don't mean to be rude, but what I have to tell you is...well, it's personal."

"I understand. But it's really for your own security that she's here."

"What are you going to do, jump my bones?"

Jon let out a nervous laugh.

"Of course not!"

"I'm sorry, that was really crude. I'm just *such* a mess right now!"

"Don't apologize, it's all right. But back to the issue at hand? You can say anything with Carla in the room—trust me, she's the soul of discretion."

That she was, but when he turned to her for affirmation she stood up.

"Actually, it's getting late for me, and Pastor Hartwell is the soul of integrity." She started walking to the door.

"Wait, Carla—"

"And I have a cat who'll pee all over my bed again if I'm any later for his supper."

That elicited a giggle from Maria.

"So I'll just say goodnight to both of you."

And with that, she was out the door.

20

ONLY A FEW SECONDS TO DO THIS.

Even with the scant traffic at this ungodly hour, someone might drive by and report her to the police. Near the edge of the Coronado Bridge, she peered down into the inky water below. Hardly a ripple or wave. How long would she feel the pain of impact? How long would she live feeling the terror of drowning while fighting the instinct to swim, to survive? How cold was the water?

Probably very cold.

Dark and cold. That was exactly how she envisioned her death, for such had been her life. Nothing would stop her now. She'd mentally rehearsed it for months. Twice in the past week she'd come close, then changed her mind. But she'd managed to get this far tonight.

No turning back.

She had to do it—now.

Just then, a seagull flew over her head and let out a plaintive cry. It drew her eyes upward to a blue rectangular sign with white lettering that read:

**SUICIDE COUNSELING
CRISIS TEAM 24 HOURS
1-800-479-3339**

Too late.

Part of her wished someone would stop their car, get out, try to talk her down. Not that she'd change her mind, she only wanted someone to know that she'd taken her own life—and why. But that would really be inconsiderate of her, subjecting a good Samaritan to such a horrible memory.

It's time.

With twitching fingers, she gripped the edge of the wall and climbed up. The wind swept matted strands of hair into her tear-stained face. She sucked in a sharp breath through teeth chattering despite the evening warmth.

Just one step forward...

Nick stood back from the ledge watching the subject, who looked utterly harmless to anyone but herself. With one foot outstretched over the sixty-meter drop, she asked the cosmic question.

"Why, God?"

Nick tried not to listen.

He hated watching this. He'd ushered the souls of many a suicide victim to the Terminus but always tried to avoid the scene just before they killed themselves. With this assignment however, he was forced not only to attend a suicide but to facilitate it.

She's just one human. If she goes ahead and jumps, it's for the greater good of millions.

Nick got up on the ledge and stood behind her—floated, actually.

The woman sobbed softly and pulled her foot back.

Was she reconsidering? This assignment was supposed to be easy. Now he had to listen in to know what she was thinking.

// I HAVE TO DO THIS. NOTHING ELSE WILL STOP THE PAIN...//

"That's right," he whispered into her ear. "The pain. There's no other way to end it."

She nodded, sniffed, wiped her nose with her sleeve. Then she looked up into the sky.

"I'm sorry. I'm so, so sorry." She stuck her foot back over the ledge.

"Make it right, then," Nick whispered. "Go ahead and jump. Maybe that'll help make up for what you've done. You'll—"

"*What?*" She pulled her foot back and started crying. "It wasn't my..." The rest of her words were muffled by sobs.

What kind of inane assignment was this, anyway? Nick listened in.

// NOTHING'S GOING TO BRING HER BACK. I'M SORRY, GOD. I KNOW YOU DON'T APPROVE OF THIS, BUT I CAN'T GO ON. //

"Go ahead and do it. It's what you want, what you need," Nick whispered, feeling increasingly uneasy about it all. "You'll finally find...peace."

"Peace, yes." She leaned forward, trembling as she started tipping over the edge.

A sudden chill wrapped around him, went through him. Not a

physical sensation, as he was not in a physical state. It had been years since he'd experienced it.

The dark vapor.

Memories flashed through his mind—questionable choices, unauthorized interventions, Sophia, Victoria Station, *Clara*…

In his dazed state Nick had taken his attention off the subject—now ready to spring, her knees bent. He thought he heard Tamara's voice but couldn't be sure if it was really her:

"No matter what, Nikolai, you will always be loved…"

With a profound gasp, the subject cried out, "I'm sorry!"

Filled with anxiety and an odd sense of familiarity, Nick rushed out and floated directly in front of her.

"Wait!"

Astonished, she opened her eyes.

Those eyes.

Those emerald pools.

But before he could piece it all together, she leapt from the bridge.

21

THE BODY. THAT WAS YURI'S FIRST THOUGHT as he peered past the wall at the Coast Guard ship whose officers were eyeing Jonas's boat through binoculars. If they were to come around, they'd find his body hanging from the deck. That would only complicate things.

Making sure he was out of their sight, Yuri pulled the knife from the sheath strapped to his ankle and began to saw away at the thick rope. He wasn't making much progress and now he heard the roar of the Coast Guard ship's engine as it began to move.

Yuri let out a grunt and slashed at the rope even more feverishly.

The ship was coming to the front of Jonas's boat and about to turn to the side where his body hung. The rope sliding in his grip as he cut it stung Yuri's fingers. Just before the Coast Guard ship rounded the corner, the line broke.

A heavy splash below. Yuri shoved the knife overboard, rolled over on his back, and laughed. Just in time.

Five minutes later, a pair of Coast Guardsmen boarded. Yuri remained on his back as if barely conscious.

"Sir?" the male officer said, crouching down at Yuri's side. "Sir, are you all right?"

Yuri groaned, slowly reached for his neck and rubbed it.

"Hmmm?"

The female officer zipped open a bag, presumably containing first aid equipment.

"Looks dehydrated."

Yuri sat up and gazed into her face with his best desperate look.

"Thank God you came!"

"I'm Chief Petty Officer Renard," she said, then nodded to her partner. "This is Seaman Apprentice Grant. Sir, are you all right?"

"It was terrible. A huge storm—you would not believe how big! I hit head..." He rubbed the back of his skull where he'd gotten bumped. "My friend Jonas...he..." Yuri moaned as he touched his neck again. He didn't have to pretend, the pain was real.

"Jonas?" Renard said, looking around.

"He was up here during storm." Yuri stood up, very slowly.

"How long were you here?" Grant said.

"I don't know. Last I remember, ship was going to sink!" Yuri peered over his shoulder and hollered, "Jonas!"

"Have you checked below?" Renard pointed to the cargo hold.

Yuri's face went cold. "Of course."

"Mind if we look?"

Dammit!

"Is slippery and dark. Come with me." He led them down the steps, grabbed the flashlight on the counter and waved its beam around in a cursory scan.

"See? Not here." He started back to the steps.

"We need to have a thorough look," Renard said.

"I looked everywhere," Yuri said. "I think Jonas maybe fell overboard during storm!"

"I think he could be down here, injured." Grant pulled out his own flashlight. "Let's make sure."

Better create a diversion.

As the other two started off to search the hold, Yuri made a gurgling noise, started to convulse, then fell on the floor with a loud thud.

"He's having a seizure," Grant said.

Renard, who had walked off a little ways, rejoined them. "Yeah, I don't think so."

She was holding the suitcase and not buying Yuri's act.

"What's inside, Sir?"

The suitcase was quite heavy with the key component he'd fully assemble with other parts in the States. Yuri opened one eye and glanced at it with concern.

"I don't know."

"Where's your friend...Jonas?"

"I don't know. Like I said, maybe he fell overboard!"

Renard huffed and spun the suitcase's combination cam lock.

"Or maybe you're a murder suspect."

"That's crazy!" Yuri said.

"Save us all the time and trouble," Renard said. "Open the case."

22

"I HOPE THIS ISN'T AWKWARD FOR YOU." Maria hugged her arms and leaned back into the chair.

"Awkward?" Jon shook his head. "This isn't the first time I've been alone with a woman—I mean..." A burning heat washed over his face and ears. "*Now* I'm feeling awkward. That came out completely wrong."

"It's okay, I know what you meant."

He twisted the lid off the bottled water and took a sip.

"So what did you want to talk about?"

For a moment she seemed to search his eyes as though seeking any hint of insincerity, any sign that he might not be someone to whom she could entrust her secrets. Jon kept his smile in place as best he could. Better not look directly at her. His eyes swept the conference room from one end to the other. The inspirational posters that read FAITH, HOPE, and LOVE atop a scenic vista seemed to him, for the first time in his seven years here at True North, clichéd, over the top.

But Maria, it seemed, had pushed past her uncertainty.

"Before I start, I want to tell you—I've been listening to you speak for over a year now. Your messages always give me...hope."

Her brown eyes, tinted with a smoky shadow and framed by fine eyebrows, gave her a look that was smoldering and at the same time innocent. The thought made him uncomfortable.

"Thank you, Ms. Guzman. That means a lot."

"Maria, please."

He smiled. "Carla told me you seemed distressed, Maria. Are you all right?"

Her smile vanished, replaced by a look that could break a heart of stone in two.

"Honestly, no. I'm a wreck."

"Tell me about it."

She pulled a Kleenex from the box in the middle of the table and dabbed her eyes.

"I know the Bible says we have to forgive those that trespass against us. But there are some things you just can't forgive!" The bitterness in her eyes and voice disturbed him. And he could see that it was hurting her, cruelly, which disturbed him even more.

"Can you tell me what's happened?" he said softly.

"It's my brother." Maria drew a deep breath and let it out. "He murdered my fiancé."

In all his years of ministry, Jon had never come across such an issue. Infidelity, financial issues, personal conflicts, yes. But murder?

"Have you reported this to the police?"

She waved the idea off as if it were a gnat flying around her face.

"I can't do that. In my family, there can never be justice. Only revenge."

Jon leaned forward. "Are you in any danger, Maria?"

"No. At least, not yet."

"Not yet? What—"

"Mister—I mean Reverend—Hartwell...Oh, can I just call you Jonathan?"

"Jon is fine."

"Jon, is everything I tell you protected by that same thing with doctors and lawyers, what's it called?"

"Privilege."

"That's it."

"Of course. Strictly confidential. But if you're likely to be a danger to yourself or others—"

"No. I just...I'm such a mess right now. I just need to talk things out. Is that okay?"

Jon kept his face neutral. It wasn't easy. But as they talked he sensed more trust from Maria, found it unusually easy to connect with her. Perhaps it was Carla's absence. Or the mutual connection they seemed to share—he could disapprove all he liked, but he couldn't deny it. The way she looked up to him, so vulnerable, so in need of his help and grateful to receive it, so unlike Elaine who had to be in charge all the time.

"Maria, how are you feeling, right now?"

She looked down to her hands, folded and resting on the table. And shaking.

"I'm scared."

"Of?"

"Myself." She pushed a lock of hair from her face and hooked it behind her ear. "Lito is my big brother. He's powerful, controlling. But I never, ever thought he'd do something like this."

"I can't imagine what you're going through right now. It must be awful."

"He saw my one chance at happiness. My ticket out of the family business."

"What *is* your family business?"

"None of yours." She held a dead serious expression for a moment, then broke it with a smile. "I'm kidding. But still, it's better I don't tell you, though you can probably guess."

Jon nodded his understanding. How sad. And how could he possibly help her? To relieve his dry throat, he took another sip of water.

"Lito won't hurt me," Maria said. "That's not the problem. It's me."

"What exactly are you afraid of about yourself? Remember, it stays in this room."

Her expression reminded him of a little girl seeking approval if not unconditional acceptance for who she was, no matter how bad.

"My emotions," she said. "When my feelings are really strong I sometimes can't control myself. It's gotten me in trouble, but never anything too serious."

"Nothing violent, I hope."

"No, but…it's not always the bad feelings, Jon." She looked directly into his eyes. "Sometimes it's the good ones."

Ordinarily, Jon would have looked away from such intimate eye contact, no matter who initiated it.

But not this time.

"Tell me more."

"I'm so angry at Lito. And I'm afraid if I don't find a way to let go of this anger…" Now she looked embarrassed, ashamed. She lifted her handbag onto the table and unzipped the opening.

A gun. He suppressed a gasp

"Why, Maria?"

"Don't worry, I only brought it for protection."

"You sure? You *did* say revenge."

"I'm not planning on killing anyone." She zipped the bag shut and put it back on her lap. "But I'm afraid of what might happen if I don't get my thoughts and feelings under control. Sometimes I get all worked up—and then, who knows? Can you help?"

What he should do right now is to call the police and have them deal with her. But that would violate privilege. And if he was going to help, he needed to know more, needed more time with her.

"I can offer you some advice, read you some scripture, pray for you. But I think you need to get some good professional counseling. And seriously consider getting the authorities involved. If you ever want to get out of this life of...Well, you'll need protection, right?"

The trust in her eyes was unmistakable, the absurd plea that *he* save her from Lito, her family, herself.

"I don't know, Jon. Could you just...pray for me?"

"By all means." He bowed his head. But just before he began, he felt warm fingers wrap around his hands, which tingled with an electric thrill he could feel head to toe. Jon opened his eyes. His heart beat so hard he feared she might hear it. *He* could hear it. "I think...this is probably not the best idea, Ms. Guzman." He stood up.

"But Jon—"

"I'm sorry, I shouldn't have let this happen."

"Let *what* happen?"

He walked to the door and opened it. Poor Maria, she came looking for help from a man of God in the most desperate of circumstances, and what did he do? Commit adultery in his heart with her.

"I can't apologize enough. If you call back in the morning, I'll have Carla refer you to someone from our female pastoral staff."

"But I don't want them, I want you." At least she stood up, but the hurt in her expression was clear.

"I'm afraid I can't go any further. Please." He stood holding the door open, trying to ignore the subtle whispers in his mind.

You haven't done anything wrong....

You deserve to be treated well, respected, adored...

No one would have to know....

Maria took his hand in hers. "I didn't mean to offend you."

"You haven't. I just get, I don't know...nervous around beautiful women."

That seemed to ease the hurt a little. She looked down to the floor. "Guess I'll be going now."

Jon pulled out his business card and a pen and jotted down a number.

"This is my cell phone. If you're in any kind of danger..." He handed it to her and she slipped it into the back pocket of her jeans.

"What time is it?"

He glanced at his watch. "Getting late—half past eleven. Let me walk you to your car. It's dark out."

A single lamp lit the parking area like a jaundiced eye observing them as they reached Maria's car. She unlocked it, Jon held the door open for her.

"You're such a gentleman."

"Is that what it's called?"

She got in and put the key in the ignition. But from the sound of it, the battery was dead or close to it.

"Oh, no." Maria let out a frustrated sigh.

"May I?"

She stepped out and let him give it a try. Nothing but a weak clicking sound. He got out.

"I'm afraid it's dead."

"Must have left the lights on."

"I wish I had jumper cables." Jon looked at his watch. 11:40 PM. If he called a towing company, he'd have to wait here with her until they showed up. "Look, why don't I give you a ride, then in the morning I'll have someone bring you here and get your car started again." He handed her the key.

"You sure? I don't want to inconvenience you."

"Not at all."

She opened her trunk and pulled out a small suitcase on wheels. He pointed to his car on the other side of the lot.

"I'm parked over there."

Standing next to him, she peered over to the far side of the parking lot, dark except for the few overhead lamps. For a few seconds neither of them said a word. Jon could hear nothing but crickets chirping and Maria's breathing.

CRACK!

Maria let out a yelp and ran right into Jon's arms.

"Get down!" He pulled her to the ground.

What he thought had been the shooter was actually an ancient pickup truck rumbling, pumping country music through its speakers. Growing up in a tough Baltimore neighborhood in the eighties had trained Jon to react to anything that sounded like a gunshot. No doubt it was the same for Maria.

"Probably a backfire," he said.

"Really?" Maria's body, still pressed against his, was shaking uncontrollably. "Sounded like a gunshot to me."

Without thinking, Jon moved the hair out of her eyes, brushing her cheeks with his fingertips in the process. She looked up at him with gratitude—which she expressed by touching his face.

It took Jon a minute to recover his perspective. But in some ways it was too late.

She knew.

He knew.

"Let's get you back." They started for his car.

Maria leaned her head against his shoulder. Jon didn't object.

"Where are we going?" he said.

"The Hotel Pacifica."

23

THEY STOPPED AT A LOCAL DINER because Maria said she was "so hungry I could eat a cow." At that late hour, nobody was around but the waitress and a few patrons as they talked. And talked. Maria didn't mention her brother, Jon didn't mention his wife—they talked about things of no real consequence that interested them, which turned out to be the same things.

Finally Jon, now feeling completely at ease with this woman he was convinced could disarm anybody, looked at his watch: it was well past midnight. Maria insisted he call her a cab.

"I promised you a ride back," he said, "and I'll not be known as the pastor who didn't keep his word."

So he drove another fifteen minutes to the Hotel Pacifica.

Where, against all better judgment, he decided that chivalry required his accompanying Maria into the lobby rather than simply dropping her off. He wasn't doing anything wrong and didn't really care what anyone thought. Not the concierge who took the keys to his car, not the woman in the lobby who seemed to recognize him. The freedom from all the expectations and limitations he'd been under so long felt good.

He enjoyed the sound of Maria's stilettos rapping against the white marble floor of the lobby. He enjoyed the feel of her arm slipped around his as they turned into the dimly lit hallway where the elevators awaited. But all good things come to an end: he stopped, gently removed her arm from his, waited for her to go on into the elevator without him.

She turned to face him.

"I can't even begin to tell you how grateful I am. I...I just can't believe someone as famous as you would take the time to listen to a nobody like me."

"You're not a nobody, Maria." It was the right thing to say, but he'd lifted her chin—gently, tenderly—when he said it.

It had been years since he'd felt that current of physical and emotional attraction running through his entire being. Years since Elaine had looked up to him with admiration, adoration, desire. Yet he'd never once let his eyes or heart wander. *So stop feeling guilty over nothing.*

And then Maria's eyes met his. She shuddered, and of course ebony hair fell half over her face. She didn't lift a finger to push it aside, just kept her eyes on his as tears rolled down her cheek. How could anyone crying look so beautiful?

Nothing wrong...you've done nothing wrong.

Jon wiped the tears softly with his thumb. The elevator chimed. Time for Maria to go—

But Jon felt a strong tug on his hand pulling them both into the elevator. It didn't occur to him to question or protest.

Nothing wrong...

24

FOR THE ENTIRE RIDE UP TO THE SIXTH FLOOR Maria was determined to keep any thoughts from taking shape in her mind. Even one would lead her to what she was doing yet trying so hard to deny: leading a man of God into—

You're a sinner and going to hell anyway. Why not?

She tried to push that thought aside, though deep down it was exactly what she felt. So the feeling must be true.

It would take serious strength to act on those feelings that raged within—without regard for consequence, indulging in the forbidden just this one time. But it also took a delicate approach. Because this situation was as brittle as a sheet of ice so thin a butterfly could fall through it into the frigid depths.

The elevator slowed. Maria smiled. She and Jonathan had avoided looking at each other the whole way up.

Jonathan didn't see the hand she put on the rail right next to his—he was looking up at the lighted numbers. Before she could talk herself out of it, Maria slid her hand under his warm fingers.

The door slid open.

Maria knew what to do. Still holding Jon's hand, she led him down the dimly lit hallway toward her room.

"Maria, you know I—"

She turned, placed a finger on his lips.

"Shhhh." Stopping short, he'd nearly walked into her. Close enough to whisper. "Better if we don't talk."

He didn't reply, but his musky scent nearly drove her mad with desire. Was it because he was so kind, so gentle? Was it his strong chest and arms under the thin cotton t-shirt he wore beneath his jacket? Or was it because he was a man of influence to whom millions listened?

Yes.

With one tingling hand still resting against the pronounced ridges of his chest muscles, she reached into the back pocket of her jeans, pulled out the key card, and slid it into the slot.

The red light turned bright green.

A quiet beep welcomed them to her room.

25

THE ROOM IN WHICH YURI SAT contained nothing but a table and chair. Prior to arrival they'd cuffed him, put him on a helicopter with an armed guard, and flown him for about an hour to a military base in San Diego.

When—not if—they opened the suitcase and saw the contents of the package, it was all over. He'd be tried as some kind of enemy combatant, sent to Guantanamo Bay, tortured...

Ironically, he loved America. This was the land of free money to anyone who could get away with it. And "as far as he knew" the materials in the package were for scientific research, right? He never asked, just did the job.

Finally, the door creaked open.

In stepped a man in military uniform. His short-cropped hair was white, but he looked like he could take on a heavyweight champion.

"Yuri Kosolupov?" Yuri nodded. "Colonel Jack Braun. You're in it up to your eyebrows, boy."

"Me and my friend went on fishing trip, that's all. Coast Guard made illegal search. No probable cause."

"That suitcase tested positive for radioactive content, Yuri. We had more than enough cause to open it. You've got all the parts for two suitcase nukes."

"*What*? You're kidding me. Maybe I pick up wrong bag at—"

"Spare me the bull! How did you ever think you'd get it into the States?"

"I want lawyer, now!"

"Look, I might be able to help you out if you tell me where you got the materials."

Yuri folded his arms and leaned back in the chair.

"Law-yer!"

The colonel slammed his hand on the desk.

"You're a damned terrorist, that's what you are. So you're not in any position to make demands."

Another officer entered the room, bent down and whispered into Braun's ear. The colonel got up and slammed the door behind him.

The client had made it clear that if Yuri failed to deliver, there would be—what was the expression?—hell to pay. He took it to mean something really awful, probably worse than incarceration on terrorism charges. Perhaps it was better to stay under the protective custody of the United States government.

After a long wait Colonel Braun returned with a man in a black suit who introduced himself as Assistant Director Neal Walker of the Central Intelligence Agency. To Yuri's surprise, he handed over the suitcase.

"You're to continue on your mission," he said.

How could this be? Not that Yuri was about to question it. But the colonel looked really pissed off at the CIA guy.

"What in hell are you—"

The CIA guy held up a hand and continued to address Yuri as if the colonel hadn't said a word.

"And you have the apologies of the United States of America for nearly compromising your mission."

"Uh...well, it's okay, mistakes happen."

"We take these matters seriously, Mister Kosolupov—"

"Then why the hell weren't *we* informed?" Braun said.

"This is highly classified, Colonel," Walker said. "The storm threw our operative's schedule off, we lost track of him, and he missed a check point. We'd have contacted you sooner if we knew where he was. Fortunately, the Coast Guard picked him up and your office contacted us. Your assistance is most appreciated."

"Gentleman, may I go now?" Yuri said, edging toward the door. Walker glanced at Colonel Braun.

"Unless you have any objections?"

"I still maintain that he's a terrorist," Braun said.

"Colonel, does the name Stanislav Lunev mean anything to you?" Walker asked.

"Soviet intelligence defector, yes."

"Not just any defector—he was the highest ranking GRU member ever to defect. His claim that Soviet suitcase nukes had already been deployed in the U.S. was true. Our man here is posing as an eastern bloc arms dealer, helping us flush out potential threats to national security. At the same time, he's taking discovered devices to classified sites for deactivation and analysis." Walker turned to Yuri. "How's that going?"

Incredible luck, but what should he say?

"I'm glad to be back on track, sir."

Walker returned his sharp gaze to Colonel Braun.

"Satisfied?"

"Marginally."

Eyes narrowed, Braun moved aside, giving Yuri a wide berth. Still incredulous at his luck, Yuri was escorted out of the building by a pair of black-suited men who handed him his wallet, cell phone, fake passports, everything.

"Thank you for your hospitality, Colonel."

26

AS SHE FELL, THE RAGGED WOMAN neither screamed nor let out any other sound. The laws of physics would try, convict, and sentence her to a watery grave. The angel laws, on the other hand…

Casting discretion aside, Nick flew down, wrapped his arms around her, and whisked her back to the shoulder of the Coronado Bridge's island-bound right lane.

Astonished, she opened her eyes, and tried to form a sentence.

"What…Who are you? I thought…"

Nick released her and stepped back, still holding her trembling shoulders.

"Easy there."

"Where did you come from!"

Nick projected the construct of a parked BMW pulled over in the outermost lane. Over his form, he'd constructed a casual pewter-colored jacket over a black T-shirt and a pair of Calvins—*zeitgeist* and all that rot.

"You're safe now," he said. But she shrugged free and tried to shove him out of her path.

"You had no right!"

"I just saved your life."

"You have no idea—why couldn't you just mind your own business?" She headed back to the edge, slapping Nick's arm away when he reached out to stop her. But when she got there, instead of making another attempt to jump she leaned against the lamp post, covered her face, and began to cry. Or laugh, it was hard to tell.

He got close. Another good look at her might shed some light on why he'd suddenly decided to jeopardize his career by saving her.

"It figures I would lose it." She felt around her neck.

"Lose what?"

"The jade pendant my father gave me when I was little. He got it from the Forbidden City in Beijing." She looked up, blew a tangle of hair away from her mouth. "Probably worth more than my life."

"Are you all right?" Nick said.

"In case you hadn't noticed, I just tried to jump from the Coronado Bridge, also known as the third deadliest suicide bridge in the nation."

"How'd you get up here? There aren't any pedestrian paths."

"For a twenty-dollar tip, cabbies don't mind dropping you off wherever you want, no questions asked."

"Hmmm." He gave her a head to toe once-over.

She too looked at herself, her tattered clothes and grimy hands, which she wiped on her pants.

"Yeah, well...I figured blowing my life savings on a cab ride to *end* my life had a poetic ring to it."

"Are you going try jumping again, or shall I tie you up?"

"I don't think so." She let out a long breath. "Not tonight, anyway."

Following her lead, Nick exhaled—a most satisfying feeling when occupying a physical form.

"Come, now. It can't be as bad as all that."

"How would *you* know?"

"Tell me."

She stared wordlessly at him for a good three seconds.

"No."

"Why not?" he said.

"I'm tired." True enough. Weariness tinged her voice.

"Of course."

She shrugged. "I don't think I could spend another night in the shelter."

"Say no more." He gestured to his construct-BMW, gently took her arm, and led her to the passenger side door, which he opened for her.

"A gentleman, no less. What are you, from the last millennium?"

He couldn't help smirking.

27

JON NEARLY LOST HIS BALANCE when he entered Maria's hotel room with her lips firmly pressed against his. In the process of steadying himself his left foot hit the door with enough force to shut it.

He found himself suddenly short of breath, his heart racing, his mind in torment. He'd only meant to accompany her to her room for safety's sake. Now every nerve, every cell in his body screamed, *Do what's natural. It's the way God created you. You want this. You* deserve *this!*

Maria leaned back and met his eyes.

"What's the matter, Jon?"

"Nothing, I just..." This was pathetic. He could never do this. It wasn't fair to Elaine, it wasn't fair to Maria. It was *wrong*.

"Maria, I'm really sorry that I..." A sudden wave of regret warmed his face, ears, neck.

"It's okay," Maria said. "We're just two people in need. Two consenting adults."

Knowing better, Jon turned toward the door. From behind she pressed her warm body against his back.

Pain filled his heart.

Pangs of guilt wrung from the agony of going too far, only to deny the release of the fire he had so foolishly kindled.

No one will ever know...

That voice, those words—he recognized them. They weren't completely *his* words. He had slipped into a state of elective moral blindness, but now that he could discern that inner voice intermingled with his own he was able to squeeze his eyes shut and pray.

Dear God, forgive me...

// COWARD! YOU'VE GOT A BEAUTIFUL YOUNG WOMAN STANDING BEFORE YOU! DO WHAT FEELS RIGHT! //

"Jon? Don't worry, okay? It's just for tonight. Nothing more." Maria smiled— which further eroded his defenses. "I'm a big girl and I won't be coming around messing up your life. One night, then I'll love you from a distance. I promise. No strings attached."

// SHE'S YOURS //

Give me strength, Lord.

He turned and gently pushed away.

"I'm sorry."

"Oh." A torturous pause. "I see."

Jon mustered the courage to meet her eyes.

"This was entirely my fault. Whatever problems I might be having with my wife, this is wrong."

She was trying not to cry, but he could imagine how humiliating it must be for her to put herself out there only to be rejected.

"You're right, you're right, I don't know what I was thinking." She sighed. Her shoulders fell. Finally she looked up and put her hand on his face tenderly. "You're such a good man. I don't deserve you."

"Don't say that, you really—"

She pulled him close and pressed her lips against his desperately.

For the first two seconds, the shock disoriented him.

For the next two, he couldn't bring himself to resist.

And for the final two seconds, he fought his emotions and hormones until, with a gasp, he freed himself. Her face was still lifted, lips parted, eyes shut.

"Just a goodbye kiss," she said. "Not sorry about that."

"I've got to go," Jon said when he could control his breathing enough to get the words out.

It was just a kiss.

He almost laughed out loud at the sheer lameness of the thought as he opened the door.

"Pray for me, Jon."

He allowed himself a brief moment of light-heartedness and smiled as if defeated by an admired opponent.

"I'm the one who needs prayer."

"I'm *so* embarrassed."

"No need," he said. "Goodbye, Maria."

As he double-timed on the carpet in the empty hallway, Jon knew he'd crossed a bridge he should never have approached. And in the process lost the right to think of himself as Elaine's victim.

It was too late for that now.

28

FOR THE ENTIRE DRIVE NICK PONDERED what he had just done. The last time anything like this happened was back in England a century ago. Hadn't he learned from that?

Apparently not.

The subject had fallen asleep slumped down in her seat by the time they arrived at the Broadmore Hotel in La Jolla. The clock on the dashboard read 3:35 AM. The streets were desolate. At this unholy hour no concierge was on duty, so he constructed one to come to the passenger door.

Nick nudged the subject gently until she awoke with a start.

"We're here." He nodded at the window.

A handsome young man wearing a white shirt and black pants opened the door for her. She lowered her face, embarrassed by her state of disarray. Nick walked around to help her out, while the concierge stepped back.

"Thank you," she said. "I feel like such a lady."

Nick nodded to the concierge. "Checking in."

"Yes, sir." The concierge shut the passenger door, got into the driver's seat, and drove the construct-car off into oblivion.

When they got to the front desk, the subject stood behind him as though hiding. Nick gently lowered his palm on the chrome-domed bell so as not to ring it too loudly. A bleary-eyed young man, probably an undergrad at UCSD, emerged rubbing his eyes but smiling as best he could.

"May I help you?"

"A room, please."

"For two?"

"Just her."

"Name?"

Nick turned around. She straightened and pushed the messy locks of hair from her face.

"Matheson. But there's no way I can afford—"

"Not a problem." Nick turned back to the desk clerk. "Matheson."

"First name?"

This time Nick asked with his eyes only. She sighed and looked straight at him.

"Hope." She smiled. "Ironic, isn't it?"

"I think it's lovely."

He handed a gold Amex card to the desk clerk.

"Not sure how long she'll be staying, so keep this on file for any and all incidentals."

"All?"

"I've got an astronomic credit limit." *More like cosmic.* "She'll stay here until we can find her something more permanent. Anything she needs, just charge it to the card."

The clerk ran the card while Nick's construct caused it to interface in a way that ensured the hotel would be paid. Then he signed.

"Welcome to the Broadmore." The clerk gave him the room's key card, which Nick handed to Hope.

"Suite 310." She took the key and walked toward the elevator. "You really shouldn't have done this, but I guess there's no point in saying it."

"None whatsoever. Go and get some rest. I'll have some fresh clothes and toiletries sent up later." Which meant they'd materialize in her room. "What are you, a size five?"

"Ha! Try eight."

"Just guessing."

"Thank you, really." She smiled. "For everything."

"Come and meet me here in the lobby in the morning—you'll be famished, no doubt. We'll have breakfast."

"I don't know what to say," she said, stepping into the light.

"How about, 'See you later?'" Just as he leaned forward to get a good look at her face, she turned around and went into the elevator.

"Later."

No doubt it was the physical form that hung on Nick like armor, but he actually felt tired. He went over to a sofa, sank into it, and found that he could actually smell the wonderful scent of leather and feel its buttery soft surface. Unfortunately, he also felt the tightening in his chest and shortness of breath. That all too familiar manifestation of stress had returned.

He'd intervened without authorization.

Revealed himself to a human.

Touched her meaningfully while perceptible.

Surely he had failed again.   How would he explain it to Lena? Through the ages, his rashness and indiscretions had...

Did he really care?

His smartphone chimed.

A text message from Lena:

> Meet me in five or ten. Construct of your choice.

29

FOR ONCE, NICK WAS GRATEFUL that despite their supernatural abilities, angels were neither omniscient nor omnipresent. Lena had no idea where he was, much less what he'd done. But where best to meet his alluring yet intimidating new supervisor?

He thought about it for all of two seconds, then appeared on a level rock that rose from the waves pounding the La Jolla shores. Upon arrival he wove a thin construct of invisibility to human perception. About half a dozen seals barked loudly and dove into the water. That was the thing about animals, they often perceived the presence of angels. Dogs always did, and they caused the most trouble.

Nevertheless, he loved this part of the planet around sunrise. Any minute now the first sun rays would strike the rolling waves.

He sat on the rock surface.

"Crikey!" A cold wet sensation in the seat of his pants jolted him to his feet. He nearly slipped.

"Aw, you're wet." Lena said from behind him. He turned to face her.

"It's nothing."

"How did it go with your last subject?"

"The crazy suicidal woman?"

"Did she do it?"

"Not exactly. Bit of a complication—nothing major." Best not to expound further. "In any case, it's only a matter of time before she tries again."

"What happened?"

"Right, well...she was there at the bridge.... "

"But she didn't jump?"

"You know, I don't understand what the hurry is."

Just then a huge wave crashed against the rock, sending frigid water over them both. Nick gasped for breath and wiped water from his face. Still drenched, he looked at Lena. She was staring at him—completely dry.

"Why are you still in your mortal form?"

"I thought I'd switched out of it," he said.

"Apparently not."

She touched his shoulder, and all the water from his hair and clothes lifted to become a myriad of drops and rivulets that sparkled like gems in the early morning light. She smiled, twirled them around Nick's face, then sent them back into the ocean.

"There. Better?"

"Thank you." Nick tried again and this time felt certain he'd exited his physical form. "I'm usually quite good at transitions."

"Of course you are." Lena slipped her arm around his and took him to the edge of the rock. The seals who'd fled were poking their heads out of the water, observing the two of them. Lena hissed at them, and they dashed off as though a great white had just surfaced. She laughed and looked at Nick. "So tell me what happened."

"Look, I know she's dangerous to the future and all that, but really, what's the rush? What harm could she possibly do?"

Lena narrowed her eyes. "Just tell me what happened!"

Nick glared back at her. "Testy, aren't we?"

"Nick!" She squeezed his arm—not with much force, but it hurt enough to make him want to groan in pain. He managed to stifle it and act as though he'd felt nothing. He *should* have felt nothing.

"At the moment just before she jumped, some man in a car got out, caught her by the arm, and convinced her not to do it."

"And you just *let it happen*? Didn't you at least try to use a construct to stop him?"

"It happened so fast I—"

"Given the scope and importance of this assignment, I'd have expected you to take some initiative, think outside the box. But you just acted like some kind of...I don't know, boy scout. Why—"

Another wave threatened. Just as it was about to crash over them, Nick captured it into a sphere of energy, suspended it above them for a fraction of a second, then shot the entire mass of sea water up into the atmosphere. It all exploded in a circular spray, misting outward around the outline of the moon, faint but visible in the daytime. The effect of the resulting millions of microscopic droplets acting as prisms was a pale rainbow halo around the moon in three concentric circles.

"Impressive," Lena said.

"I learn from the best. Though it's not quite as impressive as what you did outside of Grand Central when you sent all that red destructive energy into a nuclear explosion in the sky."

She admired the show for a while. Then, still gazing into the night sky, she sighed heavily.

"Nick, it's important you complete this assignment if you want to pass probation and start on the real work."

"I'll get her to do it one way or another, okay?"

"Wait." She stepped back and gave him a probing look. "You're not getting attached, are you?"

The word *attached* felt like an icepick stabbing him, but she mustn't know.

"Hardly! I don't think I could ever feel anything but scorn for this sort of mortal."

"What sort?"

"You know, the kind that leads millions of people astray. And looks like something the cat dragged in, you might be interested to know. And smells even worse. "

The bell of a fishing boat tolled in the distance. Briny air filled Nick's senses, soothing air. Lena smiled.

"Just focus on your assigned baddies, okay?" She made a pouty face. "I know it's difficult changing jobs so abruptly. That's why I'm going to give you a little more time to complete these assignments so you can be fast-tracked to a promotion."

"Good. I hate babysitting these humans. They can be so..."

"Irritating?"

"To say the least."

"Infuriating?"

"More often than not."

She stared out into the inky ocean as if searching for more adverbs.

"Irresponsible, small-minded, arrogant...*evil!*"

Taken slightly aback, Nick gave her a thin smile.

"Right, well...They're all made in the image of the Father, aren't they?" he said. "There's got to be *some* good in them."

For a moment her expression softened, giving way to an almost child-like innocence that seemed to transform her into someone he barely recognized.

"What is it, Lena?"

"Nothing...You just reminded me of someone."

"Really? Who?"

Sounding vulnerable—which in itself was astonishing—she whispered, "Nick, what is it you want, more than anything else?"

He gave it some thought. Despite the connection they seemed to be making, he didn't feel comfortable opening up to her.

"I don't know, really. I was hoping a job change might help me find out. How about you?"

She set her lips, didn't look at him, and when she answered him her words came reluctantly—apparently she didn't feel any more comfortable opening up than he did.

"I just want to be able to make sense of everything. I want a world where things are in order. Where the evil this entire race of humans is so capable of is eradicated. Where those who deserve to be in charge are, and those who do wrong are brought to justice."

"A tall order indeed. I suppose you've some idea about how that can happen?"

Finally, her eyes met his. "Together, we can make it happen." She put her hand on his, a gesture that felt disturbingly intimate. "It's all about being aligned."

"With what, or whom?"

"Those with the power to help." Gradually, the innocence and vulnerability ebbed like the tide pulling out. Her feisty sensual charm returned with a vengeance in her posture, her eyes, her curling lips. "You're in a good position to make a difference, Nikolai."

"That's what I'm counting on."

She put her hand around the back of his neck. Pulled his face down so close their lips nearly touched.

"But make no mistake, you gorgeous creature. If you fail, after all the latitude and special treatment you've been shown..."

She was as lethal as she was alluring. *Fight or flight.* Nick pulled away, grabbed her wrists, and held her in place.

"I don't respond well to threats."

"Mmmm...that's good, because I'd rather motivate you with rewards." She moved in close to whisper in his ear. "Go and check on your third assignment, then come back to suicide girl later in the morning. You've got till midnight to *persuade* her."

Nick could hear her laughing as she vanished from his construct.

30

MARIA HADN'T ANSWERED LITO'S CALLS for two days now. Her condo in Mission Valley looked like it had been ransacked. No sense trying to use the GPS to track her location, she knew to shut off her cell phone.

He entered the condo with his spare key. Maria never liked that he kept a copy, but since he paid for everything she couldn't really argue. And besides, he'd only used the key once, to scare off a USD college punk who had gotten the idea in his empty head that he could spend the night. For just a moment Lito was back when life was simple, when all he had to do was to punch a bully in the face to teach him not to mess with his baby sister.

Awwwwwwk!

A raven gawked down at him from the eaves dripping with last night's rainwater. It cocked its head, stared at him with one glassy eye, and proceeded to mock him. Repeatedly. Every caw seemed louder and more disdainful.

He swore and reached around his back for his gun. All the anger he felt for Alfonso coalesced for a brief moment into a focused beam of hatred aimed at the hideous raven. But the thought of awakening the neighbors at 7:15 AM with the crack of a Baretta Bobcat convinced him to restrain himself.

"Next time, little *diabolo*." He smiled. "Next time."

Lito locked the door and walked to his red 135i. Owning a Beamer wasn't something he really cared about, he only did it to keep up the image of success and power. He did like that smell of fine leather though.

But as he climbed into the cockpit, the smell brought little comfort—he was too aware of the empty passenger seat.

Got to find a replacement for Alfonso.

But who? Until he learned of Alfonso's flirting with the Suarez syndicate, there'd been no one else he trusted.

As he drove out of the parking area, the foreboding bass line palpitations from the *Confutatis Maledictis* movement of Mozart's *Requiem* poured forth from the speakers. The bright morning sun hid behind a gray cloud even as Lito put his sunglasses over his eyes, from which a solitary tear rolled down his cheek.

Rapt in the power of music, Lito never noticed the black Cadillac following him.

At the top of his lungs, he sang with the male chorus:

Confutatis

Maledictis

Flammis acribus addictis...

31

HOPE LAY AWAKE IN THE KING-SIZED BED in the hotel room so graciously purchased on the handsome stranger's dime. She stared at the rectangular glow on the wall now changing from orange to bright yellow as the rising sun cast its light through the window.

Wrapped in the sheets, she was completely naked, wishing she could simply enjoy how clean everything felt, how nice the rose-scented pillows smelled, how good her skin felt after her first shower in a week—all thanks to that generous man who'd saved her.

Had this been another time, another life, she might well have thought more about the nice man's looks: beautiful eyes, chiseled features, and oh yes, very strong arms.

But no.

She allowed no such thoughts, not since the final nail was hammered into the coffin of her soul several years ago. Never again would she allow herself to desire anything other than to escape the miserable life in which anyone she'd ever allowed into her heart had either beaten, molested, or otherwise betrayed her.

The one drop of rain in that barren desert had been taken away and along with it, Hope's will to live. Being rescued by a Clive Owen-ish hero couldn't change that—he'd only prolonged her pain.

She sighed, reached for the phone, and dialed.

"Good morning, front desk. How can I help you?"

"Couldn't sleep a wink last night."

"I'm sorry, Ms...Matheson. Is there anything we can get you?"

Clive *had* said to put everything on his credit card.

"I need a bottle of Ambien. They're sleeping pills."

"Of course. We can call in a prescription for you and have them delivered."

Prescription. Right. The last doctor she saw refused to give her any because he thought—he *knew* she was suicidal. Which was why she'd not been to any kind of doctor, even though as a homeless person for nearly a year she probably could have gotten to one through public assistance. Too complicated, too much trouble.

"Never mind," she said. "I'll be fine."

"Is there anything else, perhaps?"

"It's all right. I'll try something else." Which was to say, another method of ending it all. She hung up, hugged the pillow to her chest, and curled into a fetal position. Whoever said "it's all in your head" had no idea what it meant to be truly depressed. The physical pain radiated from her gut all through her chest—the *last* place it went was her head, though that hurt like the devil too.

She wanted to keep it from getting too messy in this fancy hotel room, what with its thick white carpet, cherrywood furniture, and pristine marble bathroom. But she'd have to go the gruesome route of mirror shards and crimson bathwater.

She'd cut herself before, so she wasn't worried about how it would feel. It was the thought of all that blood flowing from her wrists into the tub that made her stomach clench. She had to do it, though. And no point putting it off.

Hope climbed out of the bed, put on the soft white robe she'd try to keep away from any of the blood—no sense in ruining it—and looked for something heavy enough to smash the mirror.

An odd euphoria rushed through her, lightening her mood, making her heart beat rapidly.

It's almost over.

Maybe that's why she seemed almost excited.

And in the privacy of her locked hotel room, she would not fail again.

There.

On the polished desk sat an antiqued brass paperweight that looked really heavy. She lifted it: it was. This would do nicely.

She wound back her arm to hurl it at the mirror—

A knock on the door.

The paperweight slipped out of her hands and hit the floor with a thud.

"Room service," a woman's voice called out. But she hadn't—

She opened the door to find a young lady standing there with a white paper bag in her hand.

"For you, ma'am." And she left.

It was from a pharmacy. On closer inspection she saw that it was in fact a prescription for Hope Matheson. She tore the bag open and found a large orange vial with a safety cap, on its label her name printed along with the name of the drug Zolpidem Tartrate (Ambien) 10 mg and the instructions: Take as needed.

As needed?

There must have been at least sixty pills in the bottle.

Had the front desk managed to find a way to get it for her after all?

Perhaps someone was looking out for her.

Someone who understood her pain.

32

LENA KNEW WHAT SHE'D DONE wasn't appropriate. Helping Nick complete his assignment didn't represent the best method of ascertaining his capabilities or loyalty.

Having shed the appearance of the hotel's housekeeping staff, she strode out into the lobby turning more than a few heads, men and women alike. The whiny little human had been the low-hanging fruit among Nick's three assignments, the one he was close to completing without her delivering the pills. But she wasn't going to take chances with so little time before the Cabrillo Stadium event, just days away. Anyway, Morloch need never know about her helping Nick. As long as the goal was reached, what did it matter how?

Evaporating from physical perception as she walked through the exit and onto the sidewalk, Lena paused. Something didn't feel right.

She'd been watching Nick carefully since he brought Hope to the Broadmore. Though he denied it vehemently, he fancied this mortal. That was why he'd hesitated to help her meet her demise. And of course he lied about it. Lena expected nothing less from angels of his stock. They were not above subterfuge, something Lena had good reason to know all too well. That made him the perfect candidate.

With one leap, she launched herself onto the hotel's roof. It was only a few stories, nothing like a New York skyscraper but a fine spot for perching invisibly while she thought about angels who lied, angels who got entangled with humans...

This had to be a passing thing for Nick. He couldn't be developing genuine feelings for a human. How could a superior being see humans as anything but barely sentient mammals? *Cruel, filthy animals.*

A sharp pain burrowed into the center of Lena's ribs. Odd, she rarely felt pain. And it brought an irritating wetness to her eyes.

"Oh, my Lord, Punkin'!" George Walker stands at the open door and drops his lunch pail. He rushes over to his nine-year-old daughter, who sits alone at the kitchen table, dabbing cuts on her bruised face with a white towel stained with blood. "What in the world happened to you?"

"Nothing, Daddy. I...I just fell down, is all." She tries to smile but winces in pain. She's never been a good liar anyway.

"Where's your momma?"

She points at the closed bedroom door.

George takes the towel, rinses it, wrings it, then gets down on one knee to gently press it against a swollen bump above her eye.

"You so brave, Punkin'. I'm proud of you. Now you can tell me the truth." Tears stand in his eyes as he struggles to be strong for her. "It was them boys from school, wasn't it?"

"No, it wasn't."

"I said, you can tell me the truth."

"I am, Daddy. Wasn't no boys this time. It was Courtney."

"Big fat Courtney?"

"She and her eighth-grade friends. They see me coming home, minding my own business, then they go and say I'm a freak and ask me, how come no one ain't never seen your momma—you even got one? And Courtney says I got one all right, she went and married a nigger." She puts her hand over her mouth. "Sorry, Daddy. I hate that word, but that's what they say."

George pulls her tight into his arms.

"Don't you pay them girls no mind, you hear? They just need some proper education. Don't pay them no mind, and—"

"I did like you told me! I kept walking. But then Fat Courtney smacks me upside my head. I still didn't say nothing, just kept walking even though the slap hurt. But then she goes on, hitting at me and saying niggers and white folks ain't got no business making freaks like me for babies and she won't shut up and…and…"

Holding her arms, George leans back and looks her straight in the eye. "You didn't. Did you, Punkin'?"

"I didn't mean to, I swear." She sniffles, holding back a sob. "I just tried to give her a little shove 'cause she was all up in my face, spitting when she talked. But she fell down real hard and started cussing at me. That's when I knew I done wrong, so I held back how mad I was, like you always tell me to, and I didn't fight back. I just waited till they finish whupping me, then ran home."

George scrutinizes his daughter. "You hurting anywhere? Anything feel broken?"

"Nah, Daddy. You know they can't really hurt me—not that bad, anyway." Her head slightly bowed, she glances up with a little smile he doesn't like. "But I can hurt them."

"No, sweetie. Don't even think about that."

"Why, Daddy? I ain't the only one, they do this to all the black kids in

town. *And just because I'm mixed, different, they do even worse to me. I* hate
'em!"

"Now, Punkin'—"

"I do, Daddy. They're so mean."

George takes another look at her bruises and cuts. The bleeding has
stopped, the swelling has gone down a little. Still on his knees, he hugs his
daughter and nods to the sofa.

"Come on, let's sit."

A moment later, she's leaning into him on the comfortable old couch with
its plump stained cushions.

"You know, those mean kids? They all the Lord's children too, Punkin'.
And even though they do some pretty rotten things, they all been made in his
image."

"You saying God's mean?"

George laughs, something he's done rarely since her mother got so sullen
and quiet.

"Oh, no. No, that ain't what I mean at all. I'm saying everyone's got
some good in them deep down because we all made in His image. The bad
stuff? That's just garbage we picked up—from our parents, from our bad
choices. That's in our nature too."

"Is it in my nature, Daddy?" Her eyes meet his, desperately seeking abso-
lution—for what, George cannot fathom. "Am I just like them—you know,
deep down?"

Before he has to answer—which he'd rather not—the bedroom door
swings open.

"Enough, George!" Lucretia stands there, flaxen hair flowing past her
shoulders like sunlight, lovely features marred by her perpetual scowl. "Are you
just going to coddle her like that until she becomes as feeble as you?"

"Honey!"

She covers her mouth, whispers, "Sorry," and retreats into the bedroom, swinging the door shut behind her.

The buzzing hornet in her back pocket causes Lena to check the caller ID. Yuri, her eastern bloc liaison.

"You're late," she said.

"Do you know how hard it is to get this stuff out of there and into the States?"

"Not my problem. What's the current status?"

"Package is en route. One last stop for processing, then they'll be delivered."

"They'd better be, Yuri."

"Have I ever let you down?"

"There's always a first time—which would, in your unfortunate case, be your last."

"It'll be there. Ahead of schedule. I'd stake my life on it."

Lena smiled. "Your life is always at stake, always has been."

33

IN ALL HIS GOING TO AND FROM the earth, relatively few things disturbed Nick to the point of actual worry. He'd never acquired that annoying human habit. But now, as he slowly traversed the distance between La Jolla and his next assignment, his physical form was becoming more of a burden to shed. Which was, well, worrisome. What he hated about flying while fully physical wasn't so much the cold air or the tailpipe fumes on the freeway below but the queasiness and perspiration. With Lena and his assignments he was back in that state of flux, that neither-here-nor-there place.

With an important issue to resolve.

Am I actually going to push Hope back into despair and suicide?

If there were more asinine rules that said he must do whatever he was told with no adequate explanation, perhaps it was time to see if there were indeed real consequences for not blindly obeying them.

Blasted rules.

How had they worked out for him back in Victoria Station?

No.

Don't get distracted.

Stop overthinking this and complete the assignment.

For no reason other than sheer instinct, Nick looked over his shoulder expecting to find that dark vapor looming about.

Not there. Perhaps he'd be okay.

As he got closer to his third subject, Carlito Guzman, his smartphone buzzed and chimed. The proximity sensor showed him which car on the surface road below was Guzman's. The text flashed his assignment:

PROTECT CARLITO GUZMAN

There, stopped at a red light on Mission Valley Road with no other cars in the lanes next to him, Guzman's car stood awaiting the signal change. But coming from behind without slowing down was another car—a black Cadillac that changed lanes to bring itself right next to Guzman's window. And from the Cadi's passenger window a gun protruded, its muzzle aimed right at his head. Guzman had no clue what was about to happen—he appeared to be singing.

Nick made himself invisible, flew down to the street, and stood directly in the path of the bullets.

The popping sound of semi-automatic weapon fire rang out.

Nick altered his molecular density so the few rounds that hit him went blunt at the point, then fell to the asphalt clinking like steel bolts. Cars on both sides of the road blazed out of the danger zone.

The gunman kept firing at Guzman. Nick kept shielding him from the onslaught. Then he tried that trick he'd learned from Lena outside Grand Central Station. Focusing on the oncoming bullets, he absorbed them into the spiritual layers, then sent them out into the sky.

It worked. The Cadillac raced off and took the on-ramp to the freeway. Nick saw Guzman look all over his body, all around the inside of his car, astonished he hadn't been hit.

Nick passed into the car, where the cartel leader now sat perfectly still, his head resting against the steering wheel. He sat down in the passenger seat, which sank just a bit—apparently he'd brought weight and density with him even while invisible.

But then Guzman lifted his head and turned in Nick's direction.

"Holy—!"

Nick instantly re-established invisibility.

With sudden jerky movements Guzman swiped his hand over and around the passenger seat, then spun around looking in back for Nick. He finally gave up, shut his eyes, folded his hands, and began to pray.

"*Gracias a dios…gracias señor…*"

It was, of course, the first time Nick had heard his voice. He could usually discern sincerity in a human's tone, especially one who thought he was alone. Guzman, he sensed, was genuinely grateful that his life had been spared.

So what if, for a split second, the subject had seen him? So far as this part of his assignment was concerned, Nick had succeeded. He'd protected the drug lord from death. And according to Lena, Carlito Guzman would go on to do great things if given the chance.

Imagine, feeling happy for a drug lord! But saving a life rather than watching it end? That was refreshing. And judging by the look on this young man's face, Nick sensed that something wonderful was happening within him.

This felt good.

34

HOPE MATHESON WOULD BE AWAKE by now. Having muddied the waters, Nick wasn't exactly sure what he ought to do about her. For now, better teleport back to the Broadmore. But as soon as he focused on the hotel, a dull throb started in his head.

Worse, the pain intensified every time he tried to teleport.

Most annoying.

Never mind, I'll fly.

A murder of crows blackened the sky as they flew overhead heading northwest towards La Jolla. He'd have to fly in the same direction to get to his suicidal subject. Judging by the sun's height over the eastern horizon, he'd better hurry.

By human standards, traveling from Mission Valley to La Jolla in ninety seconds would be extremely fast. But compared to teleportation, the trip had seemed interminable. Now, holding two shopping bags full of women's clothing, size 8, he stood in the Broadmore's lobby shrouded from physical sight and paused to think. Wouldn't it be more enjoyable for Hope if the clothes appeared magically before her eyes?

Yet when he recalled the one time he'd tried something like that, how it worked, where it ultimately ended, he heard sounds from London at the turn of the 20th century. *The squeal of metal, the screaming train whistle—*

No. He'd vowed never to allow himself to go down that path again. And he had an assignment to complete.

With the snap of his fingers, Nick sent the shopping bags into what he called the oblivion locker, within which he could store physical items in an inter-dimensional state of limbo, to be retrieved at any moment.

He went to the elevator. He'd have to do something drastic to push Hope over the edge. But it just didn't seem right.

Something about her...

Stop it! Were those feelings not the very ones that set him on the path to that fateful day in Victoria Station?

When he reached the third floor, he stepped out of the elevator and started the long walk down the hallway toward room 310. Sunlight flooded the end of the corridor, so brilliant that Nick had to cover his eyes for a moment. Yet another odd physical sensation he couldn't re-member dealing with before.

When he opened them he thought he saw something floating around the door to Hope's room. It resembled a shadow that could not possibly co-exist with all that bright sunlight. But every time Nick blinked, it disappeared—only to reappear a few moments later.

The dark vapor.

It made him uneasy, though for several millennia it had never done anything other than hang about, as though watching to see what he would do in a situation where his choices were unclear.

But at this point Nick was fairly certain what he would do.

He'd waited all this time for a promotion and wasn't about to let the weakness of human-based emotions cloud his judgment again. At least, that's what he kept telling himself. A part of him felt differently. And that part seemed to be telling him not to do this. It was sort of like that doctors' oath—*First do no harm.*

But Hippocrates was a mere human with a limited perspective.

Nick stepped up to the door—right into the dark cloud.

Which to his surprise changed into a white vapor that rushed past him, sending a refreshing mist onto his face, and went straight through the huge glass window at the end of the hall.

That sort of thing had never happened before.

But it didn't matter. He had an assignment to complete and had already lost too much ground.

He knocked on the door of room 310. When he got no answer after several tries, he placed his ear against its smooth painted surface and listened.

No sound.

35

THE DOOR WAS LOCKED. He'd have to pass through. It used to be simple, but lately, passing through solid material felt like rubbing against sandpaper. He'd started managing it faster to shorten the pain of scraping between the physical and spiritual layers, but the benefit was small and in any case cancelled out by the fact that the pain kept escalating.

This time it felt as though his skin was peeling off, all over his body. The pain was so intense he could barely think. But finally, he passed through into the room.

Teleportation was so much simpler.

Wrapped in a white terrycloth robe, Hope sat on the bed, facing the window. In her open palm lay a pile of pills. A capsized bottle lay on the bed with its top off, more pills spilling out onto the sheets. A large bottle of Arrowhead Water stood on the nightstand.

It was the first time he'd seen her bathed and out of her filthy clothes—he wouldn't have known her. Her wavy hair flowed just past her shoulders and glowed in the sunlight. The very sight of her eased Nick's still painful skin to the point that he forgot about it.

But he couldn't forget that the beauty of a mortal had once nearly destroyed him. And he could hear Lena telling him, *You've got till midnight to* persuade *her.*

Somehow, Hope had managed to get hold of pills that were about to make his job incredibly easy for him. Which didn't make him feel any better. It made him feel something close to the despair on this beautiful young woman's face.

You're not causing her death. It's her own doing. You're just keeping her on track.

Right. Just think of how many you're saving by simply nudging her to do what she's going to do anyway. She must really be dangerous—there were no guardian angels protecting her or trying to convince her not to go through with it.

Hope let out a heavy sigh. She didn't seem like the kind of homeless person who talked to herself—there was too much clarity in her eyes—so Nick prepared to listen in on her thoughts. Thoughts he'd have to collude with in order to encourage her to go through with it and swallow the pills.

Thoughts, as it turned out, he'd never heard nor heard of in the thousands of years he'd roamed the earth.

36

PERCEIVING THE SPIRITUAL REALM IS NOT for the faint of heart.

Even if you're an angel.

But for a human unequipped and unprepared, the lifting of the veil that separates the two realms can cause sheer madness. Nick had witnessed this first-hand in England. The very recollection was like ripping open an old wound.

What he now saw pouring out of Hope and surrounding her as she buried her head in her hands was neither angels nor demons. They were people. Humans. Not their physical form but her memories of them, their essence.

First a man dressed as though he were from the 1970s stood over her and said, "*It wasn't the cancer, Hope. I died because of you. What father with such a pathetic daughter would want to live?*"

She didn't lift her head, didn't look at the man. The only sound she made was a bitter sob.

Her father's apparition faded into a bruised purple vapor and disappeared into her ear. And now sitting on the bed next to her was the phantasm of a woman, her face and arms covered with black and blue patches and cuts. *"Sweetie, if you'd been a good girl Daddy would have stayed. And Thomas wouldn't have touched you or beaten you. I deserved what I got, that's why I never said anything when he did it to me."*

Hope winced, cried out, and threw her hands up as if to block an onslaught of ravens.

Though the voices from within her were doing a fine job helping him complete his assignment, they infuriated Nick.

Others came out and accused. Finally they all surrounded her, talking over each other, stabbing prosecutorial fingers at her. The last tormentor floated out of Hope's body and stood before her. She was the very image of Hope.

"You're some kind of masochist to keep holding onto a life that gives you nothing but suffering. If there even is a God, he must hate you. Why else would he allow you to suffer like this? All those emails and phone calls to Hartwell Ministry's life-line? Nothing's ever changed, nothing ever will. You know why. Because you're worthless and your life is meaningless. Stop being a coward and end it."

These were not demons but internal thoughts, voices that resounded in Hope's soul like cymbals struck over and over. No human could face them for long without losing her sanity—it was hard enough just listening to them. All Nick had to do was turn his head, shut his eyes, even leave the room and come back to find her dead, dark reapers taking her spirit to the Terminus. Thankfully, he'd never have to deal with that sort of business again.

Hope lifted her head and stared at the handful of pills.

Nick's chest tightened. He tried to hold onto Lena's warnings like a handrail on a subway staircase slick with rain.

Nearly a dozen of Hope's inner voices surrounded her, chanting in a whisper:

"Do it...

> *do it...*

> > *do it..."*

Faster and faster they spun, all speaking at once in a dissonant cacophony that resembled a profound electrical buzz. Then, in one collective scream, they shot into her head through the ears and eyes and mouth.

She gasped.

And brought the pills to her mouth.

37

HOPE GRABBED THE BOTTLED WATER from the night stand, twisted the top open with her free hand, and gulped down the pills in her mouth. She gagged a little, and a couple of wet pills slipped out. Quickly she downed the next handful, gathered from the bed.

And the next.

And the next.

Though there were still some pills left, she'd taken most of them. She lay back in the bed, hugging the pillow.

A painful ache overtook her.

It wasn't from the drugs. It was because of the image in her mind.

Her little daughter. That one refreshing dewdrop in the desert of her life.

Hope squeezed her eyes shut. But as the sorrow enveloped her, she saw her little girl's face again.

She could barely inhale.

But as she let the breath out she whispered, "Chloe."

38

"CHLOE?" NICK WHISPERED. Yes, that was the name she'd spoken.

He rushed over to the bed and turned Hope over. Pushed her hair, still damp, from her face. Tried to get her to speak.

"Hope?"

He patted her face.

"Come on!" He picked up the empty pill bottle and patted her face repeatedly. "Hope Matheson!"

For a brief moment, she opened her eyes.

Ignoring a sharp pain piercing the center of his head, he drew on all his strength to create a mini-construct that slowed time enough for him to gaze into her eyes before she shut them again.

Just long enough to tell.

He had suspected before, but now that he'd gotten a good look at her eyes he was certain.

It *was* her—the mother of the last subject he'd taken to the Terminus, the adorable little girl who brought back such painful memories he'd had to resign from the reaper work.

Hope had emerald eyes, just like…Not for a hundred years had he felt this way for anyone, much less a mortal. Now he knew why he didn't want to let her go.

"Come on, Hope. Hang on."

But the construct fell apart even as his strength ebbed. Her eyes rolled back and shut.

Exhausted, Nick fell to his knees at the bed.

He reached out and gently cupped her face, which felt cold and moist. If he could just heal her...

You're in enough trouble as it is!

But if she died, the dark reapers would come for her.

Think. If he failed this assignment again, then broke the angelic laws against unauthorized healing, he himself might be the one taken by the dark reapers.

Tormented, he grappled with the decision.

Then, placing a hand on Hope's forehead, he reached inside her mind and projected a sliver of a construct. One that didn't task all of her five senses, just enough to cause the necessary effect.

He grabbed the trash can under the nightstand and held it at the edge of the bed.

Hope lurched forward and let out a horrendous retching sound.

Carefully, Nick lifted and turned her head so that she vomited only into the can. With each heave she tossed out a mixture of water and pills, some partially dissolved.

Nick turned away. Of all possible times to be experiencing the full extent of human olfactory senses, why did it have to be now? He looked back to check on her.

Not done retching yet, but nothing was coming up now. He patted her back, told her she'd be all right. She made a whining sound, then finished.

As she sat back, Nick grabbed a stack of tissues from the box and handed them to her. He sent a small healing pulse into her body from his fingertips as he brushed them across her face. Technically, he hadn't healed her—though his hand did glow. The vomiting had. Helping her feel better wasn't the same as healing her. Not exactly.

She looked into his face.

"Oh, my—it's you, again, Clive."

"I'm afraid so. *Clive?*"

She waved her hand. Never mind.

"How did you—?" She slapped her hand over her mouth, grabbed the trash can, and completed her sentence with a final dry heave.

"I daresay you've tossed the last of them," Nick said.

She got up, looked surprised that she'd managed it with ease, then went into the bathroom. Nick heard her running water, gargling, spitting into the sink. Then she came out and stood there dabbing her face with a white towel.

"Sorry you have to keep saving me. Really, I didn't mean to be saved."

Nick pushed aside any thought of what Lena would say if she found out. *When* she found out.

"Are you going to try again?" he said.

"I really thought I was going to die, this time."

"You nearly did."

"But somewhere in the darkness, I felt something I've never felt before. Never in my whole life." She looked down at the floor. "Well, that's not exactly true. It did happen once, on the day my daughter

Chloe died...in the..." She squinted at Nick. "In the hospital, just before..."

Eyes still on Nick, she stood.

Nick stood.

Still looking directly into his face, she walked over to him.

"It was you."

"Hope—"

"Oh, my God. It was you."

"Hope, I don't think you understand."

"I thought I was just bereft and seeing things. But even though it was for a split second, I've never forgotten that look in your eyes." She leaned closer. "It gave me a couple of seconds of joy."

"Look, you've been through a lot—more than I can imagine."

Suddenly, she wrapped her arms around him so tight he could barely breathe.

"Don't leave! Whatever you do, don't vanish again."

"I won't, but—"

"I'll really go insane if you do. Maybe I already am." She pinched his arm.

"Hey!"

"Okay, I guess you're real. But am I?" She smiled. "You pinch *me*!"

"I'm not going—"

"Fine." She reached up. As though avoiding a punch, Nick backed away. But then with both hands touched his face. Tracing the outline of his jaw, she gazed at him in wonder.

For a long moment.

At first, Nick meant to pull away. But instead, he reached up and gently grasped her fingers. A tingling sensation ran through his being.

For the first time in a century he felt the very real, very human sensation of touching, and being touched by a human.

His head felt light.

39

HE'D LOST TRACK OF HOW MUCH TIME had passed. When you haven't been touched by a woman meaningfully for over a hundred years, it takes you by surprise when it finally happens again.

Finally, Hope pushed away just a bit, averting her gaze but not for long.

"I'm *so* sorry."

"It's...quite all right."

"I don't make a habit of touching strangers like that." She let her hand slide down his neck, around the curve of his shoulder. "But you're not really a stranger, are you?"

Nick tried with no success whatsoever to collect his thoughts.

"I don't know what you mean," he said, backing away slightly.

"We met. The day Chloe died."

Still dazed by the effects of their contact, he could hardly think. How did humans bear this without absolutely losing their minds?

"Chloe...Yes, I remember."

"You touched me. We looked into each other's eyes." She took a small step back, her eyes ever widening in recognition. "But it was so brief I always thought I'd imagined it. Yet here you are."

Regaining a little of his composure, he took a wobbly step back toward the chair.

"Are you quite all right, Hope?"

"I think so." She touched her stomach, brushed his concern aside with a tentative smile. "May I ask you a few questions?"

"A few?" Nick nearly fell back into the chair. His head felt as though it was somewhere in the clouds. "I don't know if I'd make it through the first."

Hope tightened the belt of her robe, came over to the edge of the chair, and knelt so she could look up into his face.

"First question. What's your name?"

"Not sure I should tell you."

"Why?"

"Is that question two?"

She smirked.

"Okay, next. Where did you come from?" She narrowed her eyes scrutinizing him.

"That's, um…classified."

"Fine." She gave him an appraising look. "That brings us to question three."

His throat gave out a tired groan, like an old St. Bernard rolling over in its sleep without waking up. Nick had never before made such a sound, and Hope picked up on it.

"Are *you* quite all right, Clive?" she said, imitating his English accent.

"Never better." He reached for the other trash can and put his face into it, making a queer sound that was a cross between a grunt and the noise people make when punched in the gut. Of course nothing came out since he neither ate nor drank. Yet here he was, mirroring his subject.

When the feeling of nausea subsided he opened his eyes and found Hope looking at him with concern.

"You're looking awfully pale," she said.

"Are you done with your questions?"

"I have one more."

Nick placed his hand on her shoulder and sat up straight.

"Let's have it, then."

Again she looked him straight in the eyes.

"*What* are you?"

40

NO TURNING BACK NOW. Nick was committed.

And this time his rashness had forced him into a situation that sabotaged his future. Yet somehow, he didn't care.

Which was why, with Hope gazing up at him expecting a truthful answer to her final question, he decided to give her one.

"Don't you know what I am?" he said.

"I have an idea," she said. "But it's crazy."

He knew that expression on her face—part wonder and part fear. He'd seen the fear in nonbelieving humans who just found out they'd sorely miscalculated their beliefs, or lack thereof during their wretched mortal lives.

And the wonder? That was for those who'd always believed and looked forward to the next step towards eternity—about which Nick's knowledge was incomplete, since he'd never been allowed to board the trains that took souls to their final destination.

"I'm what you would refer to as an angel," he said.

"An angel. Yes." She stood up, went over to the bed and sat on its edge. "Now I understand. You really *were* there when Chloe died."

"I was." Nick went over to sit beside her. Her eyes filled with tears.

"Please, do you know if she...I have to know about my little girl."

"She's just fine," he said. "I accompanied her to the Terminus—it's where all souls go to get sorted out before they take the long trip to eternity. I'm sure Chloe went to heaven. I saw her off myself."

Hope buried her face in his chest and sobbed. For a good minute or so. Something about a beautiful woman weeping always softened Nick's heart, no matter how firm his resolve.

He put his arms around her and patted her back. Hope lifted her head and wiped her eyes with a Kleenex from the nightstand.

"Thank you."

"For what?"

"When Chloe died, all that was worth living for died with her. You just gave me a glimmer. Will I see her again?"

In the time that elapsed—which according to the clock was all of one second—Nick considered her question. Saw the purity in her eyes, the innocence, the desperate need to be rescued, protected, *loved*—how could she possibly be a hell-bound danger to humankind? And even if that were the case, hadn't *he* broken laws of his own? Was he any less a menace?

"I wish I could tell you," he said. "Just know that Chloe is safe, happy, and in the best place she could be. You and I ought to focus on the here and now."

"I suppose." She wiped her tears with the back of a hand.

"We might start by leaving this place," Nick said. "You've made a beastly mess."

"I have, haven't I?" She laughed, which brought a smile to Nick's face.

"I'll send for housekeeping," he said.

"Wait a minute."

"What now?"

Hope eyed him with the suspicion of a precocious girl he once knew, once loved dearly—arguably more than his own life. It was a look of absolute wit, sharp and quick.

"You're an angel," she said. "And I almost believe it."

"As well you should."

"But I don't see any reason why."

Nick sighed. "Truth is not contingent upon your belief, but as you mortals are so fond of saying: It is what it is. A most annoying phrase, if you ask me."

"All right, then. If you're an angel…" She put both hands on his shoulders. "Prove it."

41

THE SOUND OF MUTED SNIFFLING and whimpers woke Jon.
At first, he was disoriented. Golden light blinded him as he sat up and
opened his eyes. He blinked a couple of times before realizing he was on
the sofa at home in the study.

Elaine, sitting in his desk chair, was staring at him with eyes red-
dened by tears.

"Well?" she said.

Jon groaned and rubbed his stiff neck.

"Well, what?"

She looked angry and at the same time, wounded.

Compassion urged him to go comfort her. Anger urged him to do
no such thing—his own wounds were still fresh.

"What do you want, a detailed log of my every step?" He pulled his
cell phone from his pocket. "Aren't you already tracking me with the
built-in GPS?"

"What?" She looked bewildered. "Jon, what's happened to you?"

He got up. Thought about the mess he'd made. What if someone
saw him last night walking into the hotel with Maria or going into her

room? What if someone snapped photos with an iPhone? They might go viral all over the internet, preceding the inevitable media fallout. What was he going to do? He hadn't slept with the girl, but who would believe him?

He felt unbearably vulnerable.

Flight or fight.

"It's your fault, you know."

"Mine?" Elaine blinked several times in rapid succession. "What did I do to deserve you running out in the middle of the night and staying out until after midnight? Oh my God, Jon. I was so worried!"

"I'll *bet* you were." He swiped his jacket from the arm of the sofa and headed for the door. "You started to worry about who would pay for your Italian shoes, your designer wardrobe—"

"No! Jon, I really *was* worried about you!"

When he reached the door he turned, saw the despair on her face, and walked back to her.

"Oh, Jon..."

He came so close he could smell the scotch on her breath—occasionally, she drank when stressed out. And he'd caused her plenty of stress last night.

He reached straight over her, took the laptop from his desk, and walked out the door. But not before saying something he knew he'd regret.

"You're a bad liar, Elaine."

Back in his office, Jon shut the door and left instructions for Carla: No calls, no messages, nothing. He sat at his desk with a cup of Starbucks that had grown cold about an hour ago and gazed vacuously at his laptop screen.

Click, click, stare...

Click, click, stare...

And so it went, for the entire morning. He Googled twice for those damming pictures, but they hadn't shown up. Yet. He thought about getting on his knees and repenting but his heart was still infested with bitterness—he'd just pray that he and his family would be spared the humiliation of a disgraced televangelist. What good would another one of those do for the kingdom of heaven? And what kind of prayer was that, treating God like...

If—when—the scandalous pictures came out, Elaine would own the high moral ground. *I may not have been the best wife but I never shacked up in a hotel with some young buck!*

His chest constricted. His lungs refused to fully inflate. Jon stood up, yanked loose his necktie, and fumbled with the top button of his shirt until he gave up and ripped the collar open so he could breathe.

He went to the window and slid it open.

In came a cool gust.

He sucked in air and tried to will his chest to expand sufficiently to inhale. In the years of his ministry he'd faced protesters, death threats, media criticism, and general discouragement, but nothing robbed him of his joy like his negative feelings for Elaine. How could one woman cause so much pain, weaken him to such an extent?

// YOU WANT A DIVORCE...YOU NEED TO DO IT //

It wasn't the first time he'd heard those words whispered in his head, but he'd always pushed them away. Today, as he stood staring out at the

Pacific, the seagulls flying free in the clear skies, Jon said it out loud.

"I need to do this."

His phone buzzed—a new text-message.

Maria: Are you all right?

He didn't particularly feel like answering it, but if he didn't she might keep texting him—something he wouldn't mind in another reality but had to discourage in this one.

Jon: I'm okay. How about you?

Maria: I'm so sorry about last night.

Jon: My fault entirely. Will you forgive me?

Maria: LOL. You're a good man. Hope things work out.

Jon: What are you going to do next?

Maria: I don't know. But we should forget about last night...about everything, okay?

Jon: Thanks for understanding.

Maria: NP. Take care, Jon.

He gazed at the screen for a long moment, took a deep breath, and with his thumb pressed the DELETE THREAD button on his display. For all intents and purposes, Maria Guzman never existed.

He was still holding the phone when it buzzed again. The image of Elaine's smiling face—a picture taken from their honeymoon in Maui— was on the screen. For a moment he wanted desperately to answer, to apologize, say anything that might restore them to...to what? How many years had it been since they'd truly been happy together?

No.

He couldn't deal with Elaine.

Not now.

Not with an important speech to prepare. Next week, he'd be at Cabrillo Stadium in San Diego before tens of thousands and millions more on television. He hit a button, and Elaine's face vanished.

42

YURI GOT PAST THE MEXICAN BORDER without a problem—
his client obviously had friends in high enough places that he could pull
important strings. Through tinted windows he watched all the cars at
Tijuana's border checkpoint, marveling at how he'd gone from a potential enemy combatant to a VIP of the CIA, his cover that of a covert operative in unaccounted-for cold war nuclear devices.

The driver let him off at the designated spot when the black Mercedes pulled up—the parking deck of the Wyndham Hotel near Mission
Bay. Yuri pulled the suitcase out from the trunk and walked directly into
the backseat of the Mercedes, where a lethally beautiful brunette (code-
named Raven) sat puffing on a cigarette. She crossed her long black-
leather-clad legs and eyed him with the warmth of a glacier. She looked
exactly like she did in the photo the client had texted him, so he didn't
hesitate to enter even though she seemed beautiful but deadly, the kind
who'd kiss you then stab you in the back.

Yuri shut the door, sat with the suitcase on his lap.

The car sped off.

"It's about time, Yuri."

His ears grew hot. She was so hot he couldn't help but stare.

"So, you are Raven?"

"I am. Seems you ran into some trouble." She flicked a lock of hair away from her face, re-crossed her legs, blew a cloud of smoke into Yuri's face, and pointed to the suitcase. "Is the package intact?"

43

PROVE IT. HAD SHE REALLY just asked him to do that? Oh, well—in for a penny…

"For one thing," Hope said, "I don't see any wings."

"Oh, you mean these?" From behind Nick's back, two large wings unfurled so quickly they sent a cool gust through her hair. Nearly stretching the entire length of his body, they glowed, the feathers white as snow.

"Where'd those come from?"

"They've been there all along."

"Why didn't I see them?"

"I chose not to show them. Would've alarmed you, don't you think? Now then…" He stood up and reached out to her. "If you need more proof…"

She took his hand and stood up, pulling her white robe tight with her free hand.

The entire hotel room just…detonated in a white brilliance that gently obliterated the walls, windows, floor, and ceiling, until all that remained was light. At first it hurt too much to keep her eyes open, so she squeezed them shut. But even that did little to mitigate the overwhelming brightness.

An intimate warmth enveloped her like a down comforter. Hope didn't want to open her eyes, breathe, do anything that might disturb the moment. Beneath her feet she felt nothing, certainly not a floor. Something like a soft breeze whispered past her ear and ran through her hair like a caress. Then came the early morning scent of a meadow fresh with dew.

Eyes still shut, she took in the wonderful fragrance and smiled.

"Clive? Where are we?"

His deep-chested laughter seemed distant, a mile away across an ethereal valley. And yet he whispered into her ear.

"Who's Clive?" His warm breath tickled the back of her neck. She felt his firm chest but couldn't fully distinguish his form. It was as if he were there and yet not there.

"I'm sorry, it's just...the way you look, the way you talk, you remind me of someone. What is your name, anyway?" Hope wanted desperately to open her eyes and behold what must be the most incredible sight she'd ever seen. But it might ruin this amazing moment the way tossing a stone into the still waters of a pond sends infinite ripples, irrevocably altering its placid state. No, she'd keep her eyes closed as long as she could stand it, take in every sensation.

Nick's words came into her mind, not by hearing but by perception.

// DO YOU BELIEVE I'M AN ANGEL NOW? //

"No," she said, smiling to show she was kidding. "What's your name?"

A warm wind laced with something like the aroma of sweet olive blew past her. It was Clive, sighing.

He said, "I could tell you..."

"But then you'd have to kill me?"

He didn't get it.

"Sorry, I'm kidding. Look, if you don't want to tell me your name, that's fine. I'll just keep calling you Clive until—"

"Nikolai."

All at once she felt him surrounding her, his shoulder beneath the back of her head. A jolt—like the one she felt when she was five years old and stuck a hairpin into the electric wall socket, only not painful— passed through her body, from her heart out to the tips of her fingers.

She opened her eyes but couldn't see a thing.

Utter darkness.

But she could feel his arms holding her tight, the way she'd held Chloe when she woke up with the night terrors..

"Shhhh..." Again his hot breath spread across her neck. It comfort- ed and electrified her at the same time. "Knowing and speaking the name of an angel with whom you've had this much contact should not be taken lightly."

Part of her thought she might cry. But not from fear. She wasn't sure why.

"I—I don't understand. Can I?"

"Can you what?"

"Say your name?"

Under the veil of the absolute gloom, his chest rose and fell. His arms tightened around her.

"Can't believe I'm doing this again," he said.

"May I?"

"Yes." The vibrations from his chest resonated in her shoulders.

"Nikolai."

All around her, the darkness melted away. She caught the briefest glimpse of what lay beneath them and buried her face in his chest.

"It's all right," he said, stroking her hair. "Don't be afraid. Go ahead, look."

Trembling, Hope lifted her face and peered over his arm.

Far below—she couldn't tell how far—she saw a blue mass with green and brown patterns under a floating cottony patchwork. The earth and they were high above it. It was so beautiful she had to force herself to look and not hide her eyes.

"I'm dreaming."

"You're not."

"Then I must be dead."

"Definitely not."

She looked up to him and thought he looked resigned. But to what?

"How can we be—how can *I* be here out in space and still alive?" she said.

"Because you're not really in space. At least, not as you understand it." He winced, suddenly. Touched the side of his head.

"What's wrong?"

"Not sure. It takes a bit of effort to project a construct around you so you can experience this."

"A what?"

"A construct."

"I don't understand any of this, Nikolai." She wrapped her arms around him even tighter and gazed down at the planet. Though she didn't sense herself falling hundreds of miles to the surface, everything within her felt that if she were to let go, that was exactly what would happen.

"May I ask a small favor?" he said.

"I'm not in a position to object."

"Would you call me Nick? Nikolai is so...I don't know, nineteenth-century."

"Nineteenth—okay, whatever you say."

Any fear had given way to an odd euphoria. She was staring down at the earth! Not in an astronaut's space suit but just as she was, wearing nothing but her hotel robe, the belt of which had floated up.

"How's this possible?" she said.

"Welcome to my realm." Nick was gazing down at the giant blue marble that was Hope's home. "I don't mean that as in *my* realm where I'm the owner or master, but the realm in which I'm indigenous."

"So, you're an alien?"

He shook his head and grinned. "I've brought you to the spiritual realm."

"Not to sound skeptical, but you see that big globe down there, with the continents—North America, Africa, and all? That looks pretty physical to me."

"Of course. The physical and spiritual realms aren't mutually exclusive. They coexist, layered and woven together like a basket's distinct ribbons. But here's the part most humans don't realize. *Your* realm, the physical, is merely a likeness, a dim reflection of reality—which is, of course, the spiritual realm."

She thought of *The Chronicles of Narnia*, which her father used to read to her when she was a child.

"Like the Shadowlands."

"Precisely."

Just then, something massive overshadowed the moon's reflected light. Hope turned around just in time to see the large pair of solar panels and a communications dish mounted to the center of a huge NASA-emblazoned satellite—coming straight at them.

"Nick!" She threw herself into his arms again.

"It's okay, just relax."

She braced for the impending impact.

"Do something!" she yelled.

"Why?"

She pounded his chest. "Hello? We're going to die!"

"Get a grip, will you? Now watch. Wait for it..."

Hope turned around and looked on in horror as it careened straight at them.

"We're going to die, we're going to—Oh..My—!"

She was about to shut her eyes, but it was too late. She saw the whole thing happen, even as the satellite reached them.

She felt nothing.

In the course of a second—maybe less—the entire satellite passed through them. Or rather, they passed through *it*. Everything happened so fast Hope could barely make out what she saw inside the spacecraft the moment before it continued past them and cruised into the distance.

"What in the world?"

Nick winked at her. "Of the world, not *in* the world."

"You said I wasn't dead, but I just passed right through solid matter. Oh my God, I'm a ghost—what have you done with my body?"

"You've got it all wrong," he said. "Most mortals do, so I can't say I blame you. What was it C.S. Lewis said? 'You don't have a soul. You are a soul. You have a body.'"

"Then what happened to it?"

"You're still in it." She loved the way his eyes fixed on hers. "Think of this as another dimension—though even that would be a gross over-simplification."

"Humor me."

"Here in the spiritual realm or layer, we're free from the limitations of physical time and space. Hawking, Einstein, Sagan, all their mumbo-jumbo about quantum physics? At best, their theories are like a six-year-old's explanation of how semiconductors works."

"Well, they're all a heck of a lot smarter than me."

"Not necessarily." He took her by both hands and they started moving toward the planet. Slowly, thank God. Since there was no wind nor any sense of motion as Hope knew it, it was astonishing but not really frightening that they were hovering over the Great Wall of China in seconds.

She touched her neck and frowned.

"What is it?" Nick said, floating closer.

"Looking down at the Great Wall reminds me of my father. Before he died, he gave me a jade pendant with a dragon and phoenix carved into it. He told me all kinds of stories about it, and after he died that pendant was the only thing I had from him besides my memories."

"When did you lose it?"

"Last night, when I..." Hope lifted her eyes to meet Nick's. "When you saved me." She put on a brave face and changed the subject. "Anyway, you were telling me about the physical and spiritual realms?"

"I can tell you a lot more, but I think it's best if I show you." He pointed down. "

"Okay, I guess. The laws of physics don't apply, so I can't get hurt, right?"

"Had you been in the physical layer just a few moments ago, you'd be abstract art, splattered over the hull of that satellite by now." He took her hands and aimed headlong towards the surface of what looked like California.

"Nick?"

He turned and looked her in the eye: *Trust me.*

"Is any of this real?"

They were flying straight down as he replied.

"All of it."

44

LITO PICKED UP AN OLD PHOTO from his desk: Papi and him as a boy of eight on a fishing boat in Ensenada. He was holding a large halibut by the tail, Papi standing proudly next to him—proud because it was Lito's fourth catch of the day and the only fish he'd kept. "Toss the little fish back and go for the big ones" was a lesson Lito had finally learned.

Had Alfonso been a little fish?

What had he done with the Suarezes? And had he ever so much as hinted to Maria about the secret? Perhaps the best thing to do was to get it out in the open, tell her himself lest she hear it elsewhere—she must have wondered all these years.

Lito set the picture down and sighed. Papi would know what to do. At least, not the old man who was drunk every hour of his final days but the handsome man everyone used to come to for advice, money, and—

A light rap on the door.

"Come in!"

In came Manuel, a tall and lanky twenty-year-old high school dropout with the remarkable ability to blend into any setting—the kid was practically invisible. He was second in line to Alfonso but nowhere near as close to the family.

Following Manuel in was Eduardo, an older man who used to shadow Papi and was now Lito's advisor, since Papi had died. When he smiled he was like an *abuelo*, a grandpa, but when he scowled no one dared mistake him as anything but a vicious assassin, hence the very best protection, as well as counsel.

Back in the day, anyway.

Oh, Eduardo could still catch you by surprise and break your neck. But he just wasn't as quick as he used to be. For now, Lito chose him because he was the only person he could trust—or rather, the person he mistrusted the least.

"Manuel has some information," Eduardo said, making himself comfortable in the red leather chair at the back of the office. He lit up a cigar, just as he always had when Papi occupied this office. Lito hated the smoke, but the smell brought back the days when he read Superman comics while the two of them talked "business" here.

"What kind of information?"

Manuel looked over at Eduardo, who nodded.

Still standing, Manuel said, "It's about Alfonso." His eyes shifted to Eduardo, then back to Lito.

"Go *on*," Lito said.

Eduardo got up and slapped the back of Manuel's head. Hard.

"*Estupido!* Just tell him what you told me."

Rubbing the back of his head and glaring back at the old man, Manuel took the spoke up.

"I'm only telling you what I heard, okay? I don't really know anything and I don't want to get in any trouble."

"You will if you don't stop wasting my time like this."

"Okay, okay. Well, before Alfonso...*died*, he was telling me all kinds of crazy stuff. I thought he was just messing with me, being the new guy, you know? But then he starts telling me there's something coming and I should decide what side I'm going to be on when it all hits the fan, you know?"

Lito glared at him. "Go on."

"He was saying crap like, 'When it all goes down I'll own it all and Lito can kiss my hairy—'"

"When *what* goes down? Own *what*?"

"He said if you didn't turn over the Hernandez branch—"

"Again with the Hernandez branch! Eduardo, why am I the last to know about this?"

"Your father told me never to talk to you about it."

"How long has—" The conversation had just shifted into an entirely different gear. Lito shot the young man a sharp glance.

"Okay, Manuel>"

"Señor?"

"Get out." As soon as he'd left, Lito turned to Eduardo. "Tell me."

"I won't betray your father."

"You would betray me, then?" Lito walked over to the old man and took out his gun. He didn't brandish it or point it, just held it. To threaten him was futile, unless he planned to follow through. But killing two of his top men in the same week would send the wrong message throughout the organization: The head grows weak, insecure.

Eduardo smiled. "I'm protecting you, Lito."

"Let *me* decide whether or not I need protection, and from what."

"That's not what your father wanted in this case."

The dance grew more complex. Of course he could force it out of the old man, but that would alter their relationship. Now more than ever he needed the support of the founding members, whoever was left of them.

"My father is dead. He doesn't have to bear the burden of running this organization, doesn't have to deal with the Alfonsos in it. He never foresaw any of this."

Eduardo got out of his chair and walked right up to Lito, so close that the smell of cigar breath went straight into his face.

"He foresaw *all* of this, even how you are reacting now."

"Don't make me do this, Eduardo. You know how my family loves you."

"And I am always the friend and protector of the Guzmans. Trust me as your Papi trusted me."

Lito thought of all the times Papi talked down to him in front of men like Eduardo. *He's just a little runt, don't mind him. Lito? Never going to amount to anything. I wish I had another son, or daughter even—can't imagine Lito ever taking over for me.*

All said in jest, before he even hit puberty, but humiliating just the same. Lito had laughed along with them every time, but when he was alone he sometimes cried. Papi would find him and say, "Come on! I was just joking, Lito!" And he had been, or he'd never have passed the mantel to his son before dying. But his last words about the organization had been, "Don't screw this up, Lito."

He lifted the gun and pressed it against Eduardo's chest.

"Tell me about the Hernandez branch. What did it have to do with the Suarez family?"

The old man's bushy white eyebrows lifted and fell in resignation.

"Has it really come to this, Lito?"

"I'm sorry. I need to know."

Eduardo pushed the muzzle of the gun aside, steepled his hands, and looked heavenward.

"Forgive me, Señor Guzman. He insisted, as you said he would."

"You no longer answer to my father, Eduardo. You answer to me."

"Yeah, well...I'm going to hell because you're making me break my promise to a dead man."

"You're going to hell for a thousand other reasons, don't worry so much about this one."

"Ha!" The old man took another puff, sputtered, and slapped Lito's back. "Now, that's...funny."

"So, the Hernandez branch?"

Eduardo sighed. "Okay, sit down. This isn't going to be easy."

45

FOR THE ENTIRE DESCENT Hope clung to Nick with all her strength. Even though the wind passed right through her, she could still hear it. It made a deafening noise, louder than anything she'd ever heard in her life.

"Are we there yet?" she said.

"No need to shout, I can hear you just fine."

It was like that awkward moment where you think you need to scream above the noise in order to be heard, and then the noise stops and you're still hollering at the top of your lungs. Hope laughed, but when she saw the sandy grounds of what must have been the Mojave Desert getting alarmingly close, she buried her face in his shoulder.

"Don't you want to look?" Nick said.

"Tell me when we're there!"

"We are."

"What?" She was wrapped around him like a bear cub clinging to a tree trunk. But there he stood, his feet firmly planted in sand that stretched all the way until it touched the horizon, into which the sun was sinking.

"Oh. We're physical again." She thumped his back with her fist.

"I see you've grown quite attached. But would you mind climbing down now?"

Hope unwound herself and set her feet on the ground. It was real all right, but her sense of reality had changed somehow.

"Now do you believe?" he said, giving her a dangerous smile.

"Not sure. This could all be a dream, or a near-death hallucination." He had to be one or the other—or exactly what he said he was. Whatever the case, she wanted to experience more.

"What will it take, O ye of little faith?"

"I don't know." Deep down, she believed. But she wanted more to ground her in this reality. Her head felt light and her legs felt like they were made of linguine. She shut her eyes and sat down in the warm sand.

"Hope?" Nick came close. Without even touching her, she could feel his presence, his warmth.

"I'm just trying to wrap my head around this."

His placed his fingertips on her forehead.

"Eyes shut, please."

"Why?"

"I'm taking you somewhere." He took her hand and helped her to her feet.

"Where?"

"Think of something really significant in your life. Try to remember how it looked, what it sounded like, how it felt, the smell...everything."

When she opened her eyes, they were standing side by side. But she was now watching a younger version of herself sitting in a glider in that little apartment in Pacific Beach, singing a lullaby to the two-month-old baby in her arms.

"What *is* this, Nick? It's so real, but it happened years ago."

"It's from your mind. The thoughts you open to me are like a thread from a piece of cloth I can pull—I'm drawing on your thoughts and memories and weaving a perceptual construct for you. Angels do this to help mortals see beyond their comprehension in a metaphorical way."

"Sounds dangerous."

"How so?"

"What if the thread is attached to something really dark and frightening? What if you kept pulling on that thread until the whole mind unravels?"

Nick's eyes narrowed. "Why in heaven's name would I do that?"

"I'm just saying."

And then, in the utter nothingness, she heard it.

That doorbell. Her heart sank.

"Oh, Nick—I don't want to see this."

"What's the matter?"

"I don't know why I chose this memory." She turned away. "Make it stop."

"Are you certain?"

The fear in her muffled cry was enough. Nick was just about to end the construct when she grasped his hand.

"No, wait. Let it go on."

"You sure?"

"Yes." She sounded like a terrified child.

The construct-Hope heard the doorbell, stood up with baby Chloe fast asleep in her arms, and walked over to the door.

Hope didn't need to listen to what the two marines had to say—she could never forget the day she learned that her husband of two years and father of their beautiful baby had been killed in Fallujah when his jeep went over an IED.

She watched her younger self take the news, the papers, the al. The younger Hope Matheson saw the marines out, then sat quietly again in the glider with Chloe. But it didn't feel the way it had then, not at all.

This memory she'd avoided for so long should have torn her apart, but something unexpected happened. In the midst of reliving it, she felt the emotional and spiritual equivalent of a warm, powerful embrace. Though not in her ears, she heard a distinct, paternal voice. It wasn't Nick's, she was certain of that. It was filled with love and strength, saying, // I AM THERE //

Don't you mean, you were there?

// I *AM* THERE //

The construct faded.

They were now standing inside a white void.

Nick, who seemed not to have heard the voice, looked concerned.

"I said significant. I'm sorry, Hope—I should have asked you to think of a happy memory. Are you all right?"

"Yes, surprisingly." The memory was still there but not the devastation and despair that had always gone with it. "How about this one?"

This time when she opened her eyes they were standing with a crowd of people in the pews of San Loreno's, the church where she and her second husband had been married.

The happy couple stood before the guests outside the church and posed for photos as a storm of confetti and rice flew their way. Four-year-old Chloe stood between her mother and new stepfather, Damien Suarez.

"That's better," Nick said. "But wait, that man—"

"He was caught in the same crossfire as Chloe."

"I remember now. Forgive me, but you don't seem sad over his loss."

"Oh, Damien was charming and Chloe just loved him to pieces, and I was desperate for someone to help us out. But then he started gambling—at least I learned he'd been gambling—two months into the marriage. Behind my back he was selling my things, even some things of Brandon's I'd kept. When I confronted him about it, he...Anyway, the day he and Chloe were killed, he said he was taking her to school. But after I found out they were caught in the crossfire of a drug-related crime, I wondered how far his lies went."

She watched little Chloe in a flower girl's dress smiling, waving to the people waving at her.

"Guess we'll never know, will we?" she said softly. And all at once, like a flash flood, the memories of loss, abuse, all the things that had driven her to end her life swept over her. She held onto Nick's arms for support.

"Please, can we end this construct now?"

"Say no more."

Back into the white void.

Where, to her surprise, the same voice spoke to her soul. Now it came in a still, small whisper.

"I am there, Hope. Your past, your future, I am there."

A little more gradually this time, the pain attached to the memories of Chloe's death eased. Slow as it was, Hope sensed that this too was being lifted from her. She would be stronger than before, with a chance to overcome her past and enjoy her future—something that until now she never thought she'd see.

It helped her to focus on Nick's deep blue eyes. The face of an angel.

"Did you hear it, Nick?"

"What?"

"That voice." She shut her eyes trying to remember its pitch, its timbre. "It kept saying, 'I am there.' And when it said that, the terrible pain from my worst memories seemed to ease, as if I'd awoken from a nightmare. "

"Ah, yes."

"It wasn't you…Was it?"

"No, it was probably Him." Nick pointed upwards. "He's been known to reach through time and by His mere presence, change everything for humans. For the better, of course. You only need to be open to it, as you obviously are."

"Yes, but you led me here, helped me find...I don't know what else to call it but healing. It's like I've been set free from a prison I didn't know existed." She hugged him tight. "How can I ever thank you?"

"No need," he said, lifting her chin to look into her eyes. "I just want you to know one thing, Hope. I'm breaking all kinds of angel laws, but I'm going to say it anyway."

She fixed her gaze on him. It seemed like the sun was rising behind him, illuminating his head, his shoulders, with golden light.

"From the day I first saw you," he said, "I sensed a connection. Angels and mortals aren't permitted to share this connection, yet there it was. I had no idea I'd see you again so soon. And under such...different circumstances."

"What circumstances?"

He looked taken aback by the question, caught off guard.

"You know, meeting you at the point of despair."

"And saving me! Opening my eyes to a whole new perspective." She took his hands. "You're everything a guardian angel should be."

"I'm not a guardian." His expression sobered. "Sometimes I wonder how much of an angel I really am."

"Why do you say that?"

"I've got a past."

"We've all got one."

"Mine's longer."

She shot him a look. Remembering something that painful and still making wisecracks?

"Would it help to talk about it?" *Oh, sure. I'm counseling an angel.*

"I've never shared it with anyone," Nick said, "and I don't think talking about it will help much, right now."

"I'm sorry, I didn't mean to pry, I just—"

"But perhaps I can show you."

46

FOR OVER A CENTURY, NICK had kept his past to himself. He'd done his best to sweep that blip in history under the rug, though it was highly improbable that no one in the Angel Forces knew.

Now, having jeopardized everything to save the woman he'd been assigned to destroy, he felt the need to be known, understood. Perhaps absolved.

"Show me?" Hope's face was alight with curiosity.

"Haven't you wondered why I revealed myself to you the way I did?"

She shook her head. "I'm still trying to get my head around what you are."

"When I first saw you, back in the hospital where Chloe died, I looked into your eyes. You reminded me of a person I fell in love with and lost, tragically. And Chloe reminded me of someone just as dear to me."

"Can angels fall in love?"

"They can. And with humans, too, although that's strictly forbidden." The laws, those blasted laws. As he re-opened the wounds of the past, they returned to him.

An angel shall not become emotionally involved with a mortal.

An angel shall not become physically involved with a mortal.

An angel shall not marry or sire offspring with a mortal.

An angel shall not heal a mortal except by proper authorization...

"I shouldn't have allowed myself, but I couldn't help it."

"Who was she?"

"Her name was Sophia." Nick waved his hand, and before them the blank canvas of light began morphing into London in the early 1900s.

LONDON, ENGLAND 1907

He'd been watching her for about five years now, traveling from the mortal planes to the great beyond. Nikolai knew better than to tarry between assignments, but given the scope of eternity he didn't think anyone in the Angel Forces would notice.

He followed her invisibly with fascination and, yes, admiration—she was the loveliest young woman he'd seen over the past millennium.

Carrying on her arm a basket full of fruit from Bailey's Market, she walked at a brisk pace, easily averting a crowd of people entering the doors under the huge signs:

DISTRICT RAILWAY
VICTORIA STATION

FREQUENT TRAINS TO CITY AND
ALL PARTS OF LONDON & SUBURBS

He marveled at her alacrity. She soared past the Earl's Court Exhibition, past the R.P. Beattie Specialty in Plumbing billboard, past the row of horse-drawn cabs parked along the road.

Her eyes—topaz set in alabaster—sparkled when she saw the man seated at the bistro table down the road. He wore a black frock coat, something you saw less and less of these days, and a hat he took off as he stood and waved.

"Sophia!"

She rushed over, stopping just short of a frontal collision. Judging by the sheer joy on her face, Nick expected her to throw her arms around the man.

"Oh Albert, I'm so happy you sent for me. Do forgive this frightful basket—I had to make up some sort of excuse to convince Mother I needed to go out."

"Please, won't you join me?"

"Thank you. Lovely morning, wouldn't you agree?"

"Quite." He pulled out a chair and seated her.

Nikolai hovered about them, observing with the keenest interest. Sophia nodded her thanks as a waiter brought tea to the table, but her eyes were so fixed on Albert she never even looked at her cup. Sitting on the edge of her chair, smiling so wide it must surely hurt, she exuded excitement.

"Now, Sophia. We've known each other for about two years now."

"Twenty-five months, three weeks, two days..."

"Right. In any case—"

"And seventeen hours." She covered her smile with her gloved hand, then looked up innocently at him. "Sorry." She shuddered, then hugged her arms. "It's my nerves. I always shiver when I'm excited."

Albert did not smile. "In any case, it occurred to me that you and your family might be wondering what my intentions are."

"Yes?" she said, a little squeak in her voice.

"And so..." He reached into his coat pocket.

"Oh, yes, Albert! Yes, yes, and again, yes!" She jumped up, no doubt to throw herself into his arms—

"Yes what, Sophia? I haven't even told you yet."

"Sorry." She sat back down, still smiling. "Please, go on."

He pulled out an envelope and set it on the table.

"Sophia, I'm calling it all off."

Now the smile faded. The face fell.

"You're...? I'm sorry, I don't understand."

"Please don't make this any more difficult than it needs to be. I can't marry you. We should have seen this coming."

She said nothing. Her face, in despair, looked so different. Nikolai could hardly bear it.

Albert reached across the table to take her hands but she pulled them back, still staring into the air straight at Nikolai, as though asking him, *Why?*

"In the long run, when you're older, you'll understand. We're just not..." He looked up, also in Nikolai's direction, as though asking his help finding the word. "We're not *compatible*."

She didn't respond. Gone from her face was the joy, the innocence, all that made her who she was.

"Sophia?"

She finally turned to face Albert, and spoke. With each word her voice lowered in volume but rose in intensity.

"Thank you for your honesty, though it took you twenty-five months, three weeks, two days, and seventeen hours to come up with it."

"As I've said, in the long run you'll understand." He slid the envelope over to her. "Here."

Instead of looking at it she turned away in Nikolai's direction.

"Whatever it is, I don't want it," she said. Her veil of courage and dignity was gossamer-thin, but oh, how he admired her for it.

"Don't be ridiculous. Take it!"

"I have no interest in your...*envelope*." Sophia glanced down at the table as though it were covered with dung.

"Don't you even want to know what's in it?"

Sophia stood up. "I think I'd rather leave, Albert."

"It's a portion of the money you might have enjoyed had we—"

She snatched the envelope, opened the flap, held the envelope over Albert without looking inside, glanced up in Nikolai's direction...

Go on, now. That's my girl.

...and poured coins and bills all over Albert's head.

"What!" Albert didn't seem to know what to do with his hands. "Are you out of your mind?"

"You can keep your money, Albert." She grabbed her cup of tea and threw it in his face. "And do with it something anatomically improbable!"

Though she could not perceive his presence, Nikolai smiled and bowed as she walked away, head held high to show Albert what *she* thought of him and his pathetic attempt at appeasing what *he* probably thought of as his conscience.

PRESENT DAY

The entire construct paused like a DVR movie.

"You haven't changed," Hope said.

"Angels don't age," Nick said, wistfully regarding the young construct-Sophia. A sharp pain behind his eyes made him struggle not to grimace.

"She seems like a nice girl. What happened?"

"To make a long story short, I took an unauthorized hiatus in order to be with her. Sophia was beautiful, great fun, and a wonderful person. Over time I revealed myself to her and we did what has been forbidden since the dawn of humankind."

"You fell in love." Hope gave him a look of compassion.

"I'm afraid it's worse than that."

"Wait a minute, you mean—"

"I married her. And worse still..."

She leaned closer.

"Is that even possible?" she said.

"When I choose to take on a physical form, I'm fully human, though I still possess what you consider supernatural abilities."

"So did you have a son or a daughter?"

"I'll show you."

A little girl with golden hair and shining sapphire eyes stood smiling in front of them. A very familiar-looking little girl.

"This is...this was Clara," Nick said.

Hope knelt down and looked straight at her, knowing that as a construct, this child was just a figment of Nick's memory. Nonetheless she touched Clara's hair, ran her fingers down the braided pigtails around which little red bows were tied.

Then smiled and leapt to her feet.

"She looks like Chloe."

"The resemblance is striking. I can't help wondering if there's a reason I was assigned to escort Chloe. But since I'd been demoted to reaper, I didn't get to ask those questions."

"Demoted? What for?"

"Well, I assume that's what happened. After all, I'd broken just about every law—I was grateful it wasn't anything worse than being reassigned to the mundane work of ushering souls."

Staring incredulously at the little construct of Clara, Hope circled her while she spoke to Nick.

"Why is it so wrong for angels to fall in love with humans? Marry them, have children with them?"

"From what I've been told, certain humans and angels did have children eons ago, with dangerous results. It's all rather vague, but supposedly there's a danger of their offspring becoming highly powerful, unstable beings with a thirst for blood, some of them extraordinarily intelligent and irresistibly beautiful."

"Were they angels or human?"

"A hybrid of both called Nephilim. Several cultures cite the presence of Nephilim in their history. Outside of the Hebrew Bible, the Torah, other civilizations have their own terminology. But I've never seen one. Doubt they even exist."

"So why make such stringent laws over a matter of speculation?"

"My thoughts, exactly. Still, if Nephilim are real and have in fact abused their power to wreak all kinds of havoc on mankind, of course there's cause for concern. Believers speculate that some of history's greatest minds, most powerful rulers, and cruelest dictators were Nephilim."

"Such as?"

"Oh, there's an infamous list of Nephilim, but I consider the whole thing apocryphal. Among them are Ch'in Shih-huan-ti, Caligula, Ghengis Khan, Herod the Great, Vlad Tepes—"

"Vlad the Impaler?"

He nodded.

"Dracula was a Nephilim! And I suppose Hitler's on the list?"

"Absolutely."

Hope closed her eyes for a moment. When they opened, she pointed to the Clara-construct.

"How about her?"

"Even those who believe in Nephilim don't know if they all turn out evil—they don't even know if Nephilim are mortal or immortal. In my mind, they hold to those myths in order to justify angel laws that will deter us from intermingling with humans."

"So what went wrong with you and Sophia?" She was eager to know—he understood why and admired her for it. Now, the dread of reliving the story gave way to a need to share it with her.

"After Sophia and I married she noticed I never got ill, never looked tired, and after some years never showed signs of aging. She said I was distant, somehow—even though we were close as could be, in so many ways. She asked questions I wouldn't answer, then insisted there was something standing between us, something important, she just knew it— of course she was right.

"So I told her the truth. Then I told her I was willing to give up my angel nature and become a human to be with her. I thought she'd be happy—but the last thing she wanted was for me to renounce my angel status and lose my immortality and other supernatural attributes. No, she wanted to know all about them, even craved some of them for herself—you know, the eternal youth, the limitless energy...and in retrospect, the power."

"I can see why." Hope was eyeing him with great interest.

"I told her to let it go, it wasn't worth it. Our love was enough." Nick's voice dropped. "Only it wasn't, for Sophia. She became obsessed with the supernatural—I only learned by overhearing a conversation. She'd been secretly consulting with some kind of dark occultists about how she could tap into it. I warned her it wasn't safe—she dismissed it, saying I was just threatened by her."

"But what about Clara?" Hope said.

"Right. Well, since Sophia was never around—sometimes staying away for weeks at a time, and eventually leaving home for good—I had to raise Clara on my own. She grew into the loveliest, gentlest girl you could ever imagine. She couldn't possibly have been a Nephilim—she was sweeter than any angel I'd ever known."

Nick reached out to touch the Clara-construct, but she vanished before his hand reached it. Hope gave him a sympathetic smile.

"Did Sophia ever come back?"

From the corner of his eye, Nick thought he saw something move. He turned to look and saw nothing but the freeze-frame image of turn of the century London. But he sensed something dark and cold—and close by.

"Nick?"

"One day she did," he said, lowering his eyes. "But she'd changed."

47

WHEN THE STORM HIT, IT DIDN'T COME in the form of smartphone photos but rather a security camera video from the Hotel Pacifica. In the brief montage of clips Jon saw himself walking out of the elevator with Maria, saw Maria draping her arms around his neck and kissing him as she pulled him into the hotel room, saw himself coming out of the room, looking around—furtively—and hurrying to the elevator. One creative version put raunchy music in the background and looped the split-second moment when Jon and Maria's faces came within striking distance, just before the door obscured the view. Of course it had gone viral, getting two million hits on YouTube within hours of its posting.

Sitting in his office behind a locked door—his "Do Not Disturb" cue to his staff—Jon leaned his head back against the soft leather of his chair in an attempt to ease the tension in his knotted shoulder and neck muscles.

What am I going to do?

With each passing hour, he anticipated a mortally wounded Elaine bursting through the door and demanding that he tell her who the bimbo on the tape was. Next would be a call from his manager informing him that speaking engagements and book deal had been canceled. Divorce would give him a way out of their marriage which had all but died after Matthew's birth. It had only taken a year after the wedding for her true colors to show.

If she doesn't file, I will. But the more he thought about divorce, the worse he felt. What would happen to Matthew? And the truth was, he loved Elaine. It had only been half a day, but somehow the fact that he'd allowed himself to consider ending their marriage made him realize how much he really cared for her.

With his suitcase packed, he left the office. Might as well drive down to San Diego and check into the hotel a week early, avoid Elaine's raking him over the coals for the video.

He just needed some time away to sort things out.

Jon got into his car and tried to pray, but the words wouldn't come out. Angry thoughts kept wrenching his heart, overwhelming any sense of repentance. Four words ran through his mind as he sped down the I-5:

You did nothing wrong...

His heart, it seemed, wasn't buying it. The frustration of needing to pray, wanting to pray tormented him until, like David before Nathan the prophet who'd confronted him about his selfish pride and sin, the Shepherd King's song came to mind:

Create in me a clean heart, O God,
And renew a steadfast spirit within me.
Cast me not away from Your presence,
And take not Your Holy Spirit from me.

48

"YOU'VE NEVER HEARD OF THE HERNANDEZ BRANCH," Eduardo said, his voice like sandpaper.

"Thank you for stating the obvious. Don't make me guess."

"Lito, since you were a child, you had a reputation."

"A good one, no?"

"Well, that depends. You were always a do-things-right, play-fair type of kid. Your Papi admired you for that."

Lito huffed. "I doubt it."

"Well, okay, maybe it annoyed him a bit. But he knew you would treat people fair."

Eduardo choked on a cloud of smoke and began coughing—more and more violently. Lito cracked open a bottle of Arrowhead water and held it out, but the old man waved it off as he heaved and coughed.

"I need...a real drink."

Lito put the bottle in his hand and closed his fingers around it.

"It's all I have right now."

Eduardo took a grudging swallow and wiped his mouth with his sleeve.

"Lito, Lito, Lito. Get real. You're head of a drug cartel, not a charity."

"The drugs are just one of our revenue streams. We own other businesses—legitimate businesses—and we could have more."

The old man glared at him. "Don't let anyone in the organization *ever* hear you talk like that. They'll see you as weak, and you already got enough to worry about."

"What do you mean?"

"I tried to handle this on my own, but that idiot Alfonso went and messed everything up."

"Does any of this have to do with the Hernandez branch?"

"I'm getting to that, okay? Young people these days. So impatient."

In fact, Lito *was* losing his patience. But Eduardo was probably the only person from Papi's generation he could trust. Probably the only person, period. So he sat back in his chair, put his feet up on his desk and hands behind his head.

"I've got all day."

"Look, it's for two reasons you don't know about the Hernandez branch. First, your father didn't want you to. And second, it's too profitable an operation to risk you jeopardizing things with your boy scout ways."

"So what's the profit from? Alcohol, gambling, merchandise?"

"Some might consider it merchandise." Eduardo puffed another cloud of smoke.

"You're going to have to get a lot more specific."

"Soon as I tell you? You're going to wish I never did."

"The longer you put it off, the more you're going to wish you never stalled."

"All right." Eduardo sighed. "The Hernandez branch deals in...human assets."

"You make it sound like a temp agency."

"No, Lito. Think about it."

It should not have come as a shock, but it did. He knew other cartels had no qualms about it, and it wasn't unthinkable that Papi would do it given his lack of morals. But Lito had never imagined working in this kind of commerce.

"Don't tell me you're talking about human trafficking?"

"You say that like it's a bad thing."

"It's unacceptable!"

"This kind of thing has been going on since before you were born, before any of us were born."

"It's slavery. Do you know what they do with—of course you do. How could this have gone on all this time and nobody told me?"

The old man's considerable belly bounced as he laughed.

"Because we knew how you'd react."

"We? Who, *you and Alfonso*?" Lito was shouting.

"Your Papi and me! He made me promise not to tell you because he knew you'd want to shut it down."

Eduardo was right. Papi had known him too well.

But Lito also knew that his men would never allow him to jeopardize everything they'd worked for, sacrificed for, broken the law for—just because among all the things to which he turned a blind eye, he had a conscience about a particular trade.

He had to work his way carefully through this mine field. He relaxed his face, his shoulders, then gave Eduardo a just-kidding smile.

"So the Hernandez branch has been profitable?" he said.

"You might say that. They bring in about thirty percent of our gross revenue."

"Interesting."

"So what do you think, really? You want to shut it down, like Papi said you would?"

Lito eyed Eduardo suspiciously. "You got a personal interest in it?"

"I got a personal interest in everything we do." And he did. Eduardo was one of the organization's earliest powerful investors.

"So what was the deal with Alfonso?" Lito said. "How'd he know about this?"

"Your father told him to look after you—I was a witness to this. He also said Alfonso could never touch the Hernandez branch because it would offend you. But Alfonso either forgot or ignored the fact that *you* didn't know about it. I had him followed for three months before I found out he was trying to turn the Hernandezes on us and move them over to the Suarezes. I recently found out he almost brokered a deal with one of the Suarezes, think his name was Damien. But Damien and the little girl he was selling got caught in the crossfire. After that, Alfonso wised up and decided to lay low and work his way in from the inside."

Bile rose up in Lito's throat.

"That's why he started dating Maria."

"He was going to marry Maria and use her for leverage—get you to put him in charge of the Hernandez branch as soon as he told you about them. By then he'd have brokered a deal with the Suarezes, figuring you'd want to sell the branch off. If you didn't see it his way, Alfonso would turn on you and join them. That little—"

"I can't thank you enough, Eduardo. I had no idea he was doing this."

"I should have found out earlier, but it was *Alfonso.*" The old man shook his head. "None of us could believe it."

Lito glanced over at the picture of him and Maria as elementary school kids, Papi behind them by the big palm tree in their backyard. He tried to imagine that little girl in the picture being again ripped from the loving arms of her family—and sold as a sex slave somewhere far away. Was this really what he wanted, to run an organization that—

"So, Lito? What do you think?"

He couldn't let on what he really thought. If Eduardo had kept a secret this big from him for so long, there was no way to tell how much he could be trusted—if at all.

"It's profitable, you say. So it pays for your stuff."

"Yours too." Eduardo winked. "But hey, *you're* Señor Guzman now, not your dead father. It's your call. What you say goes."

"Don't you forget it. And the Suarezes? What's their disposition, now that we've taken out their mole?"

A wave of the hand. "Don't even worry about them. They knew Alfonso was full of hot air. Anyway, they'd have to get past me if they wanted to do anything to the Guzmans."

"They wouldn't be that stupid." But what if Eduardo himself had been compromised? Even if he hadn't, could he sense that Lito wasn't as on board with this human trafficking as he let on?

The old man sucked in another pull on his cigar and spewed out another toxic cloud.

"Now you know." He looked Lito straight in the eyes, not coughing, not smoking. "What's it going to be?"

Lito's shirt stuck to his back. He walked over to Eduardo, signaling that the meeting was over, and squeezed his shoulder.

"Business as usual, my friend. Business as usual."

49

THE CONSTRUCT RESUMED AND THE SCENE dissolved into a new one:

The terminus at Victoria Station.

Nick could imagine nothing worse than reliving this day. Yet if he didn't, the memory would continue to fester and swell like a boil. Perhaps sharing this experience with someone he cared about would help.

"You don't have to do this, Nick."

Hope stretched out her hand.

Feeling light-headed, weak in the knees, he reached for it.

"I'm sorry," he said. "It's a difficult memory."   He rested his forehead in his hand, and sighed. "Over the millennia I've confronted demons, armies, and the forces of nature at its most destructive, but none of that made me as anxious as I feel now, thinking about it."

"If it's too much…"

Nick took a deep breath.

Shut his eyes.

Gathering all his courage, he stood tall, held Hope's hand firmly, and began the memory-construct.

LONDON, ENGLAND 1913

It had been some three years since Sophia left, and he barely recognized her when she returned to their flat in London. But there she was, standing at the door, her flaxen hair now midnight black, her eyes...He shuddered. She wore a black dress, black gloves, and held herself with regal comportment. Nothing like the sweet, sassy young woman with whom he'd fallen in love and married.

"Aren't you going to invite me in?" she said.

"I'm sorry, where are my manners?" Nikolai stepped back to let her in. He couldn't believe he was treating her like a stranger. Couldn't believe she *was* a stranger.

"Hmmm." She strode into the living area, stopped, looked around. "And where is Clara?"

"At school, naturally."

"I told you in my letter I wanted her to be here when I returned."

"You're early."

She narrowed her eyes at him for a moment. "So I am." Then she giggled, but it wasn't Sophia's giggle. Not a trace of that familiar mirth.

Who *was* this woman?

"Won't you have a seat?" He stepped over to the stove, where a kettle was steaming. "Tea?"

"Thank you, yes." She sat. Odd that she'd traveled without luggage. There had to be a thousand things to ask her, but he thought it best to let her set the tone and pace. He'd assumed it would take a great deal of effort to suppress his anger over her abandoning Clara and him after he'd given up just about everything to be with her. But she was so unlike the woman who'd left him he felt no inclination to berate her. In fact, he had no idea how to talk to her.

"Thank you," she said when he placed the cup of tea on the table in front of her.

He took a seat facing her.

"You've changed," he said.

"You haven't." Her lips curled up in a smile that didn't match the coolness of her eyes. "But then, you never change, do you? Perpetually young, eternally beautiful."

He took a deep breath and let it out slowly.

"What's happened to you?"

"I've spent the last few years searching, Nikolai."

"For what?"

She put the teacup down, folded her hands across her lap, and fluttered her eyelashes.

"Why the inquisition, darling?"

"I only—"

"I would so like to see my precious little Clara. Still attending Northbrae?"

"I'll be going to pick her up there in ten minutes."

"Nikolai, why don't I go? What a splendid surprise it shall be for her to see her Mummy, waiting for her at the gate."

"Actually, I think it's best if I go myself," he said.

She came over and sat in his lap, slipping her arms around his neck.

"Darling, one might think you weren't happy to see the bride of your youth, after all this time." She lifted his chin gently and brushed her lips against his until he opened them, sending a thrill through the human form in which he'd taken up residency for the past few years.

Her hair smelled like lilacs.

She kissed him again. But it was unlike anything he'd experienced with her before. It was aggressive, intoxicating, so pleasurable it hurt. It felt horribly wrong, and yet he wanted more.

"After I bring Clara home," she said, "we can go out to celebrate our reunion at Brigham's."

Nikolai wrapped his arms around her, and she pulled him close—so close. For a brief moment, he loathed it.

Then he loved it.

He forgot where he was.

Who he was.

What he was.

"I'll go and get her right now, all right?" Sophia whispered. "Be right back."

"Go on, then." He gasped for air, having forgotten to breathe. "Come back as soon as you possibly can."

She slipped out of his arms, and left.

He barely noticed the dark vapor hovering about him.

From the second-floor apartment window he watched Sophia with waning lust as she sauntered down the street. Never had he felt so human as he did just now. Before his decision to forsake his angelic ways and pursue a mortal life with her, he'd always wanted to know, to *feel* what it was like to be fully human. But after what had just happened? Losing himself in those purely physical, loveless cravings had left him feeling like some kind of animal. She was his wife, but it had never been this way before—so raw, so pleasurable and yet so abhorrent.

As she continued down the sidewalk, a dark cloud seemed to pass through the street. It vanished so quickly that he wasn't sure he'd seen it at all. Yet at the same moment he became keenly aware of his angelic nature for the first time in years.

He began to perceive things again in the spiritual layers of reality on which he'd turned his back. And so, just before Sophia turned the corner, he noticed that a white aura encompassed her body as she walked. Small glowing lights invisible to the human eye floated around her and followed her like fireflies.

Lovely.

Yet the sight of those lovely white lights filled him with dread, with revulsion. Thanks to his reawakened angelic awareness, he knew what they were and the danger they posed.

And why they were floating about Sophia.

Demons.

And judging by the way they surrounded her and flowed through her, the demons had possessed her.

All those years she'd spent seeking the supernatural, only to find this? She must have given herself over to them in exchange for some empty promise. Demons were liars bent on destruction. They always offered humans what they desired most—which they couldn't really give, of course—at a dear cost.

The human's soul.

Nikolai hurried to the door, then remembered that as an angel he could teleport to the school...

Only he couldn't. Nothing happened.

His abilities were still there—he sensed it—but they were...frozen. He'd have to run and hope they'd thaw out before Sophia reached Clara to do...God only knew what, considering she was under the influence of demons.

It's not her, it's not her. He kept telling himself that as he raced down the stairs, down the street, and to his daughter's school. *Not her.*

When he arrived, a long queue of girls were pouring out from the gates of Northbrae. A sea of pigtails, navy skirts, books tied like parcels, but no sign of Clara or Sophia. He pushed through the crowd of mothers and nannies awaiting their children.

"Clara? CLARA!"

A huge bruiser of a man grabbed Nikolai by the lapels of his coat, and lifted him off the ground. "What're you doing, shoutin' in me ear like that?"

"Unhand me, now!"

"You'll say you're sorry first, now, won't you?"

"I'll knock you down first." Nikolai gripped his hand but could not pull it off. He craned his neck and shouted again. "Clara!"

"Quit yer shoutin'!"

"Release me or throw a punch, you filthy mongrel!"

At this, the bruiser set him down, coiled his fist, and launched it at Nikolai's face.

Nikolai braced for the pain—but didn't feel the impact. Instead, the bruiser gripped his hand as if he'd just smashed it into a brick wall and howled in pain while Nikolai got to his feet and brushed himself off.

"Best run, mate."

Which is precisely what Bruiser did. Eyes wide with fear, he ran down the street, glancing back twice as he fled. Nikolai glanced down at his hands and flexed his fingers, grateful his abilities were returning. He'd need them to find Clara.

Because she wasn't there. The last child came out, met her mother, and left.

"Have you seen Clara?" Nick asked her teacher.

"She left a few minutes ago with her mother. It was so good to see—"

"Do you know which way they went?"

She pointed in the direction of Victoria Station.

"Are you two—"

"Thank you." To his relief, he found himself hovering imperceptibly above the city streets. Down below he spotted Sophia walking briskly, pulling Clara by the hand. Past Eccleston Square, across to Wilton Street, and into the railway terminus. Did she actually believe she could simply take his daughter from him, that he couldn't track them down and stop her?

He descended upon them.

Sophia seemed to sense his proximity and rushed into the throngs coming, going, and passing through the terminus. Nikolai took human form, more out of instinct than anything else, and plunged into the crowd himself. The need to stop her became visceral.

Down by the tracks, the massive steam-sighs of trains waiting to leave filled the air. The whine of metal against metal rang out along with the announcements of arrivals and departures.

He and Sophia were perhaps ten yards apart and surrounded by strangers when their eyes met, Sophia's wide with anxiety. For a brief moment, he saw the lovely young woman he'd fallen in love with—but only for a moment. A sinister aspect fell like a veil over her face. She turned and ran with Clara in tow towards the stairs and elevated walkway above platform 12, the white lights only he could see flashing around her as she pushed through the crowd.

Nikolai heard the whistle of the train from the Brighton line approaching the station, assumed his angelic form, and was instantly behind Sophia and Clara, who were now running up the stairs to the platform.

"Sophia!"

She either couldn't hear him in his extra-physical state or she was ignoring him. The train would be there in less than a minute.

The white lights faded, and for a moment Sophia released Clara's hand. She stared at her mother, who looked stunned as she put her hand to her forehead.

An interval of clarity? Nikolai had never dealt with humans possessed by demons. But if he could reach out to her now, in human form, she might talk to him. He might even be able to save her from the demonic influence.

Feeling his feet hit the ground, he ran over.

"Sophia!"

"Daddy!" Clara called out, clearly relieved to see him.

Sophia looked up, her hair all over her face like a madwoman's. But her eyes were pleading for help.

The dark vapor, which seemed to be present around every bad turn of his existence, moved over his head and ahead of him as Nick approached his wife and daughter .

"Sophia, are you—"

She threw her hands up.

"Don't!"

He stopped a few yards away.

"What's the matter?"

"I just...can't..."

He took a cautious step towards them.

"KEEP AWAY!"

The shouting frightened Clara, who wriggled away from her mother. Sophia grabbed her arm and pulled her back—a protective rather than a threatening move, but Clara yelped.

"Daddy, what's happening?"

The approaching train let out a loud whistle.

"It's going to be all right." He took another step closer to Sophia. "I'm here, love. Just tell me what you need."

Sophia shook her head from side to side.

"No no no...It's too late."

"For what?" Another step.

Sophia's features bunched up and she began to cry.

"I'm sorry, so sorry...I can't..."

Just as the train pulled in, the white demonic lights enveloped her. Sophia's expression changed utterly, overcome by malignance. She straightened up and turned to the edge of the platform.

Nikolai ran to grab her, but he was still a few feet away.

"Sophia, no!" he shouted as she leapt onto the tracks, still clutching Clara's hand.

50

THERE WASN'T ENOUGH TIME FOR HIM to adjust his time flow in order to stop Sophia from falling under the wheels of the oncoming train, or to prevent the impact against the back of Clara's skull.

Screams of horror went up all around the platform.

Clara was in his arms. The impact had thrown her there.

Dozens of people came running, but he cast a construct around the two of them so they wouldn't be disturbed. He laid Clara down gently on the platform and knelt before her unconscious body. But for the blood on his hand and widening in a pool at the back of her head, she might have been asleep.

"Clara." Her name caught in his throat like a fishhook. From under the train, a flock of demonic lights emerged like tiny bats and fluttered by, hissing as they left, mocking him.

Nearly every emotion he'd experienced in this human expedition raged within his heart. Anguish at the loss of his beautiful bride years ago when she'd left and now when demons had stolen her soul, helpless fury that this had caused what must surely be a fatal injury to their beloved daughter.

Clara's tiny gasps grew further and further apart.

She was dying.

With his hand touching his daughter's face, he knew what he must do. It would violate the most solemn of angel laws. He might incur the most terrible of consequences. Didn't matter, it was his daughter.

He raised his right hand until the fingers pulsed with glowing energy. One touch was all it would take.

Just one touch—

Someone grasped his wrist, gently but with sufficient force to stop him from touching Clara. But no one could enter his construct except—

Of course. Kneeling beside him was a beautiful woman with flaxen hair that shone with light, its glory reflected by her flowing white gown.

"Tamara?"

She took both of his hands into hers, then stood, drawing him to his feet with her. Though she had existed before the foundations of the world were laid, humans would have put her at about nineteen.

"Tamara, please." He looked down to his dying daughter. Tamara still held his hands. "She's just a child."

A tear rolled down Tamara's face.

"You cannot heal her, dear Nikolai."

"I can—I will! I've healed mortals before, even resurrected some."

"You must not. Not without authorization."

"Then authorize it, Tamara." His voice broke. "I'm begging you!"

"I'm sorry. Such authorization comes only from the highest authority. And it has not been granted."

"You've already asked?"

She lowered her eyes.

Nikolai tried to drop down and touch Clara but couldn't free himself from Tamara's grip.

"Please!" he cried. "Before it's too late!"

Clara released her final breath.

"It has been too late for some time now," Tamara said, wiping tears with her free hand. "It *is* for the best, Nikolai. You must have faith."

"She was innocent. None of this was her fault."

"It most certainly was not. But there are consequences for violating the most sacred angel precepts. Your physical union with a human produced a Nephilim."

"Nephilim don't exist, they're just a myth."

"Truth is not contingent upon your belief, Nikolai."

"She couldn't possibly harm anyone!"

"My child, you don't know what your daughter might have become had she lived to become a fully mature Nephilim." Tamara released his hand and touched his face gently. "She may have been spared unspeakable horrors."

"So this was planned?"

"Foreseen and planned are not the same," she said. "Clara's death was caused by the demonic influence your human mate invited. Ultimately, she succumbed to it."

"You stood there and did nothing—and forced me to do nothing."

"It could have been far worse for Clara, had she lived out her Nephilim life."

But she hadn't.

"Which path will she take now?" Nikolai could only hope that a child as innocent as Clara would not be judged in eternity for something she couldn't help—his sins or her own nature.

"It's not for us to know such matters."

"Just to blindly obey," he said.

"It's a matter of faith.   Faith that the precepts are good and just, whether or not our finite minds can comprehend."

Faith that the angel laws made sense.   Which they didn't.

"I haven't any more faith," he said.

"You've changed, Nikolai."   Concern etched her features.   "What's happened to you?"

"Well, I..."   She was right, of course.   He had indeed forgotten how differently angels perceive time and existence, and was now interpreting and judging through mortal eyes.   He did *not* want to talk about it, yet at the same time he longed for the guidance and clarity only she could provide.

"I fell in love."

"I see."

"Don't judge me.   Haven't you ever felt this way before?"

"My feelings are irrelevant."

Before Nikolai could respond, the expression on her face turned grave.   Without warning, utter darkness fell over Victoria Station.   A moment later, a mighty blast of light turned the entire place white.   A blast that sounded like a trumpet caused Tamara to turn around and face the light.   She stood rigid and shielded her eyes.   He came to her side.

"What's happening?"

"Be quiet," she hissed.   "Whatever happens, don't you say a word."

A mighty warrior in mail and armor appeared in the light, a broadsword sheathed at his side.   He came into full view and stood before Tamara, who knelt and bowed her head.   Nikolai, realizing who it was, did the same.

In a deep baritone that seemed to resonate beyond the confines of the train station, the warrior spoke.

"Arise, Tamara."

She stood, pulling Nikolai up by the elbow as well. The warrior must have been more than two heads taller than he was.

"To what do I owe the honor of your presence, my supreme commander?" Tamara said.

The hairs on Nikolai's neck stood on end. He had never before seen the archangel Michael, who glared down at him then turned to Tamara.

"It has come to the high command's attention that we have a traitor in our ranks."

"True, he has violated some of the angel laws," she said.

Michael glowered at Nikolai. "Some?"

"Well, yes. Nearly all, to be precise. But he's a fledgling. His heart is young but good. He did it for love."

Now the archangel was glaring at *her*.

"For lesser crimes, angels have been condemned and cast out. There shall be no exceptions."

"He does not belong with the dark legions, sire," Tamara dared to say. "He is indeed of the light."

Michael stepped up to Nikolai, towering over him, eyes so bright and fierce he had to avert his.

"Look upon me, lad."

With no choice but to obey, he met the mighty archangel's gaze. For an eternity Michael scrutinized him, peered into his very being. Then he turned back to Tamara, shaking his head.

"By his transgressions alone, it is apparent that this one knows naught of service, sacrifice. One could argue that all he does, he does for himself, and that he cares for none but himself."

"Please, sire," she said. "Afford him clemency. I will avouch him."

The archangel's left eyebrow raised slightly.

"Do you know what you ask?"

"I do, my lord." She stood ramrod straight.

"From this point on you may not intervene or rescue him from his own choices. They alone shall determine his future."

Tamara nodded.

"You are now responsible. If he fails, that failure falls upon you."

"Understood, sire."

One last glare. Tamara didn't flinch.

Michael drew his broadsword ablaze with golden fire. He stepped over and pointed it straight at Nick's heart.

"You have been granted what few angels ever have. But because it is Tamara the True, the Faithful, who testifies to your character"—he touched Nick's chest with the burning point of his sword—"you are provisionally pardoned."

At first it felt like the sword had been driven into his heart. Fire ran through his body, and though it burned, it was a cleansing pain.

"Sire."

Michael returned the sword to its sheath and turned again to Tamara.

"'Tis a noble if foolhardy thing that you do, faithful one. Nikolai shall be reassigned rather than condemned. He shall be placed in a probationary state during which time his character will be tried. You shall neither interfere nor intervene."

"Understood," Tamara said, her head lowered.

"Pray your faith is not misplaced."

And with that, the archangel's form radiated light so brilliant that

Nikolai and Tamara could no longer actually make him out. In the next moment he was gone.

Tamara's complexion looked as white as her gown

"I must take my leave now," she said. "And Nikolai?" She turned and for the first time ever gave him a stern look. "Do not fail me—or yourself."

He turned to look upon Clara's little body and struggled not to weep. No point in giving way to his grief now. He'd just been given a second chance, was indeed lucky to still be in the ranks of the angels after everything he'd done. Yet a part of him was troubled at the idea of re-joining these beings who either issued or followed orders blindly.

"Tamara..." He turned around, but she was gone.

Kneeling by his daughter's lifeless body, he could sense that her spirit had already been taken. As he took her hand and kissed it, images of the beautiful times he and Sophia had enjoyed with Clara before everything changed flooded his mind, creating very human sensations that tore against his true nature.

He could stand it no longer.

"Goodbye," he said. He kissed Clara on the forehead, then looked wistfully towards the train under which Sophia had ended her life—whether by demonic influence or a desperate need to escape it, he didn't know.

The entire construct dissolved and he was back in the present with Hope.

51

HOPE WRAPPED HER ARMS AROUND NICK, her eyes shimmering. To think of carrying all that pain for over a hundred years!

"I'm so sorry," she said. To have witnessed his past almost firsthand was nearly as overwhelming as learning that he was an angel. Her own pain felt oddly distant, replaced by concern for his wounded heart.

"I don't even know why I—"

"Shhhh." She put her finger on his lips. But his entire body tensed up. Holding his head in his hands, he began straining.

"Nick, what's the matter?"

"I don't...know!"

But from the eyes squeezed shut, the gritting teeth, she could tell he was in great physical pain. She had no idea what to do, so she just held him, lightly rubbing his back, patting it with her fingertips. "How can I help?"

He shook his head tightly, the pain agonizingly evident. After a while, his tension seemed to diminish. His breathing became more even. Finally, he took a deep breath, and spoke.

"Sorry."

"What just happened?" Hope said.

"Not sure. Sensory overload, perhaps. I might've spent too much time in this human form." He looked up, his expression surprisingly vulnerable. Cautiously, she touched his face. This time, he didn't flinch.

"I couldn't save her." Sorrow mixed with despair, his gaze fell to the floor.

"But you saved me," she said.

"A hundred years have passed, and I still haven't come to terms with what happened, Hope." Nick's voice broke. "It just makes no sense. No sense at all."

Now he was trembling, but not as he did when he was suffering from that strange physical bout. This was much more profound.

How do you comfort an angel? All she could do was hold him, whisper sweet hushing sounds into his ear, and shed sympathetic tears.

And then, the words just came.

Straight from her heart.

"He is there, Nick. Like He said to me, He's there in my past, healing the pain—I don't know, retroactively? But I'm sure He's there in your past too."

Nick looked up, his eyes moist, but fighting to maintain a strong façade. "I don't know…"

She leaned close, bowed her head to touch his, and did the only thing she knew how to do, when all else was lost. "Dear Lord, would you please mend Nick's broken heart?" And again, she held him.

Nick's shoulders relaxed and he drew a long breath, and sighed as one who had been relieved of a heavy burden. For an infinite moment, they remained in each other's arms. Hope could almost feel the anguish draining from him.

Finally, he regarded her wistfully. "If only I could just quit everything and stay here with you."

"Can't you?"

"After all that happened back in England, I'm an empty shell." He sighed. "You deserve better."

"But Nick—"

"And I can't let my mistakes endanger you."

"Danger?"

"Everything that happened to Sophia, to Clara."

"You're forgetting one really important fact." She gave him a reassuring smile. "I'm not Sophia."

Nick looked at her intently for a long moment, then seemed to relent. He bore the aspect of someone who'd made up his mind about something important.

"Let's take it one day at a time, shall we?"

"Good enough for me." She closed her eyes as he reached out and held her hand.

When she opened her eyes, they were back in her suite at the Broadmore. She was sitting next to Nick on the edge of the bed, still holding his hand.

"Where do we go from here?" she said.

"Just stay here for a while," he said. "I'll have it all sorted out soon."

"What do you mean?"

He got up, headed for the door.

"Before we met, I was bitter about my demotion to reaper—and now you know how it happened. But none of that matters anymore. I've made a decision. Just have to tie up some loose ends before moving forward. I shan't be long."

He pointed to the television and it switched on. Then to the room service menu, which flipped open on the nightstand next to them.

"Have something to eat. Before you know it, I'll be back."

Hope looked down at her white robe.

"I haven't a thing to wear."

"On the contrary," Nick said with a glance at the sofa by the door. There sat the shopping bags and boxes full of clothing, all from the oblivion locker.

Just a day ago she was a disheveled vagabond who'd lost everything, right down to the will to live. Now here she was in a luxurious hotel, every need provided by someone she knew she could trust—someone she would love even if he had nothing of his own to give.

"You don't have to do all that for me, Nick."

"It's nothing, really." He pulled a shiny new smartphone from one of the bags and tossed it to her. "Here." He then pulled his own phone from his pocket to show her. "If you need anything, I'm on speed dial."

She giggled at the thought of an angel with a cell phone.

Nick opened the door. "Just do me one favor, okay?"

"Sure."

"Don't wander off too far."

52

WITH THE HARTWELL ASSIGNMENT ESSENTIALLY com-
pleted and Carlito Guzman's life saved, it was time for Nick to check in
and make sure there weren't any loose ends that might reflect poorly on
his performance—or on Tamara, who'd put her neck on the line for him.

In any case, a poor performance report from Lena would only hurt
his chance of success at what he was about to do. After wrapping things
up with her, he planned to negotiate the terms of his fall—a decision no
angel should take lightly.

There were two ways to fall. First, rebellion: the way Lucifer and
his followers had chosen, shaking an angry fist at heaven and being cast
out for eternity. Humans might never have known about the greatest of
all fallen angels had Milton not given Lucifer that infamous line: *Better
to reign in Hell than to serve in Heav'n.*

The second manner of falling was nothing so glorious or dramatic.
Occasionally a celestial host had faded out of the spiritual realms without
revolt or discord. Of course, superiors had to approve such petitions, but
given their infrequency, it was rarely denied. Once granted, the angel
simply became human, relinquishing immortality and all other supernat-

ural powers.

Nick had considered falling during his incognito period with Sophia. But he never went through with it: at first he seemed to be getting along so well he didn't need to—then, gradually, so badly he didn't want to. Now, as he considered the ramifications, falling seemed more complicated than he'd realized.

To be cut off from eternity, from extra-physical perception, from all he knew of existence? It was an exile from which there was no return.

And yet, for Hope Matheson he would embrace this and more.

Was it the wisest of decisions? Probably not. But it wasn't just because of his feelings for her. He had no wish to rebel or join the ranks of the Dark Dominion. But neither could he continue offering his services to a commander in chief whose angelic rules made no sense. The only way for him to be happy was to find that state where he could just live as he felt—follow his heart, as the humans liked to put it. To do this, however, he had to fall and become mortal.

Perhaps Tamara and everyone else had been right, he had indeed spent too much time among the humans. Not just time. He'd given himself over to their way of thinking, living, even their limited view of reality. And already, as he invisibly followed Lito and a bodyguard through the shadows of the Pacific Plaza mall's parking deck, he sensed his powers draining.

It didn't matter, though.

Soon, none of it would.

All that mattered was his desire to be with Hope, love her, even meet an end one day.

Lito and his bodyguard Raul had just come out of the High Concept women's fashion store—owned by the Guzman syndicate, judging by their conversation.

"I'm telling you," Lito said, "we can turn this whole thing around. Get rid of all the corruption, all the bad stuff, you know? Start doing things legit and still be highly profitable."

Raul snorted. "You going soft, Lito? What's with you, man?"

"Let's just say I had an epiphany?"

"A what?

"Never mind."

Nick knew what he meant. He'd seen the heartfelt gratitude on Lito's face for having miraculously survived the drive-by shooting the other day. Many a human reacted that way when angels were sent to intervene. Some of them even turned their lives around. Nick was happy to protect this one. *Like a guardian, again.* Finally an assignment that made sense, though ironically, it was his last.

"Don't let anyone hear you talk like that, okay?" Raul said. He nudged Lito with his elbow—which, considering Raul's size, was more like getting sacked by Junior Seau. Lito would have toppled, but Raul caught him by the arm and pulled him back in time.

"Watch it!" Lito said.

"Sorry, boss."

Lito kept glancing over his shoulder as they walked to his car. Nick wondered if he could perceive him, then heard the sound of tires screeching around the corner and realized his subject was reacting to something else.

Nick's phone buzzed.

He tried to fly over to Lito, but with each attempt he ended up back on his feet.

A black sedan was coming up behind them. Slowly.

His phone buzzed again, a text message from Lena:

ABORT GUZMAN ASSIGNMENT
LET THEM TAKE HIM OUT

If he disregarded her instructions and botched this final assignment, there was no telling how it would affect his plans to fall, and his future with Hope.

The sedan passed him. Nick watched its tinted passenger side window roll down, watched the muzzle of a semiautomatic poke through.

The order had been clear, but Lena was concerned about Nick's following through. After all, the new directive for Carlito Guzman was a complete one-eighty from the original. The powers that be were now viewing the cartel leader as a potential liability for some reason and wanted him terminated. She doubted the wisdom of switching things up so sharply with Nick, an unstable recruit, but Morloch had insisted on it. And he called the shots.

"Besides," he'd told her, "what better way to determine if Nick will be a good soldier or a loose cannon?"

Seemed like Nick was being set up for failure, though.

In any case, Lena had carried out her own orders and now must focus on more pressing issues at hand.

Such as the Event.

Perched high atop Lady Liberty's crown, where she always went to clear her mind, Lena stared up at the nearly full moon and considered everything she was about to do.

53

MOMMA HAS LOCKED HERSELF IN the whole time Daddy has been away. She's come out maybe once or twice but never to talk to her—only Daddy ever takes the time. He's working one county away—now that she's sixteen he feels secure enough to do construction work out of town.

She sits by the television set watching some white guy swinging his hips and singing like a Negro, but her eyes keep drifting to the bedroom door. Even after the show is over, the set turned off, it never opens.

The silence is the worst part of all.

That's why she watches TV, but she's had all she can stand for tonight. She's about to start reading when she hears something behind the door. It's a soft sound but it's clear.

Momma's crying.

Panicked, she runs to rap on the door.

"Momma, please! Open the door!" She's threatened to hurt herself before and Daddy says never to push her to that point. So she can't open the door. But she's sick of Momma's sulking, feeling sorry for herself all the time, being mean to her and Daddy. Yet at the same time she feels desperately sorry for her mother— she's never known anybody so unhappy. Why is she so sad, so upset with them?

Daddy gave her the number where he's staying in case of an emergency. She'll call him, that's what she'll do.

He sounds exhausted when he says hello.

"Daddy? Something's wrong with Momma."

"She come out of the—"

"She's crying."

"I'm coming back now." His voice is dead calm. "Be about forty minutes, make sure she don't—"

"I know. Hurry, please."

Just as she drops the handset in the cradle, a sound from behind sends an chill up her spine.

It's the squeak of the bedroom doorknob. She turns around slowly.

"Momma?"

She's standing in the doorway, in a dress so white it almost glows. Her beautiful eyes are wet with tears. And for the first time ever, her arms open wide to receive her daughter.

"Momma!" All at once she wants to cry, laugh, shout for joy. Is that a smile on her mother's face? Even through the tears? "Oh, Momma. I'm so happy you—"

She puts a finger over her daughter's lips.

"Shhhh..." She strokes the hair so much like her own. Can it be? Is Momma finally going to love her? And Daddy?

"Punkin'," Momma says, and her daughter's heart soars. "I'm afraid it's not what you think."

Oh, no. No! She dreads what's coming.

"I'm leaving."

Pushing away hard, she steps back—burning with rage. She can hear Daddy warning her to control it. She can't bear to look at her mother.

"I thought I could do it, my child. But I just can't. It's too...it's impossible. I am what I am, and nothing can change that."

"But why do you have to leave us?"

"This life—if it even is a life—is just too limiting. I'm meant to be so much more. I thought I could give it up for your father, but I was deceiving myself."

"But you could, if you loved us. I know Daddy says we can't force you to stay, but if you loved us you would. That's what mothers DO, they stay for their family, for their children!"

Momma shakes her head. "I would if I could. I can't. I'm sorry." She looks exhausted, and sadder than ever.

"So that's why you been so mean to us? You're bored with living like us? Or is it because Daddy's a nigger?" The provincial speech she's worked so hard at dropping has returned with a vengeance. "Why, you just like them white people, ain't you?"

"I don't expect you to understand, Punkin'."

"No! You don't get to call me that! Only Daddy does. You—you're just a selfish, stone-hearted...ugh! I hate you!"

Straightening until she stands only as tall as her remarkably tall daughter, Momma nonetheless seems to be looking down on her.

"One day perhaps you'll realize you shouldn't have judged me so harshly." She glides slowly back to the bedroom door. "After all, you're just like me. You'll see. There's no hope. Every part of you that's a freak to these human insects, every part that makes you different..." She regards her daughter with pity. "You're just...like...me."

With that, she shuts the door.

Never to be seen again.

54

ALERTED BY THE SOUND OF THE SEDAN, Lito turned and saw it coming at him, saw the gun pointed from the passenger seat window. He grabbed Raul by the arm.

"Get down!" he shouted.

Raul didn't.

Instead, he seized Lito by the arms and put him in a choke hold just as the car screeched to a halt.

"Raul, what the hell—"

He didn't answer, just tightened his grip. Lito thought he would pass out any moment.

A man in dark glasses was still pointing a gun through the sedan's passenger window. The back door opened and a middle-aged man stepped out smoking a cigarette, his beige shirt unbuttoned nearly to his considerable belly. It was Pablo Suarez, better known as Pablo the Gutter not because of his ample midsection or his foul mouth but because of his penchant for disemboweling anyone who displeased him sufficiently. He puffed a cloud of smoke into Lito's face.

"Carlito Guzman. Mind if I call you Lito?"

"Mind if I call you *hijo de puta?*" Lito struggled, but Raul squeezed harder.

Pablo chortled, then began to cough violently. When he caught his breath, he spit the cigarette out and lit another one.

"I swear, these things will be the death of me."

"In that case, please, smoke some more," Lito said.

Again Pablo coughed, but it passed quickly this time.

"Now, Lito, I'll make it simple. Things are changing, of course you know this. The Hernandez branch is all but ours now. Why don't you turn it over to us quietly, hmmm? So much cleaner, without all the bloodshed, no?"

"Why don't you go to hell, no?"

"After you." From his breast pocket he pulled a knife and pressed the point into Lito's neck. "But I think we take you there the slow way, hmmm?"

Lito's entire body stiffened as Pablo the Gutter slid the blade past his collarbone, the middle of his ribcage, then rested it just above his belt. He wanted to curse Raul for his betrayal and spit in Pablo's face, but at the moment words could no more escape his mouth than he could escape his traitorous bodyguard's grip.

"You only have yourself to blame for this, *pobre Carlito.* It's your weakness, all this trying to do good and do right. We run businesses, amigo, not charities."

Even as the tip of the blade pressed through his shirt, Lito managed to summon the strength to speak.

"If you do this, there will be a war. Too many people on both sides will die."

"Ah, but that line is not so clear any more now. You really don't know how many of yours are ready to cross the street and join us, do you? Now, that is funny!"

Lito thrashed about only to be met with increased pressure on his throat from Raul's vise grip. He couldn't breathe. All he could see through his tear-blurred eyes was Pablo coiling the knife back.

It was like trying to hold gallons of water in his bare hands. No matter how carefully Nick tried to manipulate the current state of his existence relative to the physical speed of the events unfolding before him, he couldn't keep time from plowing forward. Having watched the whole scene at a fraction of the speed of mortal perception, he realized that the large man holding the knife was within inches of stabbing Lito Guzman in the stomach. His bodyguard was holding him in place for the kill.

Nick rushed over.

Though he remained invisible, Lito was looking in his direction. It almost seemed he was pleading for help. Nick knew exactly what he was supposed to do, or rather not do. Yet another order that made no sense to him.

The expression on Lito's face wasn't so much fear as sadness. And he tried hard to hold his head straight despite being in a chokehold. Whatever the reason, this man Nick had been assigned to protect was now supposed to die. But he couldn't just stand there and let it happen the way he had with Clara.

The large man drew his knife back, then thrust it forward.

Just as the tip of the knife reached Lito, Nick reached for the blade.

Never one to worry about getting physically hurt while in his angel state, he grasped the fat man's wrist with his left hand, took the knife by the sharp edge with his right, and bent it into a curve. Then returned it to its owner.

In an instant, time resumed at mortal speed.

The fat man looked at the twisted blade in his hand, gasping in wonder. Nick yanked it out of his hand and threw it across the parking deck. The three men turned to watch it fly and clatter to the concrete about ten yards away.

Then every eye seemed to look at Nick, or at least in his direction, despite his invisibility.

Or lack thereof, as he suddenly realized when the fat man's face blanched and he let out a string of curses in Spanish.

Before he could react, Raul threw a punch at Nick's face.

He'd never had to stoop to hand-to-hand with a human, so it didn't occur to Nick that he ought to duck. When the hulking bodyguard's fist struck him in the jaw, however, he actually felt it.

Letting out a grunt, he staggered back.

His vision blurred and pain stitched his skin for a moment, but aside from that, it wasn't so bad. Then Raul came at him again, rubbing his fist like he'd punched a brick wall, but ready to strike again.

The fat man scrambled into the car, shouted to his driver, and they blazed off.

Raul, closing on Nick, didn't notice. He reached behind his back, pulled out a handgun, and flipped the safety off.

"The hell you think you are, man?" He cocked the hammer.

Nick would enjoy watching what happened to the smug look on his face when the bullets bounced off him.

Raul fired.

Nick felt a sting in his shoulder, then from behind them came a growl.

Lito.

He lunged at Raul, swinging at his face just as he turned towards the sound. Raul caught Lito's fist with his free hand, twisted it until he fell to his knees, then pressed the muzzle of the gun against his forehead.

"You had to know this was coming."

Lito squeezed his eyes shut, anticipating the inevitable.

Nick reached for Raul's shoulder.

Before his fingers even made contact, Raul threw the gun to the ground, screaming. He fell on his hands and knees, then began rolling around from side to side shrieking in agony. He got up, ran forward a few yards, threw himself on the ground and began rolling again.

Lito wasn't watching. Knees still bent, he was looking upward, his eyes filled with awe.

He bowed his head and whispered, *"Dios mio."*

"Get up, Lito."

He didn't. Instead he cast a nervous glance at Raul, still writhing and screaming like a pig being slaughtered, then looked back at Nick.

"Who...*what* are you?"

Not much sense saying he was an angel when he'd soon be a mortal, and he wasn't a hundred percent angel anymore.

"A friend," Nick said.

"What did you—? I don't understand, but I thank you."

In the distance, Raul's screams died down to a whimper. He was now balled up into a fetal position, his entire body quaking. Lito looked over in his direction and shook his head in wonder.

"If that's the sort of friend you keep," Nick said, "I'm not surprised at what kind of enemies you have."

"What did you do to him?"

"I only made his dreams come true."

"Dreams?"

"Nightmares." A dull pain nagged at Nick's shoulder. He rubbed it, then felt a slight chill. "I'm not sure what Raul fears most, but I wouldn't be surprised it's being burned alive." He had neither the time nor inclination to fully explain. And judging by that look of wonder still on Lito's face, the explanation wouldn't help much.

"What are you, some kind of hypnotist?"

"Something like that."

Lito gave him a long look, then said, "No, you're more than that. I mean, you just show up out of nowhere, mess up Raul's brain, and—wait! You look familiar."

Nick scanned the area. All the commotion was sure to draw some onlooker, no matter how remote a part of the parking deck it was. "Would you please get back into your car and get out of here?"

"Yeah..." Lito started off, then stopped in his tracks. "I remember you. We've met before!" But when he turned around, Nick had already dropped out of his perception. The words floated out of his mouth as he realized. *Eres un ángel.*

Lito walked. And thought. And made a decision.

Fifteen minutes later, he knelt before the crucifix at Our Lady of Peace in Chula Vista and from a heart filled with gratitude thanked his merciful God for the angelic visitations and protection that had spared him. He vowed to turn his life around, right all his and any of his family's wrongs he could.

He left the church feeling like a new man, not one whose life was, in fact, in greater peril than ever.

55

NICK STOOD OVER RAUL, WHO WAS still curled up in a ball and moaning. The worst thing about constructs like these was that every physical sense was engaged and tied directly to the emotions and mind. For all intents and purposes, Raul's reality was that he'd been doused in gasoline and set on fire.   Only the pain wouldn't end, as it would in death.

Nick rubbed the ache in his shoulder again and shivered. What an odd sensation. Was he feeling human chills because he was now really becoming mortal? It wouldn't be the first time an angel wish had been granted before a formal approval.

At his feet, Raul's gasps formed into words Nick could hardly make out.

"Oh, God, let me die, let me die..."

Nick made himself visible.

"No, my friend."

He bent down and touched Raul's head. Raul stopped screaming, then let out a long, slow breath.

"Gracias, amigo" he said. "Gracias."

Facing death, humans showed their true nature. Raul now revealed himself as one who had used his brutality to hide weakness. Reduced to a puddle of fear, he was pitiful. Nick shook his head and sighed.

"You will never go near Carlito Guzman again, do you understand?"

Eyes still shut, Raul nodded as the construct seeped away.

"Yes. Yes, I understand! Completely."

"You will never again engage in this sort of work. If you do, you will be visited by beings far worse than me."

Raul opened his eyes, then immediately shielded them from the blazing light Nick allowed him to perceive. For good measure, he revealed his wings and brandished a flaming sword like the one he'd used with Balaam and his donkey a few millennia ago.

"Never again. I swear!"

The sincerity in Raul's eyes was palpable. Through the ages, many had repented from their ways because an angel had touched or in this case, smote them. This had never been part of Nick's duties as a guardian. But he rather enjoyed it—he'd done something that made sense.

To him, anyway.

"Get up, Raul." Because he cared naught for his soon-to-be-defunct career, he proclaimed the heavenly injunction reserved exclusively to archangels: "Cease from your wicked ways and go pray for forgiveness."

Raul got up and knelt before him with bowed head and hands folded.

"Not to me, you idiot," Nick said. "Go on and get out of here!"

Raul straightened up and ran off.

But Nick had once again defied his orders and failed to complete an assignment. There were sure to be repercussions—that wouldn't change just because he planned to leave the angel ranks. Best to check in with

Lena now. Colin Powell was right: Bad news isn't wine, it doesn't improve with time. Time to let her know he'd failed with Hope and Lito.

He took out the smartphone Lena had given him at the beginning of this set of assignments. Oddly, it was becoming less and less tangible. He could see it, touch it, even press the icons on the screen, but it almost looked and felt translucent. Of course, it too was a construct.

He found Lena's contact icon and pressed it. Right away, he heard the three-note chime that preceded the recorded message:

"All circuits are busy. Please hang up and try your call later."

"Great." The nagging pain in his shoulder got worse, to the point that he dropped the phone and grabbed the place where it hurt. That was when he realized for the first time since the pain started that he hadn't given it a proper look. At the same time, he felt something wet on the hand gripping his aching shoulder.

When he looked, he found his palm and fingers stained with a red, viscous slime of some sort.

"Blood?"

56

THE BLOOD CAME FROM WHAT APPEARED to be a wound on his shoulder. By the look of it, the bullet from Raul's gun had only grazed his flesh. But Nick had never bled before, not even a drop.

His descent into mortality had indeed begun.

It's what you wanted, isn't it?

In any case he had to check in with Lena, who wasn't answering his calls. One day she tells him to protect the cartel leader, the next day she wants him dead. If nothing else, it would be a relief not having to work for such a fickle boss any longer.

A moment later, by mortal time, Nick was back in the lobby of the Broadmore. Too weary to cloak himself with invisibility, he walked past the front desk, covering his bloody shoulder with his hand.

"Sir, are you all right?" the concierge said.

"I'm fine." Nick kept walking.

"But your arm," the young man said. "It's bleeding."

He stopped and took a quick look. The bleeding had actually stopped, but the red stain had spread down his sleeve making it look a lot worse than it actually was. And the wound no longer hurt.

"It's nothing. I fell on some broken glass."

"Would you like me to call a doctor?"

A group of teenaged girls were staring at him. *Enough of this.* Nick planted a construct into the concierge's mind, then glanced across the lobby to the revolving door.

"Look, isn't that—"

"Justin Bieber!" one of the teenagers shouted.

The concierge double-timed over to the hotel entrance following the squealing girls.

Nick blew out a weary breath and got into the elevator. Better end the construct before "Justin" appeared to enter the lobby. Just as the elevator doors slid shut, he heard one of the girls saying, "I *know* I just saw him."

When he finally got to the room he realized that he hadn't got a key, so he knocked.

"Hope? It's me, Nick." He kept knocking, but no one answered. Perhaps she was in the shower.

The only way in was to pass through the door, something he wouldn't be able to do much longer. But as he began to alter his physical state he felt light-headed, and the door's material resisted slightly. Rather than passing through as though the door were air, it felt thick and sticky, like tar.

At one point, the resistance stopped him from moving forward. What an idiot he'd look like in the middle of a door, nose inside the room and hindquarters out in the hallway.

With a great lunge, he pushed through and fell onto the carpet inside the room. When he got to his feet, the entire room swerved counter-clockwise a quarter turn. Nick grabbed the frame of the open closet door to steady himself. It took a few long seconds for everything to settle.

Finally, he opened his eyes. Diffuse light illuminated the room through sheer curtains.

"Hope?"

He knocked on the bathroom door, which swung open revealing a tidied shower, tub, and sink.

Exhausted and disappointed, Nick went into the bedroom. On the night table he saw a small ivory envelope with his name on it. He tore it open and unfolded the note:

Gone to the village to explore. If you have any trouble finding me, I'll be at The Coffee Shack in the afternoon.

Love,
Hope

His first thought was to go and join her. But the more human he became, the more he realized how tiring it was being mortal. For the first time since his London days, the need for sleep engulfed him.

Without quite intending to, he dropped onto the bed. His eyes closed.

And the note fell from his hand.

57

THE FIRST THING LITO HAD TO DO was reach Maria. Secondary were his plans to leave the family business, but that couldn't happen overnight. Not if he wanted to survive and keep his sister from harm.

The truth was, he didn't exactly know how to make such a change, much less make it safely. But his life had been spared more than once, and by divine intervention—surely a way would become clear. In any case, he wasn't about to renege on the vow he'd made in that church last night.

I might end up in jail. Even if that happened he'd continue to do right, as best he could. Not my will but thine, and all that. Of course, he could do much more good if he wasn't locked away...

Lito waited patiently in the lobby of the Sheraton on Harbor Island. His sources had informed him that Maria had returned to San Diego yesterday and checked in. Clever enough not to use her credit card, for which he had online access, she had no doubt bought a prepaid Mastercard or Visa.

He kept his eyes trained on the hotel entrance. Coming or going, she was bound to show up sooner or later. And sure enough, at 9:07

AM she walked in wearing a black, close-fitting short skirt and stilettoes, the bag slung over her shoulder bouncing with each step.

"Maria!" He dropped his iPad into his leather courier bag, grabbed it, and followed her. For the briefest of moments she paused, nearly stopped, then resumed walking, even faster. "Maria, wait! I just want to talk."

That got him a quick turn of the head.

"I have nothing to say to you, Lito."

He overtook her, then stood right in front of her. She stepped to the left. So did he, again blocking her.

"Please, Maria. Just give me a minute, okay?"

"I swear, I'll scream if you don't get out of my way." If eyes were knives, his face would be sliced to ribbons by now.

"You have to know why I was protecting you from Alfonso—"

"You protect me by taking away the one person that made me happy?" Her voice resounded throughout the lobby. More than a few people turned to look.

"He was using you."

"You're paranoid, Lito! Admit it, you can't stand seeing someone else be my protector, provider!"

He grabbed her arm. "Alfonso was dangerous, he was about to—"

"LET GO OF ME!" Lito had already loosened his grip so that when she yanked her arm back, her newspaper and magazine went flying across the lobby. The magazine nearly struck the bellhop, who ducked just in time.

Hands up in surrender, Lito backed away and watched her storm out of the lobby. He hadn't even gotten to the reason he wanted to speak with her. No matter what happened with the family business, he wanted to make sure the secret Alfonso had threatened to tell Maria would never come to her through another person. He could no longer live with that hanging over his head. Not when a new life awaited him.

Over at the baseboard lay Maria's newspaper, a half-folded white slip of paper atop its scattered pages. Lito picked up the paper and unfolded a printout of an online receipt for an event. Jonathan Hartwell: SEIZE YOUR DESTINY.

Had to admire this guy. He never gave up the name of the girl on the video that had gone viral but failed to identify her. Nor had he issued any public apologies, though Lito had read in the paper that he would give an official statement at the event tomorrow night.

Lito sighed. If Maria was serious about her claimed faith in Jesus, she might have to forgive him. But for that to happen, they'd have to speak again. And with his radical shift from the life Papi had left him, it was only a matter of time before the clock ran out. The Suarez syndicate, the Hernandez branch, and now the power- hungry Guzman lieutenants were up to something.

But what?

He didn't know. What he did know was that like Atlas, he bore the weight of that world on his weary shoulders.

Before anything else happened, he must tell Maria the truth.

He only prayed he would live long enough to do it.

58

THE SOUND OF VACUUM CLEANERS and hotel workers speaking in Spanish woke Nick. How long had he been asleep? A quick glance out the window revealed the sky ablaze in a dazzling amber conflagration that stretched across the Pacific. He got up—and marveled. For thousands of years he'd taken such sights for granted. But now he realized how beautiful it was.

Heartbreakingly so.

Quite literally, in fact, because the sharp ache in the center of his chest seemed to have a direct line to his eyes, from which tears were trickling. He'd always wondered why humans wept at moments of beauty—a Brahms symphony, a Shakespeare sonnet, a sky like this one.

It hurt.

In a sublime way.

This was what it was like to be human—to *feel* the contrast of light and darkness, hate and love, despair and hope. He stepped out onto the balcony and leaned against the wall, fully taking in the breathtaking canvas upon which Father had once again painted one of his masterpieces.

The words of the great psalmist came to mind.

Where can I go from your Spirit?
Where can I flee from your presence?
If I go up to the heavens, you are there;
If I make my bed in the depths, you are there.
If I rise on the wings of the dawn,
If I settle on the far side of the sea,
Even there your hand will guide me,
Your right hand will hold me fast.

If I say, "Surely the darkness will hide me
And the light become night around me,"
Even the darkness will not be dark to you;
The night will shine like the day,
For darkness is as light to you.

The roar of the rushing waves, the gulls floating over the shore, the briny gusts, the thrilling sky...He sighed with pleasure. It was the difference between reading about someone you love and being with them.

How could he ever go back to being an angel?

A man on a motorcycle on the street below revved his engine while waiting for a red light. Another man in a T-shirt revealing muscles that would intimidate anyone with half a brain was about to cross the street in front of the biker. To test if he was still an angel, Nick tried to conjure up a construct that would make the man in the T-shirt look like a hot blonde in a red bikini .

"Hey babe," the biker said in a gravelly voice. "Want to ride with me?" He made kissing noises and smacked his lips.

The man in the T-shirt hit him in the face so hard he fell off his Harley.

Right. Still an angel.

He quickly ended the construct. The expression on the two men's faces caused a burst of air to shoot out of Nick's mouth and nose—a snort, followed by laughter.

His first prank. Being human was going to be fun.

It was different this time, though. So much more real and intense than in London back in the early 1900s. Perhaps that was the difference between temporary defection in which you lived as a human, and elective renouncement of angel existence, in which you *became* human. In any case, he couldn't wait to tell Hope.

As he got ready to leave, he decided he'd try to find her sans angelic powers. No supernatural surveillance, no celestial fly-bys, just human ingenuity. He pulled out his mobile phone, which felt even less physically solid than before, and texted her.

59

SITTING AT A TABLE OUTSIDE THE COFFEE SHACK in La-Jolla Village, Hope watched the fiery sky and told herself not to worry. She hadn't heard from Nick all day, but he could go anywhere and be back before anybody even noticed. He experienced time differently. For all she knew, he could be anywhere on the planet between here and the spiritual layers. She had to trust that he'd be back soon.

Since she was a little girl she'd loved watching sunsets. And now, to perfect this glorious scene, a monarch butterfly alighted on her hand and fanned its wings..

"Hello." Hope brought it close to admire the intricate patterns on its wings, the bright colors that matched the ones dominating the sunset. Hard to believe this lovely creature had recently been a creeping bug.

Well, yesterday she'd been a woman with nothing to live for. To-day, a new creation.

"Like you," she said as the butterfly flew off. "Free." Now that the burden of depression and despair had been removed, her spirit could soar with the same sweet liberty.

She took a sip of coffee that not only warmed her but tasted better than coffee had tasted in years. Her new lease on life came with a renewed appreciation for its simple pleasures.

She couldn't wait to tell Nick what had happened during her first day of freedom. After all those emails and phone calls over the past few years, she had finally been able to contact the source of light that had been there in her darkest days with a different report–an encouraging report. The conversation had led to something incredibly exciting. Nick would be so pleased.

The phone on the table chimed. Her first text message.

It was from Nick, of course.

> **Nick:** How do I get to The Coffee Shack?
> **Hope:** Are you still at the hotel?
> **Nick:** No, I'm actually...

She heard a dull, clanging thud nearby, followed by a loud moan.

"Oh my gosh, Nick! Are you okay?" She hurried over to the sidewalk, where a very dazed, a very physical Nick lay at the base of the streetlamp into which he had walked. He was rubbing his forehead with one hand and clutching his cell phone with the other. A small crowd had gathered.

"I guess that's why they tell young people never to text and walk." Hope said, offering him a hand. He was a lot heavier than she'd imagined. "You found me."

"It wasn't far."

She led him to her table, wondering how an angel could be so...well, clumsy.

"Wait a minute, Nick." She glanced around. "Can they *see* you?"

"Yes."

"And...that's okay?"

"I'll explain in a minute, all right?" He pointed to the cup. "May I?"

"Sure, knock yourself out."

"I nearly did back there," he said.

"It's an express—"

"I know. Sorry, just trying this humor thing. Need some practice." Nick lifted the cup and took a long sip. "Mmm...now *that's* good."

"My fave."

"Oh, bother. I've finished it."

"It's all right, there's more from where that came from." She reached out and slipped her hand in his. "You act like you've never had a latte before."

"If I have, I can't remember it ever tasting that good." He stopped her as she was about to signal the waitress for another cup. "Never mind that. I've something important to tell you."

"Wait, Nick! I have something to share too. Can I go first? Please? I'll explode if I don't tell you soon."

"By all means, ladies first." He sat back in the chair, eyebrows raised.

"Okay, then. A few years back, when I was depressed and hitting rock bottom—"

"Excuse me," the barista said. "Can I get you two anything else?"

"I'm good, thanks." Hope looked at Nick. "Another latte?"

"How about something stronger?"

"Espresso?" the barista said.

"Anything stronger than that?"

The barista told him the best they could do was a double espresso. Nick asked for it to go, then leaned over the table to loop a wayward lock behind Hope's ear.

"You were saying?" His touch electrified her but this time it seemed more natural. The sensation originated from within her.

"During my dark years after Chloe died," she said, "one of the only rays of light came from Jonathan Hartwell's talks on the radio. You know who I'm talking about?"

"Who doesn't by now?"

"Yeah, too bad about that scandal. I'm sure there's a good explanation, if he says there is. Guess we'll know tomorrow." She sighed. "Anyway, I used to call his lifeline a few times a year, when I needed someone to talk to, and eventually I became one of their regulars. They prayed for me, sent me care packages—they're really the sweetest people, and they did everything they could. But I stopped calling, pulled away from them once I started thinking about...you know."

"You were afraid they might talk you out of it."

The very memory of those recent attempts sent a chill through her heart. She reached out for his hand.

He took it, and smiled poignantly.

"Well, anyway, that's all the past, thanks to you. And today, after almost a year, I called them again and told them how I'd been rescued from—"

"You didn't tell them about me, did you?"

"No." She hadn't thought they'd believe an angel had saved her life and with a touch healed the pain within her.

"Good." He let out a sigh. "What *did* you say, then?"

"That God had revealed the truth to me—I mean, that's what angels do, right? Bring messages from above?"

"Um, right."

"Anyway, long story short, they called me back—thanks for this cute little phone, by the way—and told me Jonathan Hartwell loved my story and asked if I would share it at Cabrillo Stadium tomorrow at his speaking event!"

"Really?"

"Isn't that amazing?"

"That's wonderful!" he said as the barista returned with his double espresso.

60

"I'M HAPPY FOR YOU, HOPE." Nick drank the espresso, which made up in strength what it lacked in volume, and put a twenty-dollar bill on the table.

"You're a big tipper," Hope said. He stood and took her hand to help her up.

"It's just money."

"Still, you don't just throw it around like that."

He'd never given this human issue much thought. Might want to start, though—once his transformation was complete, he wouldn't be able to conjure up currency like that anymore.

Hope wrapped her arm around his as they left The Coffee Shack and walked down the sidewalk toward the shore. The sky's embers cooled to a deep violet as the moon rose and the multitude of heavenly hosts entered the stage. Enthralled, Nick stopped.

"Is it usually that beautiful—I mean, from down here?"

"The sky and the stars?" She watched with her head leaning against his shoulder. "It *is* special tonight, but yeah, it's usually like that."

"Remarkable. It's like I'm seeing everything for the first time."

"Is that a good thing?"

He took a minute to answer her.

"Yes, I believe it is." He led her across the street to a bench over-looking the foamy waves hitting the shore with a soft hiss. They sat under a street lamp and he turned to face her. The words didn't come readily, though.

"You all right, Nick?"

"Yes, of course. Why?"

"I don't know, you seem a little preoccupied."

Going from immortal and eternal to finite and human was hard on the system. But there really was no middle ground. If anything, it was only temporary.

"I've got something weighing on me," he said.

"I knew it," she said, not looking at him, her lip quivering.

"Knew what?"

"It was too good to be true, wasn't it?"

"I haven't said any—"

"Don't have to, it's written all over your face. You've done your job and angels can't become involved with mortals and you have to leave even though you don't want to and I really *do* understand, but—"

"I don't think you do."

"It's always been that way. Something good comes into my life, only to be—"

He pressed two fingers over her lips.

"Just listen to me, love. I am not going anywhere."

Then he lowered his hand, and let her speak.

"What about the angel laws?" she said.

"Applicable only to angels."

"You mean…?"

"I'm giving up my angel status to become human."

At first, she stared at him, as though trying to understand what exactly that meant. All at once, her eyes grew wide. Hope cried out his name, threw her arms so tight around his neck he thought he might suffocate. Then she became quiet for a minute. Sighed. Looked away, then back again.

"You've been an angel for thousands of years," she said finally. "Becoming human means…"

"I'll die one day. I know."

"For someone who's lived as long as you, a human lifespan will seem as short as a breath."

"And what a glorious breath that life will be if I could spend every day of it with you." She could feel his gaze deep in her soul—he sensed this with what remained of his angelic powers.

Which was beginning to weaken. It was happening—he could tell. With or without approval from above, gradually, *he was falling.*

"Do you know what you're giving up?" Hope said.

"To feel what you feel, to enjoy the sunsets, the tastes, the sights, the smells—most of all the love that only humans can fully appreciate? I'd rather live one day sharing that with you than an eternity without you."

She shook her head, tears rolling down her face.

"I…I can't let you give up your immortality for me."

"It's mine to give."

His entire past life seemed to have faded into a distant impression. All he could think of was being with Hope, right here, right now. With barely restrained intensity, he placed his hand on her face, whispered her name, and kissed her.

It seemed to have stunned her for a second, but then she returned the kiss, a tear falling from her eye and warmly onto his hand.

"Nick..."

"I've made up my mind." He kissed her again.

She held him desperately as more tears fell. He had observed such human behavior before but never quite understood the contradiction until now. Although the tears were Hope's, he was feeling exactly what she felt, and the awareness that he loved and was so loved filled him with such joy it hurt.

Try as he might, he could not suspend this moment beyond what a human would ordinarily experience. The thought that tomorrow might diminish the joy surging through his very human heart at this moment hung over him like an executioner's ax. He pushed the thought aside.

And then the ax fell.

61

SHE MUST HAVE SEEN IT IN HIS FACE, which had changed the minute his phone started ringing.

Hope let out a breath. "If it's important…"

"I'm sorry, it is."

He stepped away from the bench and answered Lena's call.

"Listen carefully, Nick—"

"Before you say another word," he said, "I need to tell you something."

"Make it quick."

"I've completed the Hartwell assignment. There were some complications with Guzman and with Hope Matheson, but it doesn't matter. I've made a decision."

"Wait, you failed to complete two of your three assignments?"

"Well, yes. But—"

"Listen to me, Nick. There's a new directive, so they've lowered the priority level of all your assignments. We need to speak in person right now."

"Now?" Nick glanced over at Hope. "Can it wait till—?"

The next instant Nick was teetering on the ledge at the top of One America Plaza, five hundred feet above the ground. He nearly slipped, then a firm grip on his forearm pulled him back.

"What's wrong?" Lena held him fast until he found his footing.

"You don't just yank a person into a construct without a warning." Never before had he felt so shaky atop a tall building.

"We don't have a lot of time, Nikolai, so listen carefully."

"All ears." He shifted his weight from one foot to another in a vain attempt steady himself.

"There's a much bigger agenda now, so I have to know if you're on board or not."

"With what?"

"If you thought getting out of the endless rut of reaper work was worth leaving your previous position, you're definitely going to want in on this."

Bracing his back against a glass wall, Nick cleared his throat. "I'm having a bit too much trouble with this construct of yours to understand what you mean."

"This isn't a construct."

She was coming so close he wanted to move away, but didn't dare risk losing his balance.

"Something wrong with you?" Lena said.

"Of course not."

"Then why are you acting like this?"

"I don't know what you're talking about." *Other than behaving like an angel on the brink of mortality.*

"Never mind. What I'm about to share with you is huge. My director doesn't know yet, but I'm recommending you for a major operation that's right up your alley."

"Based on?"

"Based on your strengths and skill set. As a guardian, as a warrior."

"That's all in the past, Lena. In fact, that's what I wanted to talk to you about."

She sailed on as if he hadn't spoken.

"You want a job that puts you on the front lines, where you can make a difference. Not on the sidelines where the Angel Forces have so unjustly abandoned you."

"Yes, but—"

"You want your talents and gifts fully appreciated and utilized, you want them to impact the mortal and spiritual realms alike."

"Lena, hold on a minute—"

"I don't want to hear any objections from you, Nick. This is the opportunity you've been waiting for." A sly grin twisted her blood-red lips. "And when you've risen in the ranks of the new order, never forget that it was I who gave you this break."

He dared not inquire further, despite the disconnect. If his suspicions had any validity he'd best play along until he could get everything sorted out.

"Sounds intriguing," he said. "But what about my assignments?"

"They're on the back burner for now. This new campaign is much more important. It's a huge step up for me; they're putting me in charge. If we're successful, I'll be managing all the major regions in the new territories."

"I see." Nick said. "You've been transferred to sales and marketing."

"Cute," she said. "Now, once I'm in charge I can't think of a better partner than you, what with your power, commitment to change, proactive personality...not to mention strikingly good looks."

"Yeah, right."

This was the part where the dark vapor should appear.

But it didn't.

Instead, the scant cotton clouds above them parted and the full moon emerged. Heart racing, Nick peered out over the San Diego skyline as a pair of ravens cawed and flew past the top of the skyscraper. He'd flown countless times over the earth like those dark birds, never fearing he might fall. But now, were Lena to let go of his arm he couldn't be certain he wouldn't lose his balance, topple, and make modern art of himself on the concrete below.

"So, Nikolai..." Each time she spoke his name he felt a little more strength ebb from him. "Are you in?"

Best act as if he knew what she was talking about. But this all felt really, really wrong. "Tell me more."

"I'll be in touch with the details. Glad you're with us."

"A bit presumptuous, aren't you?"

"I know what I want. I always get it." She loosened her grip. "Run along, Nikolai."

But Nick grasped her wrist. She obviously thought he knew about this "major operation." No matter, he'd sort it out another time. Right now his only concern was to get down from the skyscraper in one piece.

"Send me," he whispered in her ear.

"Seriously?" Lena smirked. "Why?"

He couldn't tell her that if he tried to go off on his own he might end his human life before it really began. Instead, he ran his fingertips through her silky hair and stroked her face.

"Because I like it so much more when you do it to me—transporting me the way you did today feels so...I don't know..."

"Carnal?" She lowered her voice to a seductive, breathy register. "All right, how do you want it?"

"Transport me back to the ground. It makes my toes curl."

She turned him around to face the open sky. Slipping behind him, she wrapped her arms around him, pressed her hand over his chest, then nuzzled the nape of his neck and cooed. For a brief moment, his mortal flesh was tingling. As soon as he realized it, he refocused.

He had to get away from this creature whose warm breath tickled his ear.

"Can't wait to make you come to me again," she whispered.

"That so?"

"Mmmm...Ready?"

He took a deep breath, then nodded. But curiosity got the best of him. He looked back and saw her eyes—really saw them. He was certain he'd seen eyes like that before, been the target of that ghastly expression.

"Just what kind of angel are you, Lena?"

"Angel?" She laughed as she shoved him off the ledge of the skyscraper.

62

RELIEVED THAT HE'D SUCCEEDED in getting Lena to transport him safely to the ground, Nick found himself standing on the sidewalk outside the entrance of One America Plaza. Save for a group of street-gang types loitering on the curb by their pimped-out rides, there were few people out in the city at this hour.

Which is what made the very tall, very muscular quartet in black leather and dark sunglasses stand out all the more when they appeared out of nowhere. The woman was at least six feet, and the three men at least eight inches taller and built like NFL linebackers. As they approached the skyscraper, headed straight toward Nick, the woman bumped shoulders with a street gangster who stood a bit taller than she, though definitely shorter than the men.

"Oh no you didn't!" He said, and pulled out a knife. "Whassup wit—?"

Before he could finish, the woman in black shoved her hand into his chest. He flew back with such force that his body knocked two of his friends down like bowling pins.

Without missing a beat, the leather clad crew swaggered on.

Part of Nick wanted to bolt, part of him wanted to know who these creatures were. Extraordinary humans, if they even were human.

The leader, an Asian male, stepped right up to him—towering over Nick by about a foot.

"Evening, mates," Nick said.

But they walked right past him. One of them—an African American about six inches taller than Nick—turned around as he passed, lowering his shades just long enough for Nick to recognize him as the man he'd met back in New York at Grand Central Station.

"Goliath—I mean, Johann?"

He kept walking, rejoining the rest of the crew a few feet away. Good. Nick was still invisible.

"You're late," Lena said from over their tall frames. Nick couldn't see her, but her voice was unmistakable. He whirled around just in time to catch a glimpse of the dazzling flash that enveloped the five of them, just before they disappeared.

Nick stared in wonder at the place from which Lena and her entourage had vanished. Whatever she was up to, he wanted nothing to do with it. Managing territories and all that rot—none of it meant a thing to him now that he'd committed to a mortal life with Hope.

But he had to come up with some way to bow out. Things were becoming increasingly dangerous.

Right now he was tired and wanted to go home. That meant being with Hope. He willed himself to return to her, waiting for him back at La Jolla.

Nothing happened.

He squeezed his eyes shut and tried harder.

Nothing.

A sharp pain entered his head like molten lava seeping into his eyes, his ears, nose, and mouth.

A man walking a Jack Russell terrier stopped.

"You okay, mister?"

He didn't know how long he waited to respond, but the pain had subsided. And he was visible.

"I'm fine." His nose was running, he wiped it with the back of his hand.

Blood.

Not again.

"You need help," the man said.

"No, really, I'm all right."

"Nuh-uh." He pulled out his cell phone. "I'm calling you an ambulance."

Nick started walking. "It's just a nose bleed. Get lost!"

But the guy and his now barking dog followed him.

"Mister, just hold still, will you? I've dialed 911, just...hold on!"

Not feeling strong enough to outpace them, Nick cast a construct on the well-meaning nuisance. To his surprise, it worked. Gripping his dog's leash with a shaky hand, the man froze in his tracks and began shaking and blubbering. The construct would wear off in a few minutes, by which time Nick would be long gone. But the unfortunate good Samaritan would never forget it. And that brought about a twinge of guilt.

Nick walked to the corner and flagged down a taxi. As it drove off, he chided himself for the construct he'd projected on the poor guy.

Really, Nick? Godzilla?

63

FOR GEORGE WALKER IT'S A HAPPY DAY. Not many of those since that night two years ago when he got home to find his wife and mother of his only child gone. Forever gone.

"You done good, George," Frank Jones says, "I'm real happy for you." A slap on the back and Frank starts toward the back of the bus. "You coming?"

"You go on, Frank. I'm waiting here for my daughter, we going to celebrate. My little girl's eighteen today!"

"Woo-weee! Eighteen already? Better keep an eye on her!" Frank steps through the back door of the bus, which hisses shut. George turns around in response to a light tap on his shoulder.

"Why, Punkin'!"

"Hey, Daddy! Did you get it? Did you get it?"

"How long you been watching me, all quiet?"

She looks down. "The whole time you were talking with Mister Frank."

George leans in close.

"You know what I told you about that kind of stuff. People see you pulling that, and—"

"No one saw me, not even you. So don't worry, okay?" She clasps her *hands, barely containing her excitement.* "Did you get it?"

"Not yet, Punkin'. I just got paid, I ain't had a chance to—"

"Not my birthday present, Daddy. The promotion! Did you get it?"

His eyes light up and his wide grin returns.

"Say hello to the new assistant manager!"

She lets out a squeal and throws her arms around him.

"I knew you'd get it, Daddy, I knew it!"

"Thank you, Punkin'. Now come on, I'm hungry—how about you?"

"Uh HUH!"

"I'm taking you to Charlie's, then dinner!"

"Milkshakes first? Are you crazy?"

"Guess I am," he says.

Both laughing, they walk down Carlton Boulevard as the sky turns dark. Yellow streetlights illuminate the snow beginning to fall again, slow lazy flakes. She used to catch them on her tongue.

The air around them seems hushed as the snowfall grows heavier. Ice crunching under their feet, they take a shortcut through the back alley to Charlie's. To their left and right are the windowless brick walls of factory buildings, ahead a dim glow that provides the only light.

George sees three men coming toward them. Which wouldn't necessarily be so bad, but when they get close he sees they're wearing ski masks.

And then they stop. Right in front of him.

"You must think you're one really special nigger, George," *one of them says.*

"I don't want no trouble," *he says, but at the same time his arms tighten and his fists ball up.* "I'll ask you kindly to step aside and let us—wait a minute. Larry, is that you? What the hell you doing—"

That gets him a sock in the jaw—and a terrified gasp from Punkin'.

George stands defiant, prepared to fight. But then the man he could swear is Larry draws a knife. The other two grab Punkin' by the arms. She struggles, but George shakes his head, warning her.

"You got to be the first nigger I ever heard of taking a job from a decent white man, George."

"I ain't take nothing. It's called a promotion!"

The man charges forward and drives the blade straight at George's chest. To his astonishment, George catches his wrist, stopping the tip of the blade about an inch above his heart. He twists the knife out of his grip, and throws it down the alley.

It's followed by one of Punkin's attackers—she's freed herself and thrown him all the way across the alley. As his body crashes against the brick wall George hears a thud accompanied by the sound of cracking bones.

The second goon pulls a knife of his own and slashes it straight at Punkin's face. The entire blade curls as it fails to cut or penetrate her eye socket. From the corner of George's eye, he sees her grab his wrist and twist.

The bones in his forearm snap like twigs.

He turns his attention back to Larry, who's looking for the knife. George goes after him. Before long he and Larry are wrestling for the advantage of weapon and position in the snow, and Larry is winning. He has George pinned down and is raising the knife.

Punkin' leaps over, just as it's poised to plunge into his heart. She grasps the sleeve of his jacket, slick with snow and water.

But his sleeve slips.

And the knife plunges in.

Too quickly for her to stop it.

"NO!" With both hands she seizes Larry, swings him over her head, and throws him up high against the factory wall.

His body smashes against the fire escape rail on the fourth floor.

George struggles to stay conscious, as the sound of Larry's blood dripping from the rail onto the snow sends a shudder through him.

Punkin' runs back to kneel beside him, tears streaming down her face.

"Daddy, hang on—you have to hang on, I'm going to get some help."

He shakes his head. "Forgive them...they don't know what they doing."

"How can you say that, Daddy! They're animals! I'll—"

He reaches up, grasps her hand.

"Listen to me...Lena. I love you...more'n anything. You ain't..."

"Please, Daddy, don't leave me alone here!"

His breath's growing short, the final gasps.

"Be...strong. You...ain't like..." He takes one last breath. "Like her."

She presses her face against his...

And abandons all hope.

All alone in this world full of savages, Lena Walker has no one to turn to when the rage threatens to overtake her. And now, it has grown into hatred.

Just like Momma, she will never be able to live at peace with humans. She's known but one good man among them all. And they killed him.

No longer will she restrain herself for the sake of "blending in" or to please her father. Nor is there any point in forgiving that which must be punished or avenged, if not eradicated like a disease.

"I'm sorry, Daddy...I am exactly like her."

64

STANDING IN A CONSTRUCT CREATED for the sake of her lieutenants, Lena's eyes slowly swept a black-walled chamber in which the candidates she'd chosen were seated.   Determined to impress her supervisor no matter the cost, she'd summoned the best of the best for this operation.

Each of them possessed a unique talent born of their unique backgrounds and cultivated over the ages.   These were the most disciplined and powerful, therefore the most efficient, of all the candidates.   Gunther, Johann, Dan, and Serena stood in a semicircle around her as still as trees.

She clapped her hands twice. "Look alive, everyone."

They stood at attention.

"Now, listen carefully.   We're about to meet with a powerful executive from the High Command.   None of you speaks unless I say so, is that clear?"   Four nods. "Good.   Your only job here is to instill confidence, is that clear?"

More nods, followed by dead silence.

"All right.   Here we go."

She waved her hand at one of the walls, and the area before them was illuminated with crimson light.

"We're ready," she called out, and a man in a business suit with eyes and hair black as night appeared, smiling subtly.

"You're looking well, Lena."

"As are you, Morloch."

"I see you've assembled your crew."

She glanced over her shoulder then back.

"The very best."

"Are they, now?" Like a panther, Morloch circled them slowly, scrutinizing each of them one by one, head to toe. He now bore the appearance of a military leader in combat attire. The candidates towered over him, but it had no effect on his stark demeanor.

"Are you sure you can succeed with so few?" he said.

"They're not the only ones. But you'd be surprised how much I can do with so little."

"And you're sure they can be kept under control, once it begins?"

"Absolutely. I *am* an authority on their kind."

"So you say." Morloch stopped pacing and regarded her with interest.

"To the humans, we're the stuff of folklore, to the rest we're little more than unsubstantiated rumors. The less that's known about us, the less anyone is prepared to deal with us."

"I like the way you think." He came and stood at her left side, hands crossed over his chest, feet spread. A commanding pose. "Are they all the same?"

"None of us are," Lena said. "Each Nephilim possesses a unique combination of qualities, from one end of the spectrum to the other."

No need to tell him that some were born completely human, while others could be more powerful than most angels or demons. "Since this operation is to take place here on the physical plane, I've chosen the ones with the greatest physical abilities."

"You're aware that our interests lie well beyond the physical, I trust."

"Of course," she said. "And I trust *you're* aware that you and I are here to help each other. The more effective I am in this realm, the more ground you'll gain in yours. Once I've established control of my territory, we'll simply round the humans up and send them straight to you *en masse*. It will be...symbiotic."

"I prefer the term synergistic." He stepped behind her and whispered into her ear. "But you *are* a crafty one, aren't you?"

"You're a great teacher." She regarded him with reluctant respect. "Now, I need some assurance that after I've proven myself, I'll be given the resources necessary to follow through with the new order."

"Have you any doubt?"

"I'm full of doubt. But I'm banking on our agendas being mutually beneficial."

Morloch placed his hands on her shoulders and began to massage them. It released so much tension that she started losing that sense of urgency over her concerns. *Damn him.* He always knew how to disarm her. As much as her body responded to his touch, she felt uneasy because her lieutenants were still there, though standing as motionless as monuments.

"Lena, Lena, Lena," Morloch said. "Don't let yourself be distracted by minutia. I personally guarantee you'll be given the resources you need to maintain your new global order if you're successful at the Cabrillo Stadium event."

"It's as good as done." The stadium event was an easy target, disproportionate to the payoff in which she would finally set things right. With legions at her command in both the physical and spiritual realms, nothing could stop her from establishing the new order.

"Oh, and Lena." He took his hands off her shoulders, turned her around to face him. "There's the matter of that angel...what was his name?"

"You mean Nikolai?" She said his name casually, not letting her apprehension show.

"Our records indicate that some of the assignments we issued haven't been completed. Why is that?"

Her stomach clenched. "I'm not sure what happened," she said, "but I'll make certain they're completed. I'm sure you can understand how menial tasks can get overshadowed by something as significant as this operation."

"Menial?" He regarded her with a glacial look. Lena backed away, but Morloch reached out and clutched her throat, holding her in extreme discomfort. "You ought to keep better tabs on your recruits."

"I...know, I—" His grip on her throat was so tight it was all but impossible to choke out a word.

"What do you know, really?" He tightened his grip, seemed amused as she struggled to speak. She couldn't. Finally he released her and let her fall to the ground gasping for air.

"Nikolai had no intention of joining the Dark Dominion, as you presumed," he said. "In fact, he's already begun his fall."

Lena had to cough out her words between gasps.

"This has to be a mistake."

"Your mistake. Without his supernatural abilities he'll be useless to us."

"I didn't know. I'll fix this, I swear!"

Morloch lifted her chin.

"*You'll* have to deal with him, Lena." She tried to stand, but the best she could do was get up on one knee.

"You said so yourself—he's of no use. So as a powerless mortal, he's no threat."

"All the same," he said as he pulled her to her feet, "if there's any chance he might still influence an unfavorable outcome at the event, I want him dead."

The thought of killing Nick caused her a puzzling degree of regret. But she mustn't let it show.

"Can you handle that," Morloch said, "or do you need me to step in?"

"No! I mean, yes, I can handle it and no, you don't need to step in."

"You're not likely to be entrusted with a large scale operation if you're unable to accomplish something this simple. Because those 'menial' tasks have not been completed, the event is still at risk for us. You're losing sight."

"I assure you I'm not—I just need a little more time."

"Terminating him is just one part of it. Because of his failed assignments, you'll have to try harder to stop the outbreak that will happen as a result of the Cabrillo event. That's the greater concern." He narrowed his eyes. "I trust you know I've stuck my neck out for you on this."

And without his help she'd never be able to carry out her plan.

"You have my word, it will be done."

"It had better, Lena." He pulled away and stepped back into the wall lit with the hue of blood. "Because if you fail at this event, I will disavow any involvement. Expect no protection from me, you'll be on your own when the accounts are settled."

65

THE TAXI HAD A CREDIT CARD SWIPER which Nick used to pay his fare and tip. It wasn't certain that an attempt to teleport would fail, but the pain and nausea were sufficient to discourage it. The driver pulled up and let him off at the corner in La Jolla where he'd left Hope.

She wasn't there.

A quick glance at his phone told him he'd missed a call and two text messages from her, the last of which said she was going back to the Broadmore. He called her and was instantly relieved when she answered.

"Nick? Where are you?"

"Back here by the shore. I'm sorry, they just took me away before I could tell you."

"Who?"

"My supervisor. She can be really inconsiderate."

"Everything all right?"

"Just a few loose ends." More than a few, actually.

"When will you be back?"

He thought about Lena's mysterious proposition and Johann's odd reappearance. If he were to let his guard down now, as his supernatural abilities drained away, might he be endangering Hope by associating with her?

"I'm not sure. Soon."

"It's all right, Nick. I'm exhausted and ready for bed. If you still have some work to do, go ahead. Just make sure to come for me in the morning."

"I'll try to get back before you fall asleep. But in case I don't make it in time..."

Hope let out the sweetest, most endearing yawn. It sent a warm rush of affection through Nick's ever-thickening blood.

"Good night," she whispered.

"'Night."

"Oh, and Nick?"

"Yes?"

"I love you." And she hung up, gently.

How many times had he heard humans utter those three words—casually, carelessly, emptily? But when Hope had said them, they nearly robbed him of his breath. Now he understood why, at the dawn of humanity, Father had said, "It is not good for man to be alone."

To ensure that nothing from his life as an angel would affect his new mortal life with Hope, Nick had to clear things up with Lena, make a clean break. But did he have to figure it all out right this minute? Right now, he'd much rather be with Hope. As he thought about her lying in bed waiting for him, the issue was decided for him.

In the blink of an eye, and to his pleasant surprise, he found himself standing at the edge of the bed in Hope's room at the Broadmore. She was breathing evenly in a deep slumber while hugging an oversized pillow. Taking care not to wake her, he knelt and pushed an errant strand of hair from her face. Still asleep, she smiled. Nick kissed her forehead lightly.

He wasn't sure he could still whisper into her spirit, especially in her sleep. But he had to try.

// I LOVE YOU, HOPE //

"Mmmm..." Her expression changed—ever so slightly, almost imperceptibly, but in all the time he'd known her he had never seen such contentment on her face. He *had* seen that expression on humans who'd been redeemed, been touched by grace. Would he ever know such peace?

For now, he would enjoy it vicariously through her.

Resting his head close beside hers, he kept looking at her even as a sharp pang impaled his chest. How was it possible? How could he love someone so much that it actually hurt physically? If only he could capture this moment, put it in a bottle and keep it for all—at least, for the rest of his natural life, anyway.

Still deep asleep, Hope murmured something he couldn't make out. She stirred and began to whimper, her brow pinched together. "It's all right..."

Not wanting to stir her from her dream, Nick remained still and listened.

A tiny sob broke through her words. "Don't be afraid...it's just a dream, it's all just been like a dream. We're going to wake up one day and laugh about it." She sniffed and tears drew glistening lines down her face. Was she dreaming of Chloe? "I'll see you soon...I love you."

And with that, she began to weep aloud. Nick got into the bed, wrapped his arms around her, held her close. Hot tears seeped through his shirt and onto his chest. And then she opened her eyes.

"Oh, Nick!" Sorrow laced her features.

"I'm here, love." He held her tight. "There now. Just a dream."

"I'm so sad…don't know why."

"Can you remember anything?"

"No, I just woke up crying." She leaned away from him so she could look right in his eyes. "Please, Nick. Don't let go of me, not till I fall asleep again."

"I won't." As he pulled her back into his arms, his wings unfurled from behind whatever remained of the construct of his mortal form. With them, he enveloped her while she returned to her slumber. "Ever."

For the rest of the night until the dayspring he hid her there—under the shadow of his wings.

66

WHAT WAS IT ABOUT HUMANS THAT MADE THEM turn into idiotic tools the minute they had hold of power? Lena stood in a boardroom with Miguel Suarez, Roberto Hernandez, and sons of the Hernandez branch from the Guzman syndicate. She couldn't let her contempt for them show—in light of what she'd just learned about Nick's botched assignments, she was going to need their help.

"This better be good, Miguel," said Roberto Hernandez, who was wearing an expensive Italian suit and a lot of jewelry. "I got a good mind to call this whole damn thing off."

"It's good, just listen to what the lady has to say."

Lena stepped forward. "We all want the same thing. I'm offering you something greater than you can ever imagine, if you help me with one meager annoyance. Something you've wanted for a long time."

Miguel lit a Cuban, leaned back, set his feet on the table and puffed.

"We just want all the Guzman territories. That little *hijo de puta* Carlito is messed up."

With a wave of her hand, Lena dismissed the Guzmans.

"Forget them. When this is all done, they and everything you know will be gone. If you want in on the new global order, you'll have to prove your usefulness."

"Stakes just got raised, bro," Roberto said with a wink at Miguel.

"What are you talking about?" Miguel said.

"You're sitting on your fat butts, thinking too small," Lena said. "I'm talking national and soon after that *global* control. You want in or not?"

Miguel grabbed Roberto's shoulder.

"Of course he does." Smiling at Lena. "We all do. Ain't that right, Roberto?"

Roberto shrugged his hand away and glared at the others.

"Some hot chick in leather shows up and now you're her lap dog?"

That did it. Lena's patience, paper thin to start with, had now worn through. She walked over to Roberto, who kept puffing on his cigar even when her hand reached his shoulder and slid down over his chest.

"I better be getting a lap dance soon," he said as he puffed a cloud right into her face, "or I'm outta here."

Lena opened her right hand. A KA-BAR appeared in it. She pressed its razor tip right into one of Roberto's chins.

"Whoa, whoa, whoa! Where the hell did you—"

She snapped the fingers of her left hand and pointed the Baretta 950 Jeftfire that appeared in it at the other Hernandez men.

"You boys done screwing around? I'm getting tired of all this."

Miguel wagged his eyebrows at Roberto and shrugged.

"I suggest you listen to the hot chick, eh?"

"O-kay," Roberto squeaked.

Lena took the knife from his throat and set it down on the table. She did the same with the gun, then slid both weapons over to the other two Hernandez men for examination.

As soon as the younger one got the knife, he grabbed it and lunged at her.

Without so much as turning around, Lena shot her hand out, caught him by the wrist, and swiftly twisted it with such strength it snapped.

"What the hell!" Miguel said.

The other Hernandez man picked up the Baretta and pointed it at Lena.

"All right, bitch. You think you're all that?"

"You *really* don't want to do that, Joey," Miguel said. "Put that—"

"Nah, man! She's whack! Look what she did to Mark!" His voice sounded tough, but the gun in his hand was shaking. To Lena: "You better watch yourself, muchacha!"

She blew out a sharp breath and let go of the moaning Hernandez whose wrist she'd broken. A moment later, the Baretta in Joey Hernandez's grip changed from charcoal to amber, then blazing white. A sound like a steak on a grill sizzled from the gun, along with the stench of searing meat.

"*Ay!*" Joey tried to drop the gun.

It took a few shakes—his flesh had burned onto the Baretta's molten surface. When it finally fell, wisps of smoke rose from the open palm of the charred right hand he clutched by the wrist with his left. Moaning and writhing, Joey fell to his knees next to his brother, also writhing, his hand bent at a perverse angle.

"I apologize for my sons," Roberto said. "They've always been...impulsive."

Lena snapped her fingers at them.

Before their eyes, the injuries vanished—everything was restored, every man in the room marveling.

Miguel blinked. "How did you...?"

"It's all a matter of perception. Of course I could have really hurt your boys if I wanted to.   But I want your help and I'll need you all physically in one piece."

"But that really hurt." Joey was gawking at his restored hands. "I saw it, I *felt* it."

"I made you all believe it was real. So for you, it was."

"And those?" Roberto pointed to the gun and knife on the floor. "I mean, they just appeared out of thin air."

"Oh, they're real."

"Now you ready to listen, bro?" Miguel got them all seated, then sat down at the head of the boardroom table and looked at Lena. "We'll do whatever you say, lady. Mind telling us what the hell you are?"

"I'm real, that's all you need to know. Now listen carefully..."

67

IT WOULD HAVE BEEN SO MUCH MORE FUN to roast them all like the swine they were, but Lena couldn't be bothered with picking up after Nick's shoddy work. These pigs would have to do it so she could concentrate on the big event tonight.

"Have it your way," Roberto Hernandez said. "What do you want from us?"

"First I want you to imagine a new world where things are done right, and only the right leaders get to make the decisions—wouldn't you want to be part of that group?"

"I don't know. Depends on what you call right. What's in it for us?"

"If you're on the right side, you stay in power in the new order." Of course, she was telling them what their itching ears wanted to hear—not the truth, that they'd be slaves and metaphysical fodder in the new order.

"You kidding me? You're just some chick with magic tricks."

"What I just did to your boys?" Lena snarled. "That's just a pre-view, and I've got a lot of others like me supporting my cause. It's all going down tonight. Make the right choice, you can be on our side. Otherwise..." She glanced over at the gun on the floor.

It floated up and over to touch each of the men's foreheads, one at a time, finally returning to press against Roberto's.

He scoffed. "Yeah. Right. That ain't real."

"Let's find out, shall we?" Lena said.

A bead of sweat rolled down his face as he sat silent. Joey grabbed his arm.

"Papi, come on—it's for real!"

"All right, all right!" Roberto watched the gun fall into his lap. He didn't need to examine it , he was convinced. "Okay, okay. So, what's the job?"

"Just two hits," Lena said. "One of them, Miguel's been trying to get for some time now, the other is an easy target."

"Who?"

Lena pointed to the middle of the conference table, where a pair of three-dimensional images appeared.

"Lito Guzman!" Mark pointed to the one on the left. "I capped him in Mission Valley!"

"Apparently he survived." These boys needed to be more thorough. But in all fairness Lena hadn't known what happened that morning until last night when her tracking device—the cell phone she gave Nick— enabled her to access the traffic cam footage. Either she'd trusted Nick too much or there'd been a huge disconnect between them.

"Nah, man, no way!" Mark said.

"He had some help," Lena said.

"What kind of help?"

She glared at Miguel Suarez. "You haven't explained to them yet?"

He shrugged. "Like they'd just take my word."

He was right. For these guys, the concept of a round planet would probably be a stretch. Better show rather than tell.

"All right, Joey. Pick up the gun."

He complied. Lena pointed at her chest.

"Shoot me."

"What?" Joey said.

"You want to know what kind of help Lito had, I'm going to show you. Now, shoot me."

"Whatever."

Just before he squeezed off a round, the others covered their ears to shield them from the blast of a weapon fired inside a room. At the same moment, Lena became invisible while standing in front of Miguel.

But Joey had squeezed his eyes shut and fired off three consecutive rounds. One of the bullets hit Lena's invisible and molecularly altered body, and fell to the carpet in the form of coin-like slags.

With Lena gone from his sight, Miguel spilled out of his chair expecting bullets to hit him square in the face. He hit the wall spewing Spanish expletives and scrambled backward, butt on the floor, until he realized he couldn't go back any further.

Lena reappeared, bent down and picked up the flattened rounds, then with one hand lifted a trembling Miguel to his feet.

"Sit."

Stunned, he obeyed but almost missed the rolling leather chair.

Roberto looked bewildered. "What are you saying Lito has a guardian angel?"

"Had." Lena circled the table, then stopped and confronted them all. "Well, boys—are you in?"

They all grunted some form of an affirmative.

"Excellent. Now, the first part of your assignment is simple." She drew their attention to the holographic image of Lito Guzman. "Kill him."

Another round of grunts. She brought up another image.

"This is Hope Matheson. Kill her."

"Aw, come on. A lady?" Roberto said.

Lena slammed her fist on the conference table. It split in half, the two parts collapsing into the middle as the men rolled back their chairs.

"I don't have time for this! Kill her, or join the sheep in the slaughter!"

"All right, all right!" Roberto said. "We got this, okay? We got this."

It was enough. Lito Guzman had changed sides and would no longer destroy thousands of lives. And Hope Matheson, if she lived to overcome her depression, might encourage millions to the enemy above. Starting with her speech tonight. As for terminating Nick, she wasn't about to trust these goons. She'd handle that her own special way.

"Just one thing," she said. "You've got to do it before the end of the night. My informants tell me both Lito Guzman and Hope Matheson will be attending Hartwell's event at Cabrillo Stadium." She gave them a conspiratorial smile.

Not one of them smiled back

"I got an in with Lito's sister," Joey said. "She's mad enough with him to want what you want."

"Good," Lena said. "Do this to my satisfaction, and you'll be given authority over all of southern California, reporting directly to me." She trained her eyes on Miguel: "Do you have anyone with sniper skills?"

"I'll get him there tonight. But there's a problem," he said. "We don't have tickets and I'm pretty sure they won't let us bring guns into the stadium."

Lena opened the palm of her hand. Miguel handed out the tickets that appeared. By now they barely looked surprised.

"Just show up."

68

LENA TELEPORTED TO NEW YORK HARBOR to clear her mind after her frustrating meeting with the cartel leaders.

Everything was going as planned. Serena—Raven—had reported that after the little hiccup with the Coast Guard and the Marine Corps, the package was en route to the installation site. Nevertheless, a last-minute check was in order. Lena dialed the number but it rolled over to voice mail.

She tried again. And again.

Finally, Yuri Kosolupov answered his cell phone.

"Are you ignoring me?"

"Stop calling!" His voice was barely audible. "We're in the middle of configuring the packages—there are security guards in the corridors. I'm shutting my phone off. Call you later."

"Yuri, wait!"

Click.

Lena slammed her fist down so hard it made a long crack in one of the spears in Lady Liberty's crown. He *cut her off?* After she sent one of her Nephilim to bail his sorry butt out of military detention?

Simmering in that old rage she had embraced years ago, Lena tried calming herself with the knowledge that in just a little while, the debts would come due.

There was hell to pay.

69

"GO AHEAD AND OPEN IT." The old man sat across the table from Maria in a corner of the Chula Vista public library, his hands on a walking stick, his deep brown eyes gazing at her from beneath sagacious white eyebrows.

Maria looked at the manila folder. What would Lito think if he knew she was with a representative of their sworn enemies, however ancient? But it was Juan Suarez who had contacted her, claiming he had information connected to her late fiancé.

"I have wanted to speak to you for so long, *mi cariño.*" He heaved a weary sigh. "But not until I had proof. Alfonso knew something Carlito has kept from you your whole life."

She thumbed through the pages, newspaper clippings, glossy photographs faded over time, then stopped at a middle-aged woman and a man posed on the porch of a house with a white balustrade and a red tiled roof. Sitting on the woman's lap was a little girl who could not have been more than two or three years old. The three of them seemed vaguely familiar.

"Who are these people?"

"Don't you know?"

She shook her head and stopped at a newspaper clipping. The headline read:

PABLO AND ANTONIA SUAREZ GUNNED DOWN AT HOME

"Pablo was my only son," Juan Suarez said.

The profound sadness in his eyes softened Maria's angry thought about how many Guzmans the Suarezes had killed. She looked again at the family photo. The mother's eyes were sad. The father looked like a man used to throwing his weight around, just what she'd expect from the Suarez syndicate leader. The little girl—

Maria saw it.

Something she hadn't noticed before. And the sight filled her with joy. At the left side of the patio chair a large black Labrador looked up at the little girl.

"Rosie!"

"Of everyone in the picture, you remember Rosinante?" Suarez said

"Rosi...nante?" It didn't take long for Maria's smile to fade. A sickening dread hollowed her stomach and crept up her throat.

"So you *do* remember."

She gripped the edge of the table, unable to speak the word that kept repeating in her mind: *NO! no, no, no...* She was plummeting, spinning into a vortex of emotions, memories, impossibilities as she pieced it all together.

"*Soy tu abuelo, mi querida.*" Suarez's eyes were bright with intensity, his hand quivering so violently the cane tapped the floor in an eerie ostinato.

"My...my grandfather?"

"Your true name is Maria de Los Angeles Hernandez Perez de Suarez."

"De Suarez?" The name caught like grains of sand in her throat. "It can't be. I am Maria *Guzman*! I know who my father was, my mother, even my brother Carlito!"

The old man sighed. "And yet, you remember the house in the picture and the dog I gave your father when he was a young man, do you not?"

She nodded. That was the only thing keeping her from storming out of the library, cursing this old man.

"I am sure you'll remember your Papi putting you on Rosie's back and riding her like Don Quixote's faithful steed."

It was true. She remembered it all—the house, Mama's sweet-smelling hair, Papi's strong hands that threw her into the air and never failed to catch her.

"It's so hard to believe. *How?*"

"Your mother and father..." Her grandfather's voice faltered. "They were killed in cold blood, a hit by the Guzman family. But the killers didn't know there was a two-year-old child in the house. They took you back to the Guzman's and raised you as their own."

"No..."

"They are not your true family, Maria. They executed your parents and burned down the house. Pablo and Antonia were illegal immigrants—they had no birth certificate for you, and no one outside of the Suarez family knew of you. And what with the nature of our business, no one ever told the authorities anything about the missing baby."

"Stop it! I don't want to hear any more."

"Don't you see? Alfonso told Carlito he knew the secret and threatened to tell you. For that, Carlito had him killed. The Guzmans are evil, Maria. Lito is evil."

At last Maria understood why Lito had always been so controlling. To him she was a child of the enemy, unworthy of the Guzmans' love and respect. Everything kind he'd done for her—every expression of love from him and the pretenders that styled themselves her parents—had been a lie.

"I don't know what to do," she said, her voice dropping to a dreadful whisper. The warmth of the old man's leathery hand comforted her as it wrapped around hers.

"The time has come for you to return to your true family."

"But...they all know me as Maria Guzman."

"Don't worry about that. Only one thing matters right now."

With the back of her hand Maria wiped furious tears from her eyes.

"After more than twenty years, your time is finally at hand."

"My time?" Maria hugged her arms as a chill from the air conditioning blew over her.

"To avenge your parents' death."

Ten minutes later, Maria was on her way to meet with her cousin Joey Hernandez. Lito was not her brother, after all, never had been.

He would pay for his sins and those of *his* father. And if heaven denied entry to those who honored their parents by avenging them, so be it. Her eyes were open now. After the initial shock, she could see more clearly than ever before in her life.

What she did not see was the old man walking briskly back to the silver Lexus parked in a secluded alley, reaching through the glass window to touch the head of a dead man whose likeness he had stolen, and

transforming into the white mist of a demon named Morloch just before
he vanished.

70

NICK STOOD AT THE HOTEL ROOM BALCONY, feeling wonderfully refreshed. For the first time in more than a century, he'd enjoyed a solid stint of slumber. After a satisfying stretch, he watched the gray marine layer slowly burn off, yielding a blue sky. Pelicans flying in a perfectly formed squadron swooped down to hover over the water.

He was more than ready to leave the past behind and start enjoying his freedom from cosmic burdens. First he had to square things with Lena—resign officially as an angel so she'd know his decision was final.

But something had been profoundly wrong with her the last time they spoke. Her focus and priorities seemed uncharacteristically jumbled. And there was that look in her eyes...

Those eyes. Staring through him as though he weren't even there.

Where had he seen that look before?

Finally it struck him.

Lena's eyes looked exactly like Sophia's when she returned to get Chloe.

Possessed.

Could Lena possibly be—

Nonsense. Lena was an angel just like him. Only humans could be possessed. No matter, all of that would soon be behind him.

A whole new life awaited him. Tonight, he'd propose to Hope. He intended to make the most of his time with her, even if it lasted a mere fifty or sixty more human years.

She was worth it.

In his periphery of his eye, a pelican high in the air turned nose-down like a dive bomber and drove into the water with a powerful splash. A moment later it emerged and flew off with a fish in its mouth.

You make falling from heaven look like so much fun, my fine-feathered friend.

Nick took a deep breath, then dialed Lena.

The call rolled over to voicemail.

He tried again. Same result.

He sent her a text: *It'll only take a minute.*

Lena called.

"Thanks for getting back to me."

"I was going to call you anyway." Her voice sounded uncharacteristically cold. "Turns out you really missed the mark on those assignments I gave you."

"I thought you said they didn't matter."

Lena clicked her tongue. "Everything matters."

"Well, it no longer matters to me. You see—"

"Nick, shut up for a second, okay? I'm in the middle of a meeting. Now, before you waste any more of my time, let me make it easy for us both."

"What are you on about?"

"I'm sorry, Nick." She paused for a second or two. "You're fired."

71

FIRED? NICK LET OUT A SHAKY LAUGH as he pocketed the mobile phone. Well, that went better than expected, didn't it? Perhaps word had gotten back to Tamara that he'd already taken steps towards resigning his commission with the Angel Forces. He'd never gotten details as to what such a decision involved, but if this was all there was to it, who was he to argue?

But still...could it be that easy?

To test the extent of his mortality at the moment, he focused on the rocky cliff about half a mile away across the cove. A moment later, he found himself drifting toward it in the spiritual layer. But the spirit realm felt oddly foreign, almost as strange as the physical realm had early in his career when he first reported for terrestrial duty.

He sped over to the cliff, surprised he could still fly. As his feet touched the ground, sea birds spread out—giving him a wide berth though his physically imperceptible form cast no shadow.

"Sorry, mates," Nick said with a grin as they flew off. "Just checking."

Yet again, a sharp pain pierced the side of his head. He put a hand to his temple and it stopped just as quickly as it had come. He shook his head and sighed. This could well be the last day he lived as an angel. At some point he had to warn Lito Guzman about the danger he was still in, thanks to Lena, and he wanted to check on young Matthew Hartwell, but neither of those tasks really required supernatural ability.

So what's the last thing you'll do with your powers? Through the ages, he'd never been afforded the luxury of personal needs or preferences. Not legitimately, anyway. But now, as a fallen angel—falling, anyway— he'd soon no longer have to worry about things of eternal consequence, just things that mattered to him personally.

For some reason he recalled hovering above the planet in the spirit realm while Hope gazed down wistfully at China, her fingers searching her neck.

"Brilliant," if he did say so himself. What better way to kick off his new life as a mortal? He was already planning to propose. He'd have to get a ring, of course, but he now realized how much that pendant meant to her.

He pulled out his phone and checked the time: 3:22 PM. He could go to the harbor where it had been lost, retrieve it, and return to meet Hope at Cabrillo Stadium. After Jon's much anticipated statement and her testimony, he'd ask for her hand.

Nick focused on the Coronado Bridge.

Nothing happened.

He tried again.

Nothing.

Another power lost, whether temporarily or permanently he couldn't be sure.

He decided on flying between the realms at superhuman speeds—

not a split- second trip but less than a minute for sure.

Aiming himself at the sky and over the Pacific Ocean, he leaped off the rocky cliff.

72

HE WAS ROCKETING THROUGH THE AIR when he again thought about Lito Guzman and Matthew Hartwell. A moment later, Nick to his surprise had teleported to the lobby of the Wyndham Hotel in Mission Valley, where he found Matthew playing some kind of game on an iPhone.

"Hello, Matthew."

"Hey." The boy didn't even look up.

"Where are your parents?"

"Over there." Eyes still glued to the iPhone, he pointed toward the front desk. Elaine was in line, waiting to talk to one of the staff.

He turned back to Matthew.

"We met when your puppy—"

At that, Matthew stopped what he was doing and glanced up.

"Nick?" Forgotten was the iPhone. "It's you!"

"In the flesh. Mind if I join you?"

Matthew slid over and made room, though there was more than enough on either side of him.

"How are you doing, kiddo?"

"Okay, I guess. You live in San Diego?"

"Just passing through, but I'm coming with a friend to your father's event tonight." He grinned. "So how's Riley?"

"She's staying with Mr. Greene while we're down here. I wanted to bring her with us, but Mom said no."

"Are your parents doing okay?" He wouldn't even hint at the recent media scandal—even the worst parents would have at least tried to shield their child from it.

"Dad's been away, so at least they're not fighting all the time."

Over at the front desk, Elaine Hartwell gesticulated emphatically at the young man in a hotel uniform. The fact that she was here in San Diego suggested that she and Jon might actually be trying to mend things, if only for the sake of his public image.

"Well, Matthew," Nick said, "don't know if I'll ever see you again, probably not—but I just wanted to say I know a great kid when I come across one. You're strong, you're smart, and I know you can get through just about anything."

Matthew was quiet for at least a minute.

"I don't know," he said finally. "I guess so."

"You know, when I was younger I had some pretty horrid stuff happen to me. But I learned that if you follow your heart..." He thought about how hollow this sounded. Nick had followed *his* heart back in London, and look where it got him. "Actually, what I'm trying to say is...oh, bother, what *am* I trying to say?"

Matthew laughed.

"What's so funny?"

"Grownups always act like they know what they're talking about even if they don't. You don't know what you're saying, and you *know* it!"

Nick put on an offended face, crossed his arms, and turned up his nose.

"I *do* know what I'm talking about." He winked. "I think."

Matthew laughed some more. If Nick had accomplished nothing else, at least—

From the corner of his eye, he caught a glimpse of a tall figure in a long black leather coat scanning the lobby.

Johann.

The big bad angel had come looking for him. Nick glanced around for the nearest exit—couldn't teleport and just vanish before Matthew's eyes.

"I'm sorry, I just remembered something I have to do," he said, his back to Johann. "I'll be off now."

"You look nervous."

"I look nothing of the sort." He patted Matthew on the head. "Listen, after I leave, you go and stand with your mum, okay?"

"Okay."

"Goodbye, Matthew."

"Later."

Nick got up and slipped away, eyeing exits that led to the courtyard. He looked back at the spot where Johann was standing.

But he was no longer there.

He turned back and bumped into an elderly woman who grabbed his arm to keep from falling.

"Terribly sorry, ma'am." He steadied her, but they'd drawn the attention of a tall woman standing at the nearest courtyard exit door. She started toward them.

Right away, Nick recognized her.

She was a member of the quartet that had met with Lena last night—Leatherchick, who'd launched the gangster through the air with a light shove. She pressed a tiny receiver into her ear and spoke. Nick read her lips as easily as the morning paper.

Found him.

The last thing he wanted was to deal with Lena. She'd fired him, what else was there to discuss? And why send all this muscle after him?

Leatherchick was headed straight at him, her face exuding all the congeniality of granite.

Nick did a brisk one-eighty.

But somehow Johann had managed to get through the crowd without knocking anyone down. Just a few steps away, he called out.

"Nikolai!"

No way. Caught between these two? Why couldn't they just leave him alone? With all eyes on Johann now, Nick could escape without anyone noticing. If his teleportation abilities didn't fail.

He set his mind on the Coronado Bridge. When nothing happened, he focused harder.

Leatherchick pushed past two heavy men as if they were tall blades of grass.

A group of Japanese teens rushed up to Johann, shouting "Samuel L. Jackson! Samuel L. Jackson!" and thrusting souvenirs at him to autograph.

By now, Nick should be somewhere around the bay. Nothing. *Come on!* He focused on the walkway outside the hotel.

Still nothing.

Leatherchick was just a few steps away.

Johann broke free from his fans.

Was the ability to teleport hindered by the stress, or had Nick lost it altogether?

Without a moment to spare, Nick rushed into a throng of Japanese youths. Almost instantly he reemerged as a bespectacled Asian kid with an ebony mop that fell over his eyes. Leatherchick was talking to Johann.

"Did she send you?" he watched her say.

"No. You?"

She shook her head. "I followed him. What are you—"

"Same team, Serena. Same objective."

Nick headed for the revolving doors. He would have liked to hear the rest, but in his uncertain state he didn't know how long he could maintain this construct. He also didn't know how much longer he'd be able to teleport. Assuming he could still do it at all.

Better check in on Lito Guzman.

73

HE EXPECTED THE SUCCESSFUL TELEPORTION to land him in a drug lord's lair, not a large suburban house with piles of boxes, "moving sale" signs against the walls, and no furniture but a chair and card table.

Nick stood outside the room where Lito sat speaking into his cell phone. Though he'd listened in on humans for countless years, for some reason he'd never felt it was eavesdropping.

Until now.

"You're not hearing me, Eduardo," Lito said. "I don't care if the Hernandezes go over to the Suarezes, I'm done...Then that'll just have to be on their heads on judgment day, nothing to do with me...I said no...You can do whatever you want with all the assets after I take my share..."

He laughed. "Maybe I *have* gone loco. But for the first time in my life, I'm a hundred percent sure of what I'm doing. With all due respect to Papi I have to do what's right, you know? That doesn't include selling women and children.... Of course they'll come after me, they already have. But guess what? I have God on my side...I just know, okay?

"Yes, my old friend. I'm saying goodbye to Maria tonight before I leave for London. Can you believe she asked me to come to the Cabrillo event with her? Guess she's gotten religious too."

He was quiet for a few minutes, shaking his head but listening patiently.

"I'll tell her everything, just pray she'll believe me. And forgive me. I'll try and convince her to come with me, if she won't I'll just leave." He passed a hand over his face, weary and seamed with regret. "If she refuses to leave with me, promise you'll look out for her, okay? Be especially careful about Joey...Yeah, he's the worst of them...Yeah...Sure...All right, then." He drew a lugubrious breath. "And Eduardo...Thank you, for everything."

The next thing Nick heard was a gun being cocked.

"You! Come out here with your hands where I can see them!" Lito's chair fell as he jumped to his feet, gun pointed.

Nick emerged from the shadows, his hands up.

"I'm sorry," he said. "The front door was open and—"

"You!" Lito said, lowering the gun.

"I wasn't breaking in, you know."

"Of course not, you're an angel." Lito slipped the gun behind his belt and reached out his hand. Nick took it.

To his surprise, Lito kept hold of his hand and pulled him into a one-armed man hug. The wound from the bullet graze had stopped bleeding but it still ached a bit.

"Now I know I'm doing the right thing."

There was no mistaking the sincerity in his eyes.

"What do you mean, Lito?"

"If being rescued by an angel isn't a sign from heaven that it's time to turn my life around, I don't know what is. And now, here you are again. This isn't just another sign, it's a confirmation."

"I just came to tell you..." How best to put it?

"I'll do anything you ask."

"You need to be careful. You're in a great deal of danger."

"Obviously." He smiled. "But you'll protect me, right?"

Awkward.

"Well, you see..." What good would it do to explain that in a little while he'd no longer be an angel but a human just like Lito? Better just finish what he came to do and leave. "I'm no longer assigned to you," he said. "Not sure anyone is, actually."

"What?"

Just tell the poor bloke.

"There's a bull's eye painted on your back."

"Tell me something I *don't* know."

"I'm here to warn you, because you're on your own now. I can't protect you anymore."

"Just like that, you're checking out?"

He gave Nick a thoughtful look, held his gaze for a moment, then sighed.

"Guess this is goodbye, then."

"I'm afraid so. You'd better get to London as fast as you can."

"I just have one last thing to do before I go."

"Be careful, Lito. I mean it."

"Don't worry." Lito patted the gun behind his back and mustered a brave smile. "I can take care of myself."

"Take every possible precaution." Nick put a hand on his shoulder and gave it a firm squeeze. Lito's eyes brightened. He stood taller, looked stronger. If only Nick could protect him a bit longer...

"I'd best be going now, my friend." One last handshake.

"Thank you, my friend."

"What for?" Nick said.

Lito smiled. "My life."

74

NICK LEFT THE WAY A HUMAN WOULD, through the front door and out to the sidewalk. Concealed by the shadow of a camphor tree, he focused on the Coronado Bridge until he felt the concrete vanish from beneath his feet.

A cool blast of air rushed over his face and raked through his hair. It wasn't teleporting but he was flying at superhuman speeds. He looked down to make sure he wasn't casting a shadow.

As he approached the bridge, a sharp pain stabbed his head—the effect of his supernatural powers draining away. Losing balance, he gripped his head between his hands.

The landscape spun as he hurtled down to the water below.

He felt no impact, no splash, no suffocating water in his lungs, but Nick knew he'd plunged beneath the bridge. When he regained his bearings, it became abundantly clear that he was between realms.

Sort of.

He wasn't drowning, but his clothes felt damp. The water seemed neither cold, warm, nor heavy. He drifted in it but didn't sink or float, the only sensation was the pain now gripping his skull like a vise. It overwhelmed him every time he tried to teleport to dry land.

Large shadows passed over as did the sound of motors and a cruise ship's horn. The briny dampness became tangible in his mouth, his nose, and pressed against the surface of his whole body. He was slipping through into the physical realm and uncertain he could control it.

He thought he heard someone calling him. The voice itself wasn't audible, but in his mind the earnest cry evoked images of Clara, Sophia...and Hope.

He turned his head, hit a concrete post. Before he could react, the darkness engulfed him utterly.

75

WITHIN THE BOWELS OF CABRILLO STADIUM, Yuri crimped the final wire to arm the second of two nuclear devices strategically placed under the stands of the plaza level on the north and south sides.

"There." He handed the remote detonators to Dan and Gunther, the two hulking men who'd overseen the activation. "After retina scan, use this button to arm, this one to begin countdown. Scan retina again, then press blue button to abort—"

"Abort?" Dan glowered at him.

"Just in case. I made very simple, even child could—"

"That'll be all," Gunther said. He and Dan lifted Yuri up as if he were made of straw.

"Hey!" Yuri struggled, but it was no use. In a few seconds he was in the locker room being slammed against the doors.

"What the hell? I make delivery, set up configuration. Why—"

Gunther opened the door next to Yuri's right ear, pulled out some neatly wound cord, and started tying Yuri's wrists behind his back.

"After delivery I get paid! I had deal with Lena Walker!"

"These are *Lena's* orders," Gunther said.

Dan got a roll of duct tape from the locker and wrapped it twice around Yuri's head, tightly sealing his mouth. Just when Yuri thought it couldn't get any worse, Gunther fashioned a noose around his neck and threw the other end of the rope over a pipe high above them. He started pulling on the rope.

Screams choked off, eyes bulging, heart about to explode, Yuri dared not move as the rope grew tighter.

Didn't matter.

He knew what was coming.

He shut his eyes.

Heard Sascha say *You'll never amount to anything.*

Heard himself say *I'm sorry, Mommochka.*

The last thing Yuri heard was the sound his neck made when it snapped.

76

THE IMPACT THAT CAUSED THE DARKNESS eventually end-
ed it. At first a flash of white light, then the dancing flecks that swam
around Nick's head, then the realization that he was mostly in the physical realm but not to the point that he couldn't exist under water without
drowning.

The damage from that concrete pillar felt real enough, though. As
he drifted in the depths, a sharp throbbing pain from the bump surpassed
all other sensation, which meant the pain of his draining angelic powers
had subsided.

For the moment.

Right above his head, a trio of sea creatures swam past him. From
their horizontal tail flukes, he could tell they were mammals—dolphins
or some other sort of porpoise.

How long had he been unconscious?

Judging by the scant trickles of light that made it to the murky
depths, evening had fallen. He'd spent several hours submerged at the
bottom of the bay which Hope had almost made her grave.

Time to find that pendant.

With the sand barely registering the presence of his feet, Nick trudged toward the spot closest to where he believed Hope had attempted her fatal swan dive.

He knew the prospect of finding anything but debris and fish muck in those dark depths was about as good as finding a diamond in a junkyard.

He had to try.

Even if it brought on more daggers to the skull. He focused on the image of Hope touching the place on her neck where her pendant had been. Sure enough, a skewer of pain impaled his left eye socket, which throbbed exquisitely.

A dark gray harbor porpoise swam over to watch him. Just past the sleek frame of the porpoise, he saw something shining in the distance. It looked almost like a penlight lodged in some kelp around one of the bridge's pillars.

Pushing through the ever roiling water and ever increasing pain, Nick slogged over to the flickering light, glad the porpoise was following. He was exhausted, the pain now so intense he almost released the mental image of Hope.

The porpoise swam closer to the light.

Nick took a deep breath—and a few more steps.

Just enough:

The jade pendant hung on a gold chain dangling from a barnacle. Its design was a traditionally entwined dragon and phoenix, but there was nothing else traditional about it. The pendant *glowed*—with a golden light that cast no physical rays, nor did it glint onto the face of the porpoise clicking joyfully while she remained close at Nick's side.

He reached out and let the pendant float up under his hand. In order to take hold of it, he'd have to become fully physical—his hand, at least. He wasn't sure he had the ability or coordination to do that now.

But he wasn't about to give up, now.

As he released the image of Hope, the pain lessened if only marginally. He slipped his hand into the physical layer, lifted the pendant, closed his fingers around it, and pushed it into his pocket. But the sudden compression in his chest and the saturation of frigid water in his clothes alerted him to a troubling realization: He had not been able to control his entrance into the physical realm.

He couldn't retreat to the safety of the spiritual layer without losing the pendant. Nor could he swim to physical safety if he remained in his current state. Already the pressure of the watery depths was crushing him. His eyes felt like they were bulging out of his head, his lungs were desperate for air.

He looked over to the porpoise, projected his need for help as best he could.

She swam over and presented her dorsal fin. Nick grabbed it with both hands.

// THANK YOU //

When they finally broke through the surface, the porpoise sent a heavy mist through its blowhole and swam toward shore.

Nick held on like a man on a self-propelled boogie-board.

"I suppose I'm going to have to learn how to swim, one of these days," he called out.

The porpoise clicked and chattered.

Five minutes later Nick stood on the sandy shore bidding farewell to his aquatic friend. Despite the pains he'd taken, the lingering aches and nausea, the teeth-chattering chill that ran like ice through his drenched body, he felt grateful. And amazed at his good fortune in surviving the plunge *and* retrieving Hope's pendant.

He couldn't wait to see her face when he returned it to her. He fished the smartphone out of his pocket, unaffected by the water because it was phasing out of the physical realm.

An artifact of his final days as an angel.

Just before it vanished he made a note of the time: 6:17 PM.

Less than an hour until the Cabrillo Stadium event.

77

THE AUDITORS COULD BE ANYWHERE. Disguised as humans, invisible to all but those to whom they chose to appear. There was no way Lena could tell where in the stadium they were, but Morloch never failed to deploy them.

The last rays of sunlight painted the sky red. She had once found such conflagrations beautiful, but now the scarlet streaks in the sky were bleeding out a languid death into the tomb of nightfall.

Having discreetly dispatched one of Hartwell's staff members and taken on her appearance, she stood at the west side of the stadium shading her eyes from the blazing white stadium lights. In just half an hour, some fifteen thousand people would pour into the arena like cattle into the slaughterhouse.

Serena, Dan, Gunther, and Johann joined her. With their black business suits, sunglasses, and expressionless faces, they looked like secret service agents. But they were nothing so trivial. They were Nephilim, strong and proud, and like Lena, ready to change the course of history.

"The packages are in place," Serena said, her tone as colorless as her features. "Timer's set. Yuri's been dealt with. Sniper's ready."

"Isn't this overkill?" Johann said. "Taking out your targets with a sniper rifle, only to have them fried when the nukes go off?"

"Just do your jobs, all right?" Lena gave them a reassuring smile. "Contingency plans are our friend." A pair of 2.5 kiloton suitcase bombs would more than suffice, but it was all about the spectacle. The bullets were to ensure that Hope Matheson was terminated while people could see it happen, the bombs to impress not only Morloch but his entire command chain. "Any questions?"

None.

"Keep on the lookout for Nikolai. He's fallen, but we can't be certain how much of his supernatural powers he still retains."

Lena watched with pride as they dispersed to their positions. Although none of them possessed the superior intellect for leadership, they were some of the strongest Nephilim she'd found over the years and the most effective at enforcing her will—muscle to her brains. And like her, they could withstand the blast of a nuclear warhead or better yet, slip out of the physical layer into the spiritual.

Lena headed for the secure entrance onto the field. At the gate, a security guard with a walkie-talkie in hand stopped her.

"Ms. Wright?" he said. "I've got a group here—DCM Security, they with you?"

"They're late, go ahead and let them into VIP lounge six," Lena said in the voice of the dead staff member whose likeness she'd pilfered. "I'll meet them there."

Five minutes later, she was unlocking the door of the lounge with Ms. Wright's magnetized badge and letting in four deeply tanned men in black suits with black ties and dark sunglasses.

"We don't have much time." Lena pointed to each of them in turn.

"You're Number One, Number Two...Three...Four." She then pointed to the cabinet and told Number Three to distribute the in-ear transmitter/receivers. "Which one of you is the sharpshooter?"

Number Four raised his hand.

"Over there." She nodded toward the closet. Number Four went over and took out a black bag whose contents he dumped onto the coffee table. Four Glock .38s. "Grab one each," Lena said, then led the sniper over to the window.

On the ground beneath it lay a footlocker. She unlocked it and motioned for him to pick up the Remington 700 bolt-action rifle, a case of rounds, and a pair of binoculars. Then she slid the window open over the vacant section of the stadium all the way to the stage.

"This entire part of the stadium has been cordoned off, for security measures. You'll keep the lights off and take your shot from here—the duck blind, so to speak. Your target Hope Matheson will be in the front row. She'll be speaking right after Hartwell. Make sure she doesn't get far into her speech. Afterwards, you'll wait here and we'll facilitate your getaway. Any questions?"

The sniper shook his head.

"The rest of you have seen the photos of the other targets. If any of them try to escape, they're your priority. Communicate and cover the different sections of the stadium. No one gets out. Number One, are the parking lot exits covered?"

He slid the gun behind his back and faced her.

"All according to Miguel's orders. We got twenty-five armed and standing by on their cell phones ready to jump. A lot of trouble just to keep people trapped inside the stadium to watch an assassination."

Lena glided over to the door, then stopped.

"This needs to be a high visibility kill, for a big audience. It all has to be done by seven-thirty, not a second later, understand? The bigger the spectacle the better." *As far as Morloch is concerned.* As for Lena, she cared more about the resources promised for accomplishing this mission than the faith of millions that would be shattered as a result.

"What are you?" the sniper said, "some kind of terrorist?"

"Terrorist?" What were terrorists, in the grand scheme of things? Simply means to an end. What Lena and the Nephilim under her command were about to do could not even be mentioned in the same breath. "You think too small."

78

EVENING HAD FALLEN AND ALONG WITH IT the temperature. Beneath the floodlights illuminating entrances into the packed stadium, a few stragglers walked toward the gates.

Nick climbed out of the taxi, his clothes still wet, his shoes sloshing with each irritating step. Teleporting had been intermittent, only taking him a few blocks at a time. Flying made him nauseous. Hence the cab.

Now he was late. Hope might have tried calling or texting, but the smartphone from Lena had given up the ghost. *As will my powers,* he thought, but then pushed it from his mind. Still groggy from his plunge into the bay, Nick hurried to the nearest entrance.

Along the way, he noticed a few men eyeing him. One of them spoke into a cell phone while never taking his eyes off him. As an angel, Nick wouldn't have given them a second thought. But now, becoming ever more human by the moment, he felt vulnerable.

He quickened his pace to a light jog all the way to the will-call ticket window. No one was there.

"Hello?"

No answer.

Over the speakers he heard the band finishing a number. The crowd cheered. Someone made an announcement. More cheers. In just a few minutes, Hope would step onto the stage to address the thousands filling the stadium and the millions watching on television.

"Anyone there?" Nick started to imagine himself at Hope's side, wherever she might be. But no—better not try teleporting. It was starting to feel like a thing of the past, the way amputees experienced phantom sensations in their missing limbs. Probably for the best. It would be awkward if he were to appear by her side out of thin air on live television.

He banged his fist against the window.

"I need some help here!" Another round of applause went up through the speakers.

A pair of men smoking cigarettes approached. Not far from Nick yet not too close, they looked as though they were just loitering around the ticket booths.

Or were they?

79

MARIA SAT IN SECTION 23 SEAT B, waiting for Lito. The plan was to feign a migraine after he sat with her a while, then ask him to bring the Ibuprofen from her car. Joey would see to it that he never came back. That was what she wanted, right?

But on the phone that afternoon, Lito had sounded so different. None of that put-on machismo, but instead, the gentleness he'd shown when they were kids—she the shy sister, he the protective brother. Memories of those happier days stuck to her mind like tiny barbs, no matter how many times she reminded herself that he and the entire Guzman family were dangerous strangers who'd lied to her, all her life. Nevertheless, the more she thought about her brother getting killed, the worse she felt.

No matter what happened when she was just a baby, Lito had always been her big brother.

A good one, most of the time.

"This seat taken?"

Without thinking, she stood and threw her arms around him.

"Lito!"

"It's so good to see you, Maria."

She held him close and didn't want to let go.

"We're making a scene," he said, smiling wide. "Let's sit down."

She nodded and sank into her seat, Lito to her left.

"Maria, before you say anything, I want to tell you something."

He reached over and held her hand like he used to when they were little and the wicked witch showed her ugly green face in The Wizard of Oz.

"Alfonso did make some threats against me, but the bottom line? He was using you and was eventually going to hurt you, even kill you."

The sincerity in his eyes was absolute. She believed him.

"Then why didn't you tell me earlier?"

"You were both so secretive—I only found out that day." He gave her a poignant look. "And if I *had* talked to you, would you have listened? By the time I found out, there was no choice. He had to be stopped right there and then."

He was probably right. Part of the reason she never told him about dating Alfonso was because she knew what he would say. But she could see it herself every time they went out, the way Alfonso's eyes wandered to any girl that passed by. He hadn't loved her. If she were to be completely honest with herself—which she was right now—she'd have to admit that she hadn't really loved Alfonso either. She was more in love with the idea of being in love, the idea of showing Lito he wasn't the boss of her.

"I have something else to tell you, Maria."

"What is it?"

He'd never had the slightest difficulty speaking his mind, but now he seemed worried.

The audience broke into applause as the band finished another song. Lito took his time to answer, Maria's anxiety increasing by the second.

"Something much deeper, much worse," he said finally. "I need to tell you now because after tonight I might not get another chance."

With great difficulty, he went on to make his confession. It took a while for him to get to the point where he confessed that she'd been raised by the very family responsible for killing her parents. But somehow he made their taking her sound like an act of mercy and love rather than treachery.

"Can you ever forgive me?" he said.

She touched his hand gently.

"Lito, I already know."

"You do? How?"

"I met my grandfather, Juan Suarez. He told me everything—about my parents, about how you killed Alfonso because he was going to reveal the secret to me."

"It was more than that, Maria. Alfonso was going to hurt you. And he and the Hernandezes were going to join forces with the Suarezes. If that happened—"

She held up her finger.

"Oh no, I just remembered something." She reached into her bag and pulled out her phone. "Give me a second, please?"

She sent a text message to Joey Hernandez.

> Calling it off.
> I will still pay you.
> Do not come anywhere near. OK?

She expected an immediate reply.

But when none came, she panicked. Until now she'd assumed she was in charge of this plan. But what if she were just a part of *Joey's* plan?

She got up. "We have to go, Lito."

"What's wrong?" he stood and followed her.

"Please, trust me. We've got to get out of here before it's too late."

As they edged sideways toward the aisle, Maria saw a pair of men at the far end of the bleachers talking into walkie-talkies. They could not have been security guards, not if they were who she thought they were.

"Over there, by the exit," she said. "See those guys?"

"They don't look like the religious type." He gripped her arm.

The men started walking in their direction.

"They've seen us," she said. "Hurry!"

80

AT THE EDGE OF THE STADIUM Nick detected an all too familiar pair of imposing figures—Johann and Serena, both of whom had foregone leather and now looked like Secret Service bodyguards. Their presence made one thing clear: Lena was near. Which might have meant they were looking for him, too.

With Hope so close by, though, he had to know what Lena was up to. And besides, being seen with the likes of Johann and Serena had its advantages. No one would mess with him if they were near. He might even be able to convince Lena to help him get inside. One last favor, for old time's sake.

A strong hand grasped his shoulder. He noticed a slight flash of light behind him, then spun around. Blocking his view of just about everything, Johann glared down at him.

"Be still. Listen carefully. You need to know what's happening."

"What—"

"Trust me," Johann said, bending down to whisper. "Impersonate Lena, then talk to Serena." He vanished.

Craning his neck, Nick saw Serena turn in their direction. He wasn't predisposed to trust Johann, but his plan made sense. Cloaking himself in a construct to resemble Lena just as Serena stepped over, Nick scanned the area.

"Where is he?"

"Who?" Nick's disguised voice leapt an octave.

"Johann," Serena said.

"Doing what I asked."

Serena glanced left, right, then signaled to someone in the distance.

"I thought I saw Nikolai," she said.

"And you just stood there?"

Serena narrowed her eyes to lethal slits.

"You *said* not to kill him until I told you first."

"That's right. Good job." A torrent of disturbing thoughts flooded Nick's mind. *You need to know what's happening*, Johann had said. "We'll deal with him later, give me an update."

Just then the two other large men who had met with Lena that night joined them.

"Dan, Gunther—status?" Serena said.

"Sniper's in place, Hernandez's and Suarez's people are armed and posted at every exit."

"Nukes are set to detonate in ten minutes and twenty seconds. No one's leaving here alive tonight."

Nick's innards twisted into knots, his mouth went bitter dry.

"Excellent," he said, struggling to maintain Lena's coldness. "And how do I deactivate them?"

All three spoke at once, but the voice he heard was Gunther's.

"We just spent all this time arming them, why—"

"Are you *challenging* me?" The sound of Lena's threatening voice coming out of him was disturbing. "I need to know that you've set every-thing correctly. It's conceivable that the timing might change. Now, review the protocols for disarming!"

"Retina scan." Dan came over to Nick and pointed at what he perceived as Lena's right eye. "The only way to arm or disarm the nukes is to have your retina scanned for the first device, Serena's for the second."

"Are they in the correct locations?"

"Sublevels C and B, as ordered," Dan said. "Koslupov's...hanging out down there in B."

Gunther snorted. "Not that anyone will find him before it's all turned to ash."

Hope.

Nick had to get her out of there. But he had one more question.

"Confirm the sniper's instructions and target."

Serena threw her hands up. "Why are you wasting time reviewing everything? Is *this* Lena Walker, the legendary Nephilim just one step down the command chain from Morloch? "

Nephilim?

"Answer the damned question!"

Serena's eyes blazed, but Nick stared her down.

"A few minutes into the onstage speech," she said, "the sniper will take out the target Hope Matheson from VIP Lounge six."

"It's almost time," Gunther said. "We still have to find Nikolai."

Nick was having a hard time maintain Lena's chilling calm.

"All right. Spread out and do it."

"Dan, you search the stands and manage the Suarez men." Serena said. "Gunther, go through the sublevels."

They went off—except for Serena.

"You're unfit, Lena," she said. "Whatever the Dark Dominion saw in you is beyond—"

"GO!"

She went, leaving Nick to fight his ever-increasing nausea.

The Dark Dominion?

The assignments made sense now. He understood why they'd wanted to stop Hope, distract Jonathan Hartwell, protect Lito then kill him once he turned. From the start, Lena had recruited him for the Dark Dominion. He should have known better, but she and Harold Morloch had hooked him with everything he thought he wanted. Now, like it or not, he was party to the horrific death and destruction about to take place.

From the center of the stadium, the band's final chords faded. A round of applause went up, and over the loudspeakers, an announcer spoke.

"Ladies and gentlemen, please welcome Jonathan Hartwell."

81

NICK MANAGED TO TELEPORT INTO THE HALLS of the stadium. Like a dying light bulb, his disguise as Lena flickered. The queasiness abated. And once he released the Lena construct he started to feel better.

He barely heard the man introducing Jonathan Hartwell. If only he had a visual image of VIP Lounge 6, he might still be able to teleport there and stop the sniper.

He drew a deep breath, rested a hand on the wall. As best he could he focused on the concept of VIP Lounge 6, the image of a sniper....

Nothing.

Eyes shut tight he tried again, this time focusing on the image of a rifle. The pain spiking through his brain suggested it wasn't going to work. But when he opened his eyes, he found himself in another section of the stadium. The lights were dim and gave him no clue where he'd teleported.

He wiped the moisture under his nose—it wasn't perspiration.

It was blood.

Again.

Thin though the blood was, it probably meant his angelic powers must be about to expire. Couldn't they last just one more day? How could he stop an armed man and two nuclear explosions without them?

He'd never felt so desperate. Or so determined. No matter what, no matter how, he had to keep the sniper in VIP Lounge 6 from killing the woman he loved.

Up ahead, a stronger overhead light fell on a wall sign. Nick ran over to it, relieved to find a map framed behind a Plexiglas window that showed the stadium's levels, restrooms, exits, and...

VIP lounges, two levels up.

But they were on the opposite side of the stadium.

Another attempt at teleporting struck back like a blow to the head with a steel pipe. The pain itself seemed to inhibit his ability.

And so, though his progress would seem ridiculously slow, Nick started running as fast as his mortal body could stand.

"Hello, San Diego!" Jon called out. The cheers and flashing lights almost blinded him, his vision was blurred by tears threatening to spill. "Thank you all for coming tonight." You'd have thought he'd said something brilliant, judging by the crowd's reaction and how long it went on. He looked down to the front row, grateful but not surprised that Elaine was there, next to Matthew. The surprise had come when she believed his tearful phone confession.

"Let me begin by saying to everyone I have hurt—the wife I love, the young woman I failed, my staff, church, and everyone I've disappointed—I truly regret the pain and embarrassment I caused. I have since asked and received my wife's forgiveness, I've asked forgiveness from my church and staff, and now I earnestly seek yours.

"This lapse in judgment has shown me that I am not above temptation. Although nothing sexual transpired, I was nevertheless wrong for allowing this to happen, and failing to keep myself above reproach. I have no one but myself to blame, I take full responsibility, and am grieved by my failure.

"But I think to be forgiven, grief over the sin is just a starting point. Action is required in the form of repentance, as well as the renunciation of my pride, anger and fear, which led me to make excuses and rationalize doing what I knew I must not.

"In the scripture, God says, 'If My people who are called by My name will humble themselves, and pray and seek My face, and turn from their wicked ways, then I will hear from heaven, and will forgive their sin and heal their land.'

"Tonight, before you and before God, I humble myself in repentance, I commit myself to turning from the slightest hint of impropriety, and from my selfish and hurtful ways.

"Now, I believe it is in the best interest of everyone that I step down from this ministry, trusting you not to allow my failures to change your view of the God who loves every one of us, who always forgives. He never changes, never gives up on us, however much we deserve it—I deserve it. As I have always preached, put your hope in Him, not in man." He was quiet for a moment, as if considering his next words.

"Not in me."

Nick had to stop running. Winded, the only thing he heard was Hartwell's voice over the wall mounted monitors.

"Will you pray with me that God would create in me a clean heart, and renew a right spirit within me?" Hartwell turned his face to the domed

ceiling as though it were open to the evening sky. *"Dear Lord, cast me not away from Your presence, and take not Your Holy Spirit from me. I pray my failure will cause no one to stumble and fall away from You. In Jesus's name..."* He wiped the tear rolling down his cheek.

"Amen."

Like a great sigh, a collective "amen" floated up to fill the stadium, followed by applause so loud it seemed to be coming from all across the country. Nick, having caught his breath, continued running to the VIP lounges as Hartwell began speaking again.

"Friends, in just a moment you're going to meet a remarkable woman and friend of the ministry. She's going to share a remarkable testimony—it's brief but I know it will encourage you, no matter what you're going through.

"Her name—most serendipitously—is Hope. Let me tell you just a little about Hope Matheson."

82

"YOU GOING TO TELL ME WHAT'S GOING ON?" Lito said as he and Maria raced up the steps toward the nearest exit.

"No time to explain, come on!" As soon as they were out of the bleacher area and into a corridor, she spotted another pair of men way across at the opposite end—Joey Hernandez and some other guy. Joey shouted something and started running towards them.

Lito needed no urging. He ran with her until they reached a door that read Authorized Personnel Only. He pushed the door which, to his relief, wasn't locked. Maria looked for a way to lock it behind them, gave up and followed him down the zigzagging stairs, her feet pounding on the concrete. She couldn't believe this was happening, couldn't believe she'd reached out to Joey in the first place.

"What's going on?" Lito said when they reached the end of the stairwell. "Why are the Suarezes and Hernandezes—"

"It's my fault," she said, her voice desperate. "I led them to you because..." She fought back tears. "Because I wanted you dead! Especially after my grandfather talked to me. It was like I was under some kind of influence. All I could think about was revenge. "

He grabbed her by the arms. "And now?"

"I don't know what came over me. I was furious with you, yes. But you're the only family I have now. You *are* my brother and I don't want to lose you!"

"What about the Suarezes?"

"Guzman, Suarez? Are any of them good, are any of them my family? All I know is that you've always been there for me, even though I haven't always appreciated it. I didn't realize this until I really thought about what it would be like if they actually killed you."

"Glad you had a change of heart." Lito stared up to the stairwell. "They may have seen us come down this way."

They would probably want to kill her too, now that she'd backed down on delivering her brother for an easy execution. Lito pointed to another stairwell and started walking down.

"Listen, Maria," he whispered. "Something's happened to me."

"What?"

"I've seen the light, so to speak. I'm getting out of this business, even though it's against Papi's wishes."

"You can't just walk away, you know that."

"God will protect me."

"How can you be sure?"

She gave him a wry look.

"What are you going to do?"

"I'm going to England. Why don't you come with me? Let them all kill each other fighting over the territories. We can live a quiet life out there, start fresh."

She stopped and let Lito walk a few more steps before he turned back.

"After what I've done? You still want me around?"

"Of course." He extended his hand to her. "You're my sister."

For the first time in a long while, her head was clear of the clouds that obscured her thoughts and judgment. She took Lito's hand, and he pulled her in for a hug.

"So, everything's falling apart here, what do you say? Will you come with me?"

She looked up and smiled. "Assuming we get out of here alive, first."

"That's right."

Above them the sound of a door kicked open resounded through the concrete stairwell, followed by pounding footfalls and the click of gun hammers cocking.

Maria tightened her grip on Lito's hand.

"Here they come."

83

THE DOOR WAS LOCKED.

Dim light pooled into the empty corridor, just enough falling on the door for Nick to read the placard.

VIP Lounge 6.

Whether from running like a madman or the thought of a sniper taking his shot at Hope soon after Hartwell finished his introduction, Nick's chest was pounding so hard he thought it might explode.

No point in attempting to teleport. It drew blood and threatened to crush his head with pain—and would only waste time if it failed, which in all likelihood it would.

Perhaps he could pass through the door. He pressed his hand against it, but the door's physical properties resisted. He strained, pressing with all his might.

"Come...on!" He felt with his fingertips for the loosening of the door's molecules. But even the memory of how to do this seemed to be eluding him. He stopped straining, took a deep breath, and pressed against the door as if he were absolutely sure he could pass through it.

Then, it happened.

First the fingernails.

Then the tip of his forefinger.

And then his entire hand passed through the door.

He turned the handle. The door still wouldn't open.

Deadbolt.

He reached up and unlocked it, then pulled his hand back through the door and opened it.

The lounge was pitch black save for a sliver of light piercing the blinds a little ways ahead—sufficient to illuminate the man in dark clothes propped up against a window sill with a rifle.

Hartwell's voice rang out. *"Please welcome Hope Matheson."* Waves of applause went up.

The sniper aimed. Took a breath...

And fired just as Nick rushed him headlong.

84

TO THE APPLAUSE OF THOUSANDS, Hope had ascended the steps to the stage. Where was Nick? Was she really going to have to do this without the one most responsible for the healing she was about to share with the audience?

But share it she must. Overwhelmed with the welcome by these thousands she'd never met, she nonetheless felt a kinship with them. She walked to the podium and stood there until the applause subsided.

She was ready.

"Hi, everyone...Wow!" She smiled and wiped a tear before it could roll down her face. "You know, it was only weeks ago that I could barely pull myself out of my cot in a shelter each morning without thinking I had nothing to live for, my life was miserable, the universe hated me...And I'll tell you, it really did feel that way.

"You see, I lost my father to cancer when I was a little girl. A bit later, I was abused over and over again by my stepfather. Brandon, my first husband—the love of my life—was killed in Iraq just after my daughter Chloe was born. My second husband turned out to be a gambler who got himself and Chloe killed. After that I just gave up on everything.

"I eventually tried to end my life by jumping from the Coronado Bridge, but I was rescued—just as I jumped." She could almost feel the collective gasp. "The scriptures say we should 'show kindness to strangers, for by so doing some have shown kindness to angels without knowing it.' But in my case, God sent an angel who showed *me* kindness.

"Nevertheless, even after that rescue, I tried to take my life again. You see, I kept listening to the enemy's accusing voices and lies. This time I nearly succeeded. But somehow, the pills I took didn't stay down. And by God's grace, I saw my past through an entirely different perspective.

"This time as I relived those painful events, I heard God saying, 'I am there, Hope.' I thought, 'You mean, you *were* there, don't you?' But God corrected me. "I *am* there. In your past, your future, I am there.'

"Right there, I realized that He exists outside of time, that I was not alone during my darkest hours. And although I still remember the awful things that happened, the pain from them eased. I'm not saying it went away completely, but it stopped hurting me, its hold on my life was broken.

"I don't know how else to explain it, but some of you know what I'm talking about, right? Some of you have been healed before like this, can I get a witness?"

Shouts of amen, and applause rose up.

"Tonight, I just want you all to know. We have a good God. He's powerful, omniscient, omnipotent, and omnipresent. He holds time in his hand. That's why he can be in our past, present and future simultaneously. He is the same yesterday and today and forever.

"So whatever you're suffering from, no matter how dire the situation, how deep the pain, God wants you to know that He has come to bring good news to the afflicted, to bind up the brokenhearted..."

She'd never considered herself eloquent enough to speak in public, but the rapt audience didn't intimidate her. And the words, the scriptures she never knew she'd memorized seemed to just flow out of her.

"He's here to proclaim liberty to captives, freedom to prisoners...to console those who mourn, to give them beauty for ashes, the oil of joy for mourning!

"Tonight, whoever you are, wherever you've been, it's not too late. Even if you're suffering the consequences of your own mistakes, your own failures, He's got healing for you."

From the corner of her eye, she could see the tears on Jonathan Hartwell's face. His wife held his hand and dabbed the corners of her eye with a tissue.

"Whether it's the pain of the past, the hurt you're feeling now, the worries about tomorrow, He's saying to you right now, "I AM THERE!" She turned and pointed to the crowds in each section of the stadium, saying each time, "with you, and with you, and you!"

As she turned back to the camera, a flash of light from the shadows of the private boxes caught her eye. A half-second later, something hot whisked through her hair just above her ear.

That was when the screaming began.

85

THE FIRST THING NICK FELT AFTER HE CHARGED at the sniper was the butt of the rifle slamming into his gut. His stomach felt like it was imploding. Flat on his back and stunned, he could hardly breathe. But he was pretty sure he'd disrupted at least one of the sniper's two shots.

He swung his rifle around at Nick's head. Nick managed to block it with his arm, then tried to stand.

But the distinct *clack* of a round being chambered stopped him.

"Who are you?" The shooter's voice was intense but quiet. He pinned Nick's shoulder down with a heavy foot and pressed the rifle's muzzle into his chest.

"Wait," Nick said.

The hammer cocked.

Nick squeezed his eyes tight, grit his teeth against the pain, and focused on the cold barrel through which a bullet was about to end his mortal life, short as it had been.

Just as the shooter pulled the trigger.

The gun vanished.

"What—?"

A fraction of a second later, it reappeared—somewhere near the door, judging by the flash of light and loud shot. Nick swung his foot under the astonished sniper's legs, collapsing them behind the knees so that he fell back with a thud.

His whole body throbbing with pain, his powers pulsing intermittently like a dying star, Nick thrust his hand down on the sniper's forehead as he struggled to get up. Whether he was human or Nephilim, Nick couldn't be certain.

He only hoped his next move would work.

The shooter became deathly still. Then he hugged his chest, shaking violently while emitting a wheezing sound meant to be a scream. Nick's construct made him experience the terror of a coiling forty-foot python crushing the life out of him. Every breath he took would cause the huge serpent to squeeze harder.

But his pain, unlike Nick's, wasn't real. Battling the nausea and pain from the latest flare-up of his failing supernatural power, he focused on the podium where Hope had been speaking and prayed he wasn't too late.

86

IT SOUNDED LIKE A FIRECRACKER. But Jon knew someone had fired a gun when he saw one of his wife's security guard's chest erupt in a crimson spray.

"Elaine!" He ran to her and Matthew, throwing himself over them without a thought for his own safety.

Another shot.

Something hit him between the shoulder blades.

His head hit the ground as he fell.

A scarlet puddle widened around him.

The last thing he saw was his wife and son kneeling over him, Elaine crying, Matthew screaming.

"Daddy!"

87

NICK HAD TELEPORTED TO THE STAGE, but the pain was so intense he could barely see past the glowing flecks swarming his vision.

"Oh my God, Nick!" Hope gripped his arms and buried her face in his chest. He thought she was crying—hard to hear with all the chaos on the stage. He put his hands on her shoulders and turned her to face the steps where people were fleeing.

"We've got to get out of here."

She pointed down to Jon. "What about Pastor Hartwell?"

He lay motionless, the white shirt under his navy jacket soaked with blood. The bullet must have gone straight through his chest.

Nick went over and knelt by Jon, who grasped his hand with icy fingers.

With a gasp, he uttered his last words.

"Elaine...Matthew..." But the remaining security staff had rushed them away, out of the line of fire. Nick had taken care of the sniper, but he hadn't succeeded completely. The rage and sadness he felt rivaled the pain in his head. Lena's heartless machinations had taken the first victims. Had he his full strength as a guardian, he might rather enjoy destroying her as he had so many of the Dark Dominion's more formidable agents. But time was running out, as were his powers.

And if Lena hadn't seen Nick by now, her cohorts surely had.

He had to get Hope to safety.

"There isn't much time." He grabbed her hand rushed her over to the steps at the edge of the stage, and crouched behind a wall of equipment crates. Catching his breath, he said, "We're going to have to leave unconventionally."

"Nick, what's happening?"

"I'll explain later, first I've got to get you out of here before..." He glanced up at the thousands scrambling to leave the stadium. Lena had recruited mortal and supernatural help to kill them all with the bombs. There was no way any of them could simply walk out.

"Before what, Nick?"

It wouldn't be a complete lie if he told her that hers was the only life that mattered to him. But the thought of leaving all these innocent people to die troubled him.

"Hope, listen. I'm losing my powers even as we speak. I might have just enough to take us to safety before..."

Throughout the stadium, the sound of automatic gunfire rang out. Hernandez and Suarez men brandished assault rifles and blocked the exits, every passageway a narrow tunnel of death. A couple of brave fools rushed the gunmen but were shot before they got within striking distance.

The lights in the entire stadium went out.

Terrified screams filled the air.

Save for dim ambient light coming in from the translucent panels of the stadium dome and cell phone cameras acting as flashlights, the entire place was dark.

"Before *what*?" Hope said.

"They've got the stadium rigged with nuclear explosives."

He couldn't see her reaction, but he did hear her gasp.

"Why would anyone—who's doing this?"

"My former supervisor. Can't tell just how many humans and angels—or demons, rather—she's got working with her. It turns out I was one of her unwitting recruits."

Hope was speechless.

"We need to go, now!" A spike of pain that struck his head kept him from saying more.

The sounds of panic grew louder. Gunshots, screams, cries for help. Hope was shaking, her breathing staccato.

"All right," she said. "Let's go."

But even in the darkness, their mutual pause confirmed that it was not so simple as leaving.

"Hope..."

"Are you thinking what I am?" she whispered.

"I must be insane."

It didn't take supernatural abilities for either of them to know how the other felt.

Or that they agreed.

88

THE PAIN IT COST NICK TO TELEPORT with Hope to a corridor across the stadium was excruciating. He could barely pick himself off the concrete with the daggers impaling his skull through his eyes and ears. Another power surge. Slightly weaker than the last one but agonizing nonetheless.

"You're bleeding." Hope pulled a tissue from her pocket and blotted his upper lip.

"Part of the process," Nick said. "The more mortal I become, the more it hurts to use my powers. Especially teleporting." He put his head in his hands. "Any idea where we are?"

As she looked around, screams and gunshots echoed through the corridors.

"All I can see is a big letter C painted by the doorway."

Sublevel C.

"Good." He steadied himself against the wall.

"Do you hear that?" Hope whispered.

"What is it?"

"Shhh!" In the curved concrete corridors, rapid footfalls grew louder. "Someone's coming."

Nothing but the blood-red glow of emergency signs lit the area. Nick got in front of her and leaned up against the wall.

"Stay close."

"How much time do we have before the bombs go off?"

"A few minutes."

"Do you know where they are?"

"Not exactly. I heard something about—hold on." He felt a draft. It reminded him of the dark vapor that used to appear like a portent when he was an angel. Probably just air coming through a vent. He glanced up and saw a sign with an arrow pointing to LOCKER ROOM C.

"Come on," he said. Hope didn't move.

"That's the direction where they're coming from!"

She was right, and they were getting louder.

"If we don't hurry, it won't matter," Nick said. "Nothing will."

They ran until what looked like a pair of shadows stopped short a little ways ahead of them.

"Don't shoot!" a trembling female voice called out.

"*Cállate!*" a man said.

There was no mistaking that voice.

Nick stepped into the red light.

89

"NICK? IS THAT YOU OVER THERE?"

Lito Guzman stepped into the light.

"Yes," Nick said, straining to see. "What are you doing here?"

"Who is this guy, Lito?" The young woman with him emerged from the shadows.

Hope came to Nick's side. "What's going on?"

"It's going to be okay now," Lito said to the young woman. Then to Nick: "This is my sister, Maria." To Maria: "This is Nick. He's the angel that—"

"The situation is much worse than you can imagine," Nick said.

"What's worse than a bunch of armed Mexican drug lords trying to kill us?" Maria said. "It's only a matter of time before they catch up."

"We've no time for this," Nick said, as he led them down the hall to locker room C. "There are two nuclear devices, one here and one in locker room B. We're going to try to stop them from—"

"Nukes!" the former cartel leader said. "What's going on?"

"Lito, you've got to get yourself and Maria out of here." They were now in Locker Room C, where an open suitcase sat brazenly on the floor by an open locker. The device inside was beeping quietly and rhythmically while the yellow LED of its timer ticked down.

8:59...

8:58...

8:57...

Maria and Hope stared at the suitcase, too panicked to speak. Lito, however, began to mutter. About the only phrase that came through clearly was, "Why, Nick?"

"It's an angels and demons thing, okay? Get out of the stadium, now!" Nick's voice boomed through the curved concrete corridors. In the silence that followed, they heard the sound of running feet.

Lito grabbed his arm. "You're a freakin' angel, Nick. Can't you just beam that thing out into space?"

"You think this is Star Trek or something? I'm losing my powers and getting weaker. There are two bombs. And the Suarez and Hernandez men are out there, armed and coming for us." The running steps were close now.

"Can't you do what you did last time and mess with their heads?"

"All right, Lito. Time to go—there may be another exit behind us, I'll see if I can buy you some time."

"No way," he said. "You saved my life, I'm not leaving you on your own. Maria, you go and—"

"If I'm going to die," she shot back, "I'll do it helping, not running." She and her brother exchanged a quick nod, then Lito turned to Nick.

"Tell us what to do."

Nick scanned the locker room and pointed to an exit at the opposite wall.

"Downstairs. Locker Room B. Find the other nuke."

"And do what, exactly?" Maria said.

"I don't know yet. First we have to—"

He stopped, because the running steps had stopped.   A cold gust from behind—the locker room door was open.   He turned around to face the cartel members.

It wasn't them.

Lena and her Nephilim stood before them.

"Nikolai, Nikolai, Nikolai," she said. "I'm disappointed in you." She glared at him with aloof eyes, which was perhaps her most dangerous look.

Nick leaned over to Lito and whispered, "Run."

90

IT DIDN'T TAKE LONG. Lito and Maria dashed through the exit while Nick put himself between Hope and Lena. Serena and Gunther stood on either side of their leader. More pounding footfalls sounded in the corridor, no doubt the cartel members.

Lito and Maria fled.

Lena showed no interest in them.

Nick tried to stall while trying to come up with a plan. If only his head wasn't spinning so wildly. If only Lena didn't look like a panther about to pounce on its prey.

"You've been a bad angel, Nikolai."

"And you're what, a good demon?"

"Don't insult me. I only work with demons when it suits me."

"So what are you?" He backed up toward the beeping detonator, keeping Hope behind him.

"Nephilim, sweetie." She stopped, just as he could retreat no further, and touched his face tenderly. And then she delivered a vicious slap—so hard flecks of light swam in front of his eyes. Had his angel powers not faded he'd have kept to his feet. But he lost his balance.

As he fell to the floor, Hope leapt at Lena.

"Hope, don't!" Too late. Lena nodded to Serena, who lifted her hand and without even touching Hope caught her by the throat and held her suspended in the air, gasping for breath. Lena stepped over to them.

"You have no idea how much trouble you've caused me, Hope Matheson. You were ready to die, I made it so easy for you. Why didn't you just go and do it?"

Hope couldn't speak. She just looked down at Nick, silently urging him to flee. He got up slowly, approached Lena and Serena.

"Let her go." He glanced over at the timer. Less than seven minutes left. But all that mattered now was to rescue Hope from Serena's grip. "Don't do this, Lena."

She turned to her other Nephilim, then pointed her chin at Nick.

"Rip his limbs off."

Before Gunther got to him, the cartel members burst in, guns drawn.

An idea came to him.

A long shot, but worth a try.

He cast a construct at the gangsters, causing Lena's Nephilim to look like Lito, Nick, and Maria. Not only did it work, he was still able to impersonate Lena's voice. "Kill them all, now!"

Lena whirled around.

Distracted, Serena lost her invisible grip on Hope and dropped her next to Nick. With his arms wrapped around her, he tried to cloak her with his invisibility, though it was uncertain to work against Lena or any of her half-angels.

The automatic weapons fire opened up.

Lena shouted for them to stop, but they couldn't hear her.

Before Gunther could react, a bullet hit him in the back. He turned around and plucked it out as if it were a burr. Then, like a bull with rage issues, he rushed the men who were still firing. Their rounds struck him but didn't draw blood—some of the slugs just popped out of his shirt. He grabbed one of the men's assault rifles and used it like a baseball bat. The gunman's head being the ball.

"What are you doing?" Lena cried out. "Stop!"

Nick reached over to the suitcase with the bomb and the small black timer—a simple device, but the colorful tangle of wires more than made up for it. On its front panel, something resembling an infrared computer port lay to the left of the countdown clock.

The retina scan.

Lena and company could teleport away in a second. And if Nick were to have any chance of stopping the nuke's detonation, he'd have to scan one of her eyes.

The cartel members were still firing on the Nephilim.

Serena growled. She didn't bother shouting orders at the humans mistaking them for their targets and shooting at them. Instead, she turned to confront them.

At once, they learned what her terrifying Nephilim power was.

91

LENA HAD BEEN OFF BALANCE since the operation gan. Morloch hadn't checked in even once before the Cabrillo Stadium event. She wasn't sure if that was a good sign or not. And what about her every step being scrutinized by those agents of the Dark Dominion known as auditors?

They were one of the few beings in all of existence she feared.

Though she'd never seen one, she sensed they were near. They gave off a coppery odor, like blood, faint but just enough for her to notice. During her training years with Morloch she'd watched them in action, or rather activated by high-ranking demons against anyone over whom they had authority.

They were here now, in the bowels of the stadium.

She could smell them.

Distracted by the bullets raining down on Gunther and Serena, it took Lena a moment to understand that those idiots wouldn't listen to her and call off their attack. Just as she figured out what was happening, Serena metamorphosed into a huge canine creature.

Lena called out, "Serena—it's all Nick's construct, we just have to stop him!"

Too late. Serena was now a wolf that even standing on all fours was at least six feet tall.

Most of the men fled.

The remaining few froze before the snarling wolf. With two strokes and a hideous snarl, she batted the men around, sending them crashing headlong into the concrete wall. Bones and skulls cracked with a sickening report. Blood-curdling screams had replaced the cacophony of weapons fire.

Lena spun around, searching for Nick. Gone. And now Hope was missing as well.

The nuke's timer continued its countdown.

6:53...

6:52...

6:51...

Gunther was holding a gunman while the wolf tore off his flesh. All the Hernandez and Suarez men who hadn't fled were dead, their body parts strewn throughout Locker Room C.

"Gunther!" Lena shouted.

He turned around, eyes blazing—Nephilim like him and Serena could not help but give into their craving for bloody carnage. Lena herself struggled to keep from succumbing to this powerful lust.

She waited a moment for him to calm down enough to comprehend an order.

"Go to Locker Room B," she said. "Make sure that nuke is secured."

For a second he looked like he was about to attack her. Then he grunted and winked out of sight.

Serena, still in the form of a giant wolf, snarled. Her knife-sized fangs dripped with blood, with scraps of clothing and flesh. She glared at Lena through the exact same blue eyes as in her human form.

"Locker Room B!" Lena commanded.

A low-pitched growl.

"Get a grip, Serena. We don't have time for this." The coppery essence of auditors mingled perversely with the smell of fresh human blood and viscera.

The wolf came closer, baring its fangs.

Lena sneered at it. "Seriously, Serena?"

She lifted her hand, which began to glow with the crimson hue of destructive energy.

The wolf backed away and resumed her natural form as Serena, along with her attitude.

"You're weak."

"Then why haven't you tried to kill me?"

"Who says I won't, later?"

"Get down to Locker B with Gunther and find Nick and his people."

"You're losing it, Lena. Watch yourself." Serena punctuated her warning with a nasty laugh. As she passed by she bumped Lena's shoulder, then vanished.

"Presumptuous bitch!"

The lights went out.

In the utter darkness Lena sensed something in front of her face. Shuffling noises behind confirmed that she'd gotten distracted again. Furious, she lit up the room with fire from her fingertips.

The suitcase had been tossed to the floor, its wires and components a mess. The nuclear device was in a shambles. The retina scanner was missing—detached. She clenched her teeth at the sight of the severed wires.

The timer was frozen at 5:57.

Nick was growing weaker, but he was still resourceful. He and perhaps Hope had killed the lights, scanned her retina in a split second while she found her bearings, and disarmed the nuke.

"Dammit!" Lena roared, then focused her teleportation power on Locker Room B. There was still one more nuke, and she wasn't about to let this entire operation fail because of one faltering angel.

92

AS HE RAN WITH HOPE DOWN THE STAIRS, Nick considered the grim irony. Nephilim were real, after all. But they seemed disorganized and easy to confuse. Must be all that raging blood-lust that blinded them to Lena's commands.

"I can't believe that retina scan worked," Hope said.

"There's one more, which can only be disarmed by Serena."

"Is her being a wolf some kind of construct?"

"I can't really tell. She's a Nephilim. They're all Nephilim."

"I thought you said—"

"I was wrong."

They reached the bottom of the steps and pushed open the door, expecting the worst. But the entire hallway was pitch black.

A wave of pain and dizziness struck Nick.

"It's happening—too fast." He faltered and would have lost his balance had Hope not steadied him.

"*What's* happening?"

"Becoming human. The pain will pass, but every time it happens I lose more of my powers." He took in a sharp breath. "Take my hand." Sliding on the cool concrete wall, his other hand found a door, slightly ajar. Just enough light came through to illuminate its placard: LOCKER ROOM B.

But he could barely stand, even though that last wave had ebbed and some of his strength pulsated.

"Hope, please. They almost killed you. Stay out here and wait."

"Try and stop me."

He looked at her in wonder. "You're nearly as stubborn as me." He put his arm around her, cloaked her with him under an invisibility construct, and prepared for the struggle of passing through the door. To his surprise, they slipped through easily. If his powers were going to leave him, they were going to drive him batty doing it so inconsistently. Though he was grateful now to be inconsistently re-blessed with the ability to teleport, and pass through solid matter—with a hitchhiker, no less.

The sudden change of darkness to bright fluorescent lights stung his eyes.

Hope gasped.

Nick quickly covered her mouth.

Then he looked up and saw it.

The corpse of a man hung from the locker room's ceiling pipes, eyes bulging, blue tongue sticking out. Thank God it wasn't Lito!

In the mirror, however, Nick caught his and Hope's reflection.

Not invisible.

Blasted, unreliable powers!

From behind a row of gunmetal lockers, Lena emerged. Then Serena, back in her human form, and finally, Gunther.

Each of them with a hostage's neck in a chokehold.

"Running out...of time!" Lito grunted, looking to the timer on a suitcase in Lena's other hand. In the crook of Gunther's elbow, his neck looked ready to snap like a dry twig. Maria struggled in vain to free herself from Serena's grip.

"Aren't you the brave fool?" Lena said to Nick. "Should have joined me while the offer was still open."

"You're about to kill thousands of people, for what?"

"I have someone important to impress," she said. "In fact...let's do this out in the open. High visibility and all—it'll only take a few minutes." She glanced down at the timer. "Four, to be exact."

In an instant, they were all standing on the artificial turf in the field. Most people had fled and were crowding into stands, while others shouted and otherwise contributed to the commotion. Occasional gunshots, whether warning or fatal, rang out.

Suddenly, spotlights came on illuminating Nick, Lena, the Nephilim holding Lito and Maria just a few feet from them, and Hope, who looked more dazed than frightened.

"Four minutes and fifteen seconds," Lena said with a glance down at the digital clock. Of course she'd wait until the moment before the nuke detonated, then teleport away leaving the blast to complete her dirty work.

Nick had to grab that suitcase.

If ever he needed to draw upon every bit of supernatural power within him, it was now. He swung a fist straight into her face.

Lena blocked the blow with her left arm. Judging by the surprise on her face, she hadn't expected him to react so violently.

Nick threw another punch, this time at her midsection.

She caught him by the forearm and twisted.

Searing pain.

Jaw clenched, Nick ignored it. With his free hand he grabbed Lena's hand—the one grasping the suitcase—and twisted it with all his might. The crimson glow of destructive energy enveloped them, pulsing like a star about to supernova.

The suitcase fell to the ground between them.

He was drawing from her power and feeding it back upon itself, like opposing magnetic charges forced into a confined space. Lena was becoming as immobilized as Nick.

"You're staying right here with the rest of us!" he said.

For the first time since he'd met her, Lena's eyes exhibited fear.

"Serena!" she called out.

For a moment, Serena didn't respond. She and Gunther were staring at what appeared to be the eye of a cyclone, standing vertical some ten yards away. Tendrils of lightning flashed out from its center. Nick didn't have time to wonder what it was.

When Lena called out again, Serena released Maria, who fell to the ground.

From over Lena's shoulder, Nick saw Serena transform into a huge wolf again and charge at them. With his strength draining at an alarming rate there was no way he could keep his hold on Lena and withstand the creature's attack.

There was only one thing he could do, and he wasn't at all sure it would work.

93

JUST BEFORE THE WOLF POUNCED, Nick grabbed Lena by the shoulders, threw her to the ground, then grappled and tumbled around with her.

But he'd cast a construct taking on her exact likeness, and apparently it had worked. When the wolf landed on them it seemed confused, the growl rumbling in her throat barely audible. Nick held still.

Hope watched in terror, her eyes moving from the struggle in front of her to the swirling vortex. Lightning crackled around its opening, sending a jolt through the stadium.

The wolf turned to look at it, then back to the two Lenas. With a hideous snarl, it lunged and clamped its jaws around the real Lena.

"Wrong one!" she cried out.

The wolf either didn't believe her or didn't care. It picked her up like a rag doll and shook her from side to side.

Nick rolled out of the way and opened the suitcase. Not realizing that his construct had disengaged and he no longer looked like Lena, he fumbled with the controls, trying to get to the retina scan module.

Gunther threw Lito down and rushed over to leap at the wolf, who released Lena and raised its head. It caught Gunther in its jaws, hurled him toward the vortex, then ran from it as fast as it could. What happened next took only a second or two, but the sight of it was horrific. The outline of Gunther's physical form remained intact while his spirit essence was ripped out of his body and pulled into the vortex, leaving a shriveled mass that fell to the ground like mummified remains.

Nick found the retina scanner.

The timer on the briefcase read: 3:00...2:59...

He got up, but a heavy blow to the head knocked him off his feet.

The scanner fell out of his hand.

Lena stood over him, breathing heavily. Bloody gashes scored her clothes and skin. She kicked the suitcase aside and jabbed Nick's chest with her sharp heel. She glanced over to the vortex, which howled like the frigid winds of Siberia. "I don't believe this," she muttered.

Another power-draining pulse hit Nick. It would result in a short surge of supernatural abilities, followed by more of its loss. But it began with overwhelming pain and nausea. He was too weak at the moment to move under Lena's foot.

A large hunting knife appeared in her hand.

She glanced around, then back at Nick as she prepared to plunge the blade down.

"Such a pity..."

She thrust the knife straight at Nick's throat.

He anticipated the cold penetration of steel into his neck.

A flurry of gray and white fur flashed before his eyes, instead. The wolf knocked Lena away and pinned her down with its forepaws. She grabbed the wolf by the neck, undeterred by its bared fangs, and threw a punch straight into its snout.

The wolf staggered, its jaws snapping.

Lena sent another blast of destructive energy into the wolf's body. It began to tremble as though it were being electrocuted.

Chest heaving, Nick sat up and called to Hope, who was crawling over to him.

"The suitcase!" She picked it up and tossed it to him.

The wolf rolled over onto Lena, then got up and clamped its jaws around her midsection.

"Why are you doing this, Serena!" Lena cried.

Again she sent another jolt of energy at the wolf. It snarled and dropped her.

Right in front of Nick.

Nick set the suitcase down, picked up the knife that had fallen from Lena's hand, knelt and held the blade to her throat. On the ground, gasping for air, barely moving, she was too weak or stunned to teleport away, or she'd have done it by now.

"Do it, Nikolai!" Snarling, the wolf loomed so close he could feel the heat, smell the blood emanating from her canine breath. "You're finished, Lena."

Lena strained. "It's just a matter of minutes before that nuke—"

"Do you think Morloch *cares* about the bodies, the carnage? He wants their souls."

Lena's eyes widened with fear. "*You're* the auditor?"

"Don't move," Nick said.

"Lena, you've failed to stop Hope Matheson," the wolf said. "The accounts must be reconciled."

One hand on the knife, the other on the suitcase, Nick had to try and get the retina scan over to Serena, though he wasn't sure it would work on a wolf's eye.

"Slash her throat open, Nikolai." Serena said. "Before her strength regenerates. Kill her and I'll disarm the nuke."

A quick glance at the clock.

2:20...
2:19...
2:18...

94

NICK PRESSED THE KNIFE AGAINST LENA'S NECK. Its handle felt warm in his hands.

"Do it, now!" Serena growled. "You know she wouldn't spare *you*."

True, but could he trust this wolf in human clothing?

Before him, just above his eyes…the dark vapor. The wolf stood over him.

"Nick…" Lena's voice sounded faint. Her eyes sought no sympathy. They did, however, bare the look of someone lost and resigned to her fate.

With just over two minutes to go, he had to act.

Now.

In one swift move he spun around and plunged the blade into the mass of fur standing over them. He wasn't sure where he'd stabbed the wolf, but it backed away, snapping its jaws at his face. For reasons he couldn't quite understand, he grabbed Lena's hand, pulled her up, and pushed her away.

"Get out of here."

The vortex swelled. A thunderous crack of lightning made the wolf back away further, still eyeing Nick and Lena. It stopped baring its fangs and used its teeth to pull the knife out of its shoulder.

Lena was staring at Nick. "Why—"

"Never mind why. Go!"

With a perplexed look, Lena said, "May you live to regret this." Then she vanished.

The timer!

A minute and ten seconds...

If only he could get close enough to Serena.

The wolf wasn't there.

Dammit, where is she?

The answer came from behind—tearing through his shirt with blunt claws. Glaring at him with Serena's terrifying eyes, the wolf snarled, its fangs red with blood.

Then something astonishing happened.

Using its fur as handholds, Hope scaled the wolf's back, the hunting knife's handle between her teeth. She then proceeded to stab at its neck, over and over. The wolf spun around and tried to snap at her but couldn't reach. It started writhing violently. Any minute now, Hope would be thrown off.

But before that could happen, a pale vapor appeared and instantly resolved into the form of a tall, dark-haired man.

Harold from Angel Resources.

He did not look pleased.

Serena, though more than twice his size as a wolf, backed away, oblivious to the vortex raging behind her.

"Morloch..."

"Where is she?" he said.

"Forget Lena, she was never—"

"I will determine how the accounts are settled!" The Serena-wolf backed even further away. "You were supposed to apprehend her if she failed. Now it is *you* that has failed."

Serena stopped just a few steps from the vortex, which began pulling at the fur on her back.

Hope held on but was starting to rise up in the wind. Nick called out to her.

"Get down!"

She rolled off the wolf's back and pointed to the suitcase, then to her eye.

The retina scan.

59...

58...

57...

Morloch lifted a finger—pulsing with a crimson glow—and pointed it at the wolf.

"The accounts must be reconciled."

"Morloch, please—" Serena said as he disappeared. The vortex expanded, charged lightning spider-webbed into the air. The wolf dug its claws into the ground, forelegs trembling with exertion, snapped at Hope, and clamped its fangs on her midsection. As she lifted her off the ground, Hope let out an agonizing scream.

"Hope!" Nick shouted.

She stabbed wildly with the knife. The wolf thrashed about with Hope impaled on its teeth. But the vortex began to pull its physical body backwards into the blazing aperture. Just as its hind legs entered, Hope stabbed the knife into the wolf's left eye socket, and dug furiously.

It opened its mouth, dropping Hope to the ground.

A howl filled the stadium, then died as the vortex swallowed the wolf completely. All around, cries of pain and terror rang out. All throughout the stadium, spirit forms were being sucked out of the Hernandez and Suarez gunmen, and into the vortex.

But Hope, lying on the ground, held out Serena's bloody eye to Nick in her right hand.

He knelt down with the retina scanner.

> 15...
> 14...
> 13...

"Oh, God. Hope!"

"Hurry..."

He took the eyeball from Hope, pointed it at the retina scanner.

> 10...
> 9...
> 8...

"It's not working...the lens is cracked!"

Hope's eyes fell shut. With a sigh, she dropped her head.

And then Nick remembered something he'd learned from Lena. A long shot, but his only chance.

"Hang on!" He backed up a couple of steps.

> 06...
> 05...

Please, just one last surge. He focused every bit of remaining energy into what he was about to do.

> 02...
> 01...
> 00...

95

THE NUKE DETONATED. Searing heat blasted through Nick's entire being. With every bit of strength remaining, he contained the explosion within a globe of his own destructive red energy. He had never experienced such intense pain and burning before, but he would not release it. Not unless his own body turned to ash.

Limbs shuddering, Nick fell to his knees.

Outside the red energy dome, Hope lay on the ground, bleeding, dying.

He started to feel himself lose containment of the nuclear energy.

No! Not yet!

Then he felt it.

The sharp pain in the eyes.

The nausea...

The final surge.

Nick looked up at the stadium roof. Envisioned the stars above.

Focused on a spot about 100 miles from the Earth's atmosphere.

But the strain was overpowering him.

Just keep it together...a few more seconds!

He found that familiar spot, the one between the layers, between the realms. It wasn't as simple as transporting water, or solid objects like a rifle or bullets, this was infinitely more difficult. But he had to do this before he became fully mortal.

Even if it killed him.

The nuclear energy was about to burst out of his containment field.

Nick started to lose all sensation.

Oh God, he was going to die.

First, the blinding light overwhelmed him.

Then it all went black...

96

FALLING...IT SEEMED TO GO ON FOREVER. Blindly hurtling downward.

Nick's shoulder, arm, and entire right side struck something hard.

The stadium floor.

His vision cleared.

Just in time to behold a wide column of red light blasting through the glass dome of the stadium. Through the gaping breach, he saw a fiery ball launch into space. A second later the night sky lit up, bright as noon.

It worked!

He rolled over, struggled to his knees and let out a triumphant grunt, despite the pain and nausea nearly overwhelming him.

"Hope!" Fighting the pain, he crawled to her and knelt over her. Shards from the dome lay around her. Terrible wounds from the wolf bled all over the grass. He touched her face gently.

She was alive, but just barely.

"You did it, Nick..."

"Shhhh. Don't talk right now."

She smiled, her eyelids fluttering. "It's...okay..."

"No, don't let go." If he could muster the last remnants of his abilities to divert a nuclear explosion, surely he could do this, in his last moments as a supernatural being.

"Nick..." Her breaths grew shorter, quicker.

"Hang on, Hope." He placed his glowing hand on Hope's wounds.

As expected, the dark vapor appeared. So did Lito and Maria, who watched but held back while Nick brazenly broke angel law for the last time.

"Come on, come on, come on..."

The wounds started to take on the healing glow.

"That's it, love! Just—" His voice broke. "It's going to work!"

But the wounds weren't closing properly. The glow was fading from his hands.

"No!" Nick lifted his hands, willed them to work. "I can do this!"

The glow was gone.

The dark vapor descended.

Nick flexed his fingers, trying desperately to conjure up the healing, but he knew—this time absolutely.

All his powers were gone.

He became aware of skin peeling from his hands, of radiation burns searing his body.

He had become fully human.

Still on his knees, he fought the agony of his burnt flesh and reached into his pocket.

"Look." He placed the jade pendant into her hand.

Hope's struggled to keep her eyes open. "You found it..."

"You see? You *have* to stay." He grabbed her hand, which was disturbingly cold, and kissed it. "I know it's not an engagement ring, but...Hope Matheson, I love you. Will you make me the happiest man in the world and marry me?"

She tried to keep her eyes on his, and managed to say, "Yes, oh yes," then her gaze went a million miles away and she smiled as if she'd just seen something unutterably beautiful. Her eyes closed, but the smile on her face didn't fade. "Nick...don't be afraid...It's just a dream, it's all just been like a dream. We're going to wake up one day and..."

"Hope...don't."

A look of perfect peace fell over her.

Nick kissed her, and wept softly.

He'd failed as an angel.

And on his first day as a mortal, he'd failed the woman he loved.

The dark vapor fell over him.

Enveloped him.

97

IN THE ABSOLUTE BLACKNESSS, Nick felt neither cold nor warm. He felt no pain. In fact, he felt nothing at all. *So this is what death is like for a mortal.*

How long before the dark reapers came for him?

An eternity—at least that's what it seemed like. He'd lost all sense of time.

Whatever happens, face it with dignity. Like a guardian. Like the warrior you once were.

The darkness began to lighten, gradually turning from dark to pale grey to bright white. Nick rubbed his eyes and looked around, but with no discernible point of reference he couldn't tell where he was.

A thin strand of black smoke wove through the air, growing longer and wider before him. He soon recognized it as the dark vapor, yet he didn't fear it. The thought of its constant presence at pivotal moments in his existence comforted him. And then, for the first time in all the thousands of years it had followed him, it transformed into something.

Or someone.

"Johann?"

As usual, the tall angel didn't speak. His dark glasses concealed his eyes—no way to tell if he came as friend or foe. Or otherwise. He stretched out his hand and gestured to the side, where a dark portal opened.

"I see." With Johann at his side, Nick approached the portal. "You're a dark reaper, aren't you?"

Johann didn't respond. He didn't even look at Nick. He just accompanied him into the tunnel through which Nick had taken countless human souls to the Terminus. Only this time, he was the one getting on the train.

With a dark reaper.

"Right. Let's get this over with, shall we?"

A moment later—it could have been centuries, hard to tell in this realm, now that he'd experienced life and death as a mortal—they arrived at the Terminus. Only it wasn't quite the construct he'd created every time he escorted a soul. No, this was an amorphous sea of light and consciousness. Rather unnerving, actually.

"Would you mind?" Nick said. "A construct, please?"

Johann turned his head to face the expanse and there it was, the construct.

Nick's construct.

Victoria Station, 1907.

Johann motioned for him to go through the open doors of the train waiting on the platform.

For the entire ride, he sat across from Nick without word or expression. No one else was in the car they occupied, so it was quiet. Nick could not stop thinking of Hope, though a multitude of thoughts crowded his mind.

"You know, for as long as I can remember," he said, "I've always wanted to take one of these rides, see what was on the other side." He shook his head.

The corner of Johann's mouth twitched ever so slightly.

At last, the train stopped.

The doors hissed open.

Face it with dignity. Nick took a deep breath, stood up, and left the train with Johann.

Once again, an absolute void. The train doors slid shut behind them and left them there, alone in the dark save for a narrow beam of light that drew a circle on the wall where they were standing.

"What are we waiting for?" Nick said.

Johann became the dark vapor, and vanished.

"Brilliant."

The circle of light on the wall grew wider and wider, revealing a great gate on either side of which stood a magnificent creature. Their wings rose high above their shoulders, and the swords in their hands blazed. Nick resisted the impulse to fall at their feet.

Before him stood the archangels Michael and Gabriel.

He held his head high, prepared to face the same judgment as Lucifer and his demons.

98

THE GREAT GATE SWUNG OPEN without a sound. A figure emerged and came forth. Nick could not have described it because the light emanating from it overwhelmed his sight. Its presence caused him to fall to his knees and bow his head. No angel of his stature had ever stood so close. That was reserved strictly for the holiest.

Or those facing eternal damnation.

Nick could barely speak. But he did, with fear and trembling.

"Father."

"Nikolai." He didn't exactly hear the voice, he perceived it. And the voice didn't just resound—it rippled through the universe. "You stand before the judgment seat, having touched humanity, having intervened and taken on their likeness and nature. What have you to say for yourself?"

"I make no excuse, Father. I'm ready to accept the consequences of my actions."

"Have you no advocate?"

Michael stepped forward, scowling down at Nick.

"There is one, Father."

The dark vapor appeared again.

Nick drew a sharp breath. *Not Johann.*

The vapor became Johann, then it evaporated into a glowing cloud which coalesced into...

"Tamara?"

The dark vapor? Johann? They had been Tamara all along?

"I vouch for Nikolai, Father," she said.

"Then you have taken full responsibility for his actions," Father said.

"I have."

"May I speak?" Michael said. Father nodded, whereupon Michael proceeded to cite each count of Nick's "flagrant" disregard for protocol. "And the most grave of all: He was found to be in collusion for a time with the Dark Dominion."

Though Nick hadn't realized it was them until it was too late, there was no use trying to explain. It would only make things worse.

Father passed his hand before Nick, who now found himself wearing what appeared to be the dress uniform of an officer in the British Army, circa 1900. The medals on it and the sword at his side evoked his glorious stint as a decorated guardian.

Now, before his cosmic hanging, he would have his medals stripped, his epaulets torn from his shoulders, his sword broken in half over Michael's knee.

Father's eyes were fixed on him with a look both terrifying and compelling.

"Come forth, Nikolai."

Nick obeyed, his back ramrod straight.

Michael held out his hand.

Nick turned over his sword.

Tamara removed his coat.

"Bow, Nikolai," Gabriel said.

Nick bowed. Down on one knee, face to the ground, he awaited the final blow that would send him into the fiery pits, to suffer everlasting torment as a mortal.

99

NICK CONSIDERED ABANDONING HIS PRIDE and throwing himself at Father's mercy, and begging for forgiveness. He never got the chance.

"Arise, Nikolai."

When he lifted his head, Father stood over him, shining like the morning, a brilliant smile spread across his magnificent countenance. Nick got up—and Tamara put a purple robe over his shoulders. Michael handed him a shining sword.

"I...I don't understand." Nick looked all around.

"My son, do you not see?" Father placed His hand on Nick's head as though in blessing. "Once you were lost but now are found. Once you were dead but are now alive."

"But I chose to defect. I broke the law."

Father laughed, the sound of it remarkably like thunder.

"Did you really think any of what you did could go on without my knowledge?"

"Well, no, but..."

"You are loved with an everlasting love, my son."

Nick glanced over to Tamara—she'd told him that, the day he resigned. Or thought he'd resigned.

"I know your character," Father said. "After all, I created you. I knew the path you would take given the settings and conflicts in which I set you. And you have developed just as I hoped."

"Have I? Then why did you—why did I have to become human?"

"Ah, that *is* the question, isn't it?" Another of those brilliant smiles. "You were destined, Dear Nikolai, to be a champion of my children, the humans. That is why you overcame your limitations and sacrificed everything to save them from that nuclear blast. And that is why you could never serve the purposes of the Dark Dominion. You love the humans."

Nick raised an eyebrow.

"Well, you may have gotten a bit too close to them, but I'll overlook it. I have the authority to do that, you know."

"Of course," Nick said, unsure if he should smile.

"You were allowed to become human so you could learn compassion for those you protect, empathize with their struggles." He leaned down to Nick's ear and whispered. "I've done it too, you know."

He straightened up and resumed speaking in what Nick perceived as his normal voice.

"And now, having been a human, you can understand them, see them as I do. My son, it takes more than might and power to be their guardian. You need my spirit." He touched Nick's forehead and he immediately felt his strength return. Stronger than ever before. "And now, you have it."

"Father," Nick bowed his head. "I am not worthy."

"You have been made worthy. Behold, I make all things new." He placed his hand under Nick's chin and lifted his head. "Well done, good and faithful guardian."

"Did you say *guardian?*"

"Supreme Guardian, in fact. You have proven faithful in lesser things, I will put you in command of much greater things." He nodded toward the gate, which still yawned open. "Enter now and partake of my joy."

Taking it all in, Nick couldn't stop the tear that fell from his eye. He'd not only been reinstated as an angel, he'd been promoted.

Tamara came over and embraced him. "Congratulations, Nick."

"Thank you, but all along, you were there—the dark vapor, Johann?"

"*And* the harbor porpoise who helped you with that pendant."

"That was you?" Nick said, laughing incredulously. But the mirth didn't last. He remembered the pain and suffering Hope had experienced in her last moments. "Alas..."

"That term does not exist here," Tamara said. "Look over there."

"Hope!"

Beaming with joy, she ran into his arms. She was whole, not a scratch or blemish. In fact, she seemed a bit younger than he remembered. Nick lifted her off the ground and spun around, his heart filled with unspeakable joy. They kissed for as long as it took—time was irrelevant.

"Humans and angels," Tamara said. "What will the neighbors say?"

More laughter.

But then Nick's jubilant expression turned somber. He touched Hope's face tenderly.

"Did you suffer, love? You know, before you..."

"You mean before I died? What an odd concept." She gave him that smile. "My entire mortal life was like a dream I barely remember.

Now, it's as if I just woke up and am back in the real world."

"That's how most humans describe it when they get here," Tamara said.

"To tell you the truth," Hope said, "Nick is the one who helped me understand all this."

"Me?"

"You see, mortal life is all just a construct of this, the *true* reality."

"Not a very good one," Nick said, taking her hand. "But I see what you mean."

"There are a couple of people who'd very much like to speak with you," Tamara said.

From behind her, a radiant young woman came up to him.

"I'm so happy to see you again!"

"I'm afraid you have me at a disadvantage," he said. But something about her eyes seemed more than familiar.

"Thank you for taking care of my mother."

"*Chloe?*"

She nodded. "You were so kind when you brought me here, I'll always be grateful."

Before he could fully grasp it all, another beautiful young woman approached.

This time, he knew right away. As she ran into his open arms, he didn't even try to hold back the tears.

"Daddy!"

"Clara!" He held her for a long time, both of them crying softly in each other's arms. Nick finally released his grown daughter and turned to Tamara. "So all along, you knew?"

"The rules were there for a reason. Had you healed her back in Victoria Station, she would have turned out like Lena."

"I can never thank you enough, Tamara." He took her hands in his. "You've done so much for me."

"And I'd do it again."

A deep thundering sound approached and caused them to turn their heads. It was Michael, mounted on a war horse, another one at its side.

"Don't get too comfortable just yet," he said. "Your work as a Supreme Guardian is just beginning. There's a whole world that needs our help, and I've just gotten word that the Dark Dominion is gearing up for a heavy offensive. We have to go now."

"I see." He turned back to Hope, Chloe, and Clara. "Seems I just got here."

Hope kissed him. "Duty calls."

"I'm afraid so."

"Go on, then. We'll be waiting."

"It could take some time," he said.

"We've got all the time in—well, you know."

"Indeed." Nick mounted his steed. "I'll see you soon."

Drawing his sword with a blazing flourish, he rode off at Michael's side, the entire First and Second Legions in all their supernal glory following them out of the city gates and off to the ongoing war.

The Dark Dominion was a formidable enemy. And although he had fought many battles in the natural realm, direct conflict in the spiritual realm would be far more deadly. But Nick had faith all would end well.

It was only a matter of time.

ACKNOWLEDGEMENTS

There are so many people who supported me and contributed to the completion of this book that I fear I will not be able to mention each one by name. For that, I ask your forgiveness and that you know just how much I value and appreciate your presence in my life.

First off, I would like to thank Renni Browne, editor extraordinaire, whose unparalleled gift for helping me tighten up the manuscript with the necessary surgical cuts have—in this author's opinion—made this book fit the Hitchcockian criteria of a great story: *Life, without the boring parts.*

I would also like to thank my fellow writers Susan Wingate and Michael Angel, who both encouraged me early on with *Terminus* to press ahead with this genre.

Of course, I could not do anything without the love and prayers of my friends and family, especially those in my connect group: Tom and Trish Vesneski, Farshid and Marisol Farokhi, Charles and Toni Covello, and many others in my church, as well as William and Ckristina Sutjiadi and Michael and Patricia Goh.

A special shout out to the fantastic members of Team Graham for your constant support and encouragement. You're a secret society and you know who you are <cryptic wink.>

Of course, I wish to thank my awesome kids Alex and Maddi for your patience and understanding whenever Daddy is on a deadline. Your willingness to set hamsters and RC jets aside and wait for me to have time again to play with you again really helped.

And finally, my beautiful wife and muse, Katie: I truly could not have written this book without your love, support, perspective, and all those long hours talking about and looking over my work with your unwavering honesty, and affirming words.

A NOTE FROM THE AUTHOR

Dear friend,

The key thing to remember in any novel is that it is a work of *fiction*. Axiomatic as that may seem, I think it important that I make the following statements:

First: *Terminus*, while some of its premise stem from my personal beliefs, is a story, a parable even. It is not to be taken literally as Christian biblical doctrine on the topic of Angels, Heaven, or the afterlife. Rather, like Christ's analogies of the Kingdom of Heaven being like a fishing net, a mustard seed, yeast, etc., this book's concepts are for the purpose of illustrating greater truths in a way in which we humans can more readily identify. Like a "construct," so to speak.

Secondly: though this book is a work of fiction, the issues of despair, suicide, emotional bondage to the past, are real. If you or anyone you know suffers from any of these, I implore you to reach out to trusted friends, qualified counselors or clergy, and by no means try to deal with it alone. Healing and freedom is available to those who seek it.

Remember, "You are loved with an everlasting love." No matter how dire the situation, there is hope. This is one reason I chose to name one of the main characters in this book HOPE. Having someone hear you, understand and/or pray for you can be life-changing. Whatever your lot, don't give up, and don't go it alone.

Thank you for taking the time to read *Terminus*, it means more to me than you can imagine. If you enjoyed it enough, would you kindly spread the word and tell your friends and family about it?

I'd love to hear from you, so please feel free to contact me through my website: www.joshua-graham.com/contact

And while you're there, please sign up for my occasional newsletter where you can receive updates, exclusive previews and content here: http://joshua-graham.com/newsletter

And please connect with me on facebook:
www.facebook.com/J0shGraham
and Twitter: www.twitter.com/j0shuagraham

Thank you, and until next time, be blessed!

Joshua Graham

ABOUT THE AUTHOR

#1 Bestselling author Joshua Graham has won multiple awards for his thrillers DARKROOM and BEYOND JUSTICE. He holds a Master's Degree from Juilliard, and a Doctorate from Johns Hopkins University. His books have been called "thought-provoking page-turners." Many of his readers blame him for sleepless nights, arriving to work late, neglected dishes and family members, and not allowing them to put the book down.

Made in the USA
Lexington, KY
04 March 2014